DÉZAFI

CARAF Books

Caribbean and African Literature
Translated from French

Renée Larrier and Mildred Mortimer, Editors

DÉZAFI

A NOVEL

Frankétienne

Translated and with an Introduction by Asselin Charles

University of Virginia Press
Charlottesville and London

Originally published in Kreyòl by Éditions Fardin, Port-au-Prince, Haiti
© 1975 by Franketienne
Translation and introduction copyright © 2018 by Asselin Charles
Afterword © 2018 by the Rector and Visitors of the University of Virginia
All rights reserved
Printed in the United States of America on acid-free paper

First published 2018

ISBN 978-0-8139-4138-7 (cloth)
ISBN 978-0-8139-4139-4 (paper)
ISBN 978-0-8139-4140-0 (ebook)

9 8 7 6 5 4 3 2 1

Library of Congress Cataloging-in-Publication Data is available for this title.

Cover art: Les zonbis, Franketienne, 2000. (Photo by Marie Andrée M. Etienne)

CONTENTS

TRANSLATOR'S ACKNOWLEDGMENTS

Mèsi anpil, as we say in the native tongue, to family, friends, and colleagues for their unflagging support, active help, and encouragement. In Canada and the United States, warmest thanks to Ketty, Gérald, Jonassaint, Baba Yaw. In Haiti, my gratitude to Franké- tienne and Marie-Andrée Étienne, and to Cary Hector, *de regret- tée mémoire.* In Taiwan, *xiexie* to Peter Lee, who kindly steered me to the University of Virginia Press, and to Taiwan Hua, always. *Ayibobo* to the memory of the incontrovertible Haitian literary scholar Maximilien Laroche, who unstintingly shared with me his vast erudition and critical insights as I labored on this translation.

Publication of this translation of *Dézafi* was made possible thanks to a generous subsidy from Lin Tzuyi of Taiwan, enthusi- astic connoisseur of Franchétienne's writings and paintings.

INTRODUCTION

Jouk lan ginin, paròl natifnatal donnin sou lang-nou, brasé trip-nou.
Kòd lonbrit-nou boujonnin: youn latriyé flè-péyi lévé sou tout kò-nou.

All the way to Guinea the native speech flowers and fruits on our
tongues, moves us to our very entrails. Our umbilical cords have budded;
countless native flowers bloom all over our bodies.

—Frankétienne, *Dézafi* (1975)

El original es infiel a la traducción.

The original is unfaithful to the translation.

—Jorge Luis Borges, "Sobre el Vathek de William Beckford" (1943)

While Haiti's birth and survival against great odds as an independent polity has been her signal political exploit, the Caribbean
nation's literature may well be her major cultural achievement.
In a relatively brief period of two centuries, generations of Haitian poets, novelists, playwrights, and essayists have created one
of the most distinctive literary traditions in the Americas, and a
bilingual one at that, contributing to the global literary treasure
house a variety of works, many of which will undoubtedly stand
the test of time. Among the authors whose writings continue to
enrich Haiti's literature today, the most original, in the eyes of
many a literary scholar, is arguably the poet, novelist, and playwright Frankétienne. With his large corpus of avant-garde literary
creations in both French and Kreyòl,[1] the dean of Haitian letters
has been praised not merely as "l'écrivain le plus novateur d'Haïti"
(Haiti's most innovative writer) but also as "l'écrivain le plus novateur du monde" (the most innovative writer in the world), and "un

de ces géants qui ont marqué et marqueront les littératures améric-aines" (one of those giants that have marked, and will continue to mark, the literatures of the Americas).[2] A prolific author who has produced some fifty novels, plays, and poetry collections inspired by Haiti's complex realities and reflecting on the human condi-tion, works that have consistently impressed critics and scholars with their esthetics and brought him renown among the masses with their sociopolitical pertinence and cultural resonance, Frank-étienne truly deserves the title of "national treasure" recently be-stowed upon him by the government of Haiti.

That a writer of this stature was little known outside Haiti for much of his half-century-long career, that is, from the early 1960s to the late 1980s, is imputable to at least two factors, one struc-tural and the other circumstantial. On the one hand, the global political economy of publishing and the international system of promotion and distribution of cultural products do not favor art-ists, writers, and other creators from small and poor nations, and Frankétienne's country is one of those places marginalized in the marketplace of ideas and creation. On the other hand, Frank-étienne learned and practiced his craft during the long Duvalier re-gime,[3] self-publishing his works, stubbornly rejecting the option of emigration, and never traveling outside Haiti until he was already well into his fifties. The international critical spotlight during those years being on the émigré Haitian writers in Canada, France, the United States, and various Francophone African countries,[4] his works as a writer based in Haiti were simply neglected. Thus it is only two decades ago that the best-known and truly popular au-thor in Haiti, the only one whose writings in the country's two lan-guages have reached both a French-speaking educated public and a large unilingual Kreyòl-speaking audience, became a presence on the international stage.

DISCOVERING FRANKÉTIENNE

While Frankétienne had occasionally been profiled in foreign French-language publications, discussions of his works outside Haiti started in earnest only with the 1986 publication of a special issue of the Montreal-based literary journal *Dérives,* entitled "Franketienne, écrivain haïtien" (1986/87),[5] to which contributed a stable of Haitian and international scholars and critics, including the journal's founder and editor, Jean Jonassaint. Franketienne would come to the attention of a wider circle of readers and literary scholars in the Francophone world several years later, at the turn of this century, when French publishers reissued his great early works: the breakthrough novel *Ultravocal* (1972; 2002); his first work of fiction, *Mûr à crever* (1968; 2002); his novel *Les affres d'un défi* (1979; 2000), a French re-creation of his masterly Kreyòl fiction *Dézafi* (1975); and a new edition of *Dezafi* (2002) using the standardized Kreyòl spelling established in 1980. The release of these works through influential Parisian publishers, which followed Franketienne's nomination in 1999 for the Nobel Prize in literature, raised the Haitian writer's international profile, and further recognition would come with awards from the French government and from UNESCO.[6]

Franketienne's renown in the English-speaking world has yet to spread beyond the relatively small number of literary scholars who research his writings and teach his works in university courses. Though some of his poems and excerpts from his novels had appeared over the years in journals and anthologies, the first full English translation of one of his works was my English version of his popular Kreyòl play *Pèlin-tèt* (1978). Meaning "head trap" and entitled *The Noose* in English, the translated play about two Haitian immigrants in New York was staged at the New York Immigrant Theater Festival in 2001 and published two years later in the translation journal *Metamorphoses* (2003), albeit in slightly truncated form.[7] Since then, an English translation of *Mûr à crever* (*Ready to Burst,* 2014) has been released in the United States, and the impending publication of a translation of *Ultravocal* has been announced by a New York publishing house.[8] To these three major works, the play and the two novels, available in English, we are now adding this translation of *Dézafi,* perhaps the most important in the Franketienne canon for its historical significance as the first published novel in Haitian Kreyòl,[9] on the one hand, and for its conceptual and stylistic originality, on the other. In addition to these translations, along with articles and essays scattered in various academic journals, some important critical volumes in English about Franкétienne's writings have been released in recent years. Most notable among these are a special issue of the *Journal of Haitian Studies* (Spring 2008); a study of the author's rewritten versions of some of his works (*Franкétienne and Rewriting: A Work in Progress,* 2009); and a book on the Spiralist novel spotlighting Franкétienne's fiction as well as the works of his two contemporaries Jean-Claude Fignolé and René Philoctète (*Haiti Unbound,* 2010).[10] In *Dézafi* a larger discerning Anglophone readership will finally discover, like the critics and scholars, one of the greatest contemporary writers, an innovative novelist endowed with a most fertile imagination and a master stylist.

Known today as Franкétienne, the future poet, novelist, and playwright was born in 1936 and was christened Jean-Pierre Basilique d'Antor Franck Etienne d'Argent. There is in this long birth name an exquisite equilibrium between the expansiveness of the noble-sounding and rather exotic patronymic and the rooting centrality of the name d'Antor, one of the manifestations of that quintessentially Haitian *lwa*,[11] the Vodou goddess of love Èzili Dantò. In the course of his itinerary, the writer would progressively shed all these appellations, signing his early works as Franck Étienne and later conflating the two into the single moniker Franкétienne, a name that encapsulates the essence of the man who would achieve international renown as a writer and artist while remaining rooted in the soil of his native land. Enracinated in the deep culture of the peasants and workers who make up the overwhelming majority of the population, he was, and is, to use the Kreyòl epithet applied to him by the publisher Dieudonné Fardin in the preface of the first edition of *Dézafi,* a natif Dayiti-Toma, an authentic son of Haiti.[12]

An unmistakable Haitianity radiates from every aspect of content and form of Franкétienne's writings in both languages, but even more so in Kreyòl. All his works in the vernacular exhibit a masterly proficiency in the Kreyòl language in all its registers, especially in what George Lang calls "deep Creole,"[13] the language spoken by the masses as opposed to the heavily French-inflected speech of the educated middle and upper classes. His "atavistic fluidity in the language"[14] is manifest in his effortless summoning of an extensive vocabulary in his plays and in the novel *Dézafi;* in his Shakespearean knack for coining arresting neologisms; in his maestro's modulation of the rhythm and sonority of Kreyòl; and in his keen apprehension of the esthetics of the language. Frankétienne's Haitianity expresses itself also in his encyclopedic display of the major referential elements of the culture—the collective historical memory, the Vodou religion, the oral tradition, and the shared symbolic code. There is, as well, in his writings the evidence of his intimate knowledge of the works and days of the common people, of their concerns and aspirations, of their modes of thinking, and of the Haitian ethos. There is, finally, his identification with the country's urban and rural landscapes, an almost carnal attachment to the land. It is all that which Frankétienne calls upon in the making of his poems, plays, and novels, all that which he transforms through his writer's imagination and renders into words. Thus it is Haiti, *le pays profond,* the heartland, that has nurtured Frankétienne, the man and the writer, as he confides to the Cameroonian critic Guy Tegomo: "I am essentially, and this is not demagoguery, a Haitian Negro. . . . So, when I say that it is Haiti that has given me everything, I mean that as a writer I have been molded, shaped, formed by this land, by its everyday life made of pain, joy, myth, lies, fantasies, everything."[15]

THE MAKING OF A WRITER

Although Frankétienne's immersion, by social background and upbringing, in the culture of the Haitian masses shaped his worldview, esthetic sensibility, understanding of the country's social and cultural realities, and fluency in the vernacular—in sum, provided him with both the raw materials and the basic tools of his writer's craft—it is through formal schooling that he came to the French language, the tongue in which he penned his first works, indeed, the majority of his oeuvre. In the postcolonial context of Haiti, where the language of the former metropole is still considered both the site and vehicle of high culture, it is naturally through the French language that Frankétienne would come to the world of written literature. His encounter with "the second tongue" on his first day in the formal setting of school was, as he has often told it, a traumatic experience.[16] Mocked and humiliated by a classmate who already spoke the language at home, the unilingual Kreyòl-speaking boy would subsequently endeavor to master the alienating tongue, establishing a rapport with French that is at once intellectual, psychological, and sensual: "I discovered the musicality of that language"; Frankétienne elaborates, "there were tender words, sweet words, violent words, acidic, sugary words. . . . This is why my rapport with words—which may surprise those people who think I'm in seventh heaven—is a physical, concrete, sensual rapport."[17]

One of the keys to Frankétienne's writings is precisely his complex rapport with language in general and his ability to negotiate the structural tension between French and Kreyòl in a sociocultural context in which the two languages coexist both in symbiosis and in antagonism. Thus, beyond the dizzying stylistic pyrotechnics and lexical luxuriance of his French writings, one senses a certain ambivalence toward a language acquired through great exertion, mastered as a prize, and wielded with exuberance. In this regard Frankétienne comports himself like earlier and contemporary Haitian writers, handling the second tongue if not with reverence at least with a mix of respect and pragmatism, even as they inflect it with an infusion of the leaven of the mother tongue either in a transgressing spirit or in order to ground their writing in the local soil. But such ambivalence disappears when Frankétienne writes in Kreyòl, passionately embracing the mother tongue and rejecting the subaltern status in which it is customarily held in society. Aware of the genius of the language, he considers Kreyòl a superb instrument of literary creation to the same extent as French and deserving of the same respect as French. As a writer, he would strive to exploit the full range of the esthetic possibilities of Kreyòl and allow it to wield its full power of expression: "I realized," he tells an interviewer, "that I was to adopt that same attitude, that same rapport with my own language, because writing in Kreyòl presents the same difficulties as writing in French. With *L'oiseau schizophone* I realized that I could not allow myself to treat my mother tongue as if it were some wild field where I could feel free to scatter all sorts of stupidities. No, one must have respect for one's language."[18]

While social, cultural, and educational forces and personal circumstances play a significant, indeed a determinant, role in shaping an author, they are not sufficient to explain his writings. Certainly a writer's creations articulate aspects of his society and culture, subliminally or overtly. However, no matter how formally and ideologically idiosyncratic a literary work might be, it is necessarily also written out of other literary works, in dialogue or in contestation, tacit, implied, or explicit, with those works. It is a truism therefore that a writer learns and practices his craft in direct or indirect interaction with other writers, past and contemporary.

Franquétienne thus apprenticed as a writer through exposure to works in two languages, French and Kreyòl. His apprenticeship in the literature of French expression took place through his reading of authors belonging to two distinct yet intertwined literary traditions, the French tradition and the Haitian tradition. French literature from the Middle Ages to the twentieth century being a required secondary school subject, educated Haitians normally would be acquainted with several of the major classics in the French canon. Those with a literary bent would continue reading the French writers, especially as a certain familiarity with metropolitan authors is considered a badge of culture. Franquétienne's readings are certainly consistent with this pattern, and he has acknowledged the influence of French authors such as Rimbaud on his youthful efforts and the impact of more contemporary French literary trends on his more mature writings.[19] But the influence of French literature on Franquétienne's writings plays itself out according to a very Haitian scenario. The Haitian literary tradition in French has evolved historically as a process of distancing from the French literary models and of enracination in the Haitian sociocultural reality, resulting in the indigenization of the literature, as it were, through a series of creative strategies centered around thematic choices, the modulation of the French language, and the projection of a specifically Haitian worldview. Commenting on the appropriation and domestication of English for literary creation in Asia, Edwin Thumboo makes an observation that most aptly describes how Haitian writers have historically handled the French language: "In a sense the language is remade, where necessary, by adjusting the interior landscape of words in order to explore and mediate the permutations of another culture and environment."[20] Naturally, then, as Maximilien Laroche, among other critics, has observed, Franketienne's writings in French, avant-garde though they be, carry those typically Haitian literary markers and creative strategies invented by the country's writers in the postindependence period, crystallized in the works of the writers of the Indigenist literary school of the 1920s and 1930s, and further developed throughout the twentieth century.[21] Thus in Franketienne's fiction it is possible to identify several of the formal elements typically found in canonical Haitian literary texts in French such as the mélange of social realism and *réalisme merveilleux* (marvelous realism); the culturally grounded imagery; and the storytelling techniques evocative at times of the folktale and of the *lodyans,* a narrative genre combining the characteristics of the tall tale and the conventions of the modern novel favored by such early twentieth-century fiction writers as Justin Lhérisson and Frédéric Marcelin.

But Franketienne's apprenticeship also took place in interaction with contemporaries who had been seeking a rupture from certain aspects of Haitian writings since the late 1940s, especially the overemphasis on sociopolitical themes and the pervasiveness of old Indigenist tropes. The most notable among those writers were the members of Haïti Littéraire, the short-lived group founded in 1960 by five young poets who were to become recognized Haitian émigré writers during the Duvalierist decades: Davertige, Serge Legagneur, Roland Morisseau, René Philoctète, and Anthony Phelps.[22] This core group of young poets had a loose association with such older writers as the poets Léon Laleau, René Bélance, and Jean Brierre; historians Jean Fouchard and Roger Gaillard; literary scholars Pradel Pompilus and Ghislain Gouraige; and novelist Marie Chauvet, who held a literary salon in Port-au-Prince where the group met for poetry readings and discussion of art, literature, and politics. Gravitating around the Haïti Littéraire group were a number of coevals, writers and artists, among them Franketienne, who shared the group's passion for poetry and literature in general, a

wary attitude toward the Duvalier regime, vaguely leftist sensibili-
ties, and the desire to create new forms of Haitian writings. Although he moved in the circle of the Haiti Littéraire poets, Frankétienne did not embrace all their views, certainly not the modernist
concept of a politically detached art or the notion of a literature
unmoored from tradition and social reality.[23] The influence of
Haïti Littéraire and early 1960s Haitian writers on Fran/kétienne
resides ultimately in his judicious absorption of some of the intellectual and artistic zeitgeist. Recognizing the imperative to develop
novel forms of expression, he shared the group's attitude toward
writing as a craft that demanded attention to detail, meticulous
facture, and a heightened awareness of language in all its aspects in
the process of literary creation, but he remained committed to the
notion of writing as a means of exploring social reality.

THE SPIRALISME BREAKTHROUGH

The radical rupture from the Haitian tradition in literature and the
ideological and esthetic reorientation sought by the poets of Haïti
Littéraire were to be achieved a few years later by Fran/kétienne,
who was only a "satellite" of the collective, to use Anthony Phelps's
designation; by René Philoctète, one of the five members of the
group; and by the novelist Jean-Claude Fignolé.[24] In the late 1960s,
these three writers began to publish conceptually and formally
avant-garde texts based on an esthetic paradigm that would at the
same time be grounded in the Haitian literary tradition, transcend
it, and move it in a new direction. Their works realized the ideological, formal, and creative breakthrough that was to be known
as Spiralisme. Fran/kétienne, primus inter pares, stands as the foremost theorist and practitioner of this innovative form of fiction,
the *spirale,* as he dubbed *Ultravocal* (1972), a novel in which cohere the distinctive ideological and stylistic elements of the Spiralist narrative, first sketched in *Mûr à crever* (1968) and brought to
full fruition in *Dézafi* (1975).

Spiralisme is both an ideology or way of seeing, in the Lukác-
sian sense of the term, and an esthetic blueprint for representing
the world and human experience in and of the world. The Spiral-

ist narrative strives to render reality in a manner that conveys its chaotic and nonlinear nature. Spiralisme posits the coexistence of the ordinary and the extraordinary, the conflation of the quotidian and the magical, multiple realities that are yet perceived and experienced as unitary, fragments that contain the whole as in a hologram. The Spiralist novel seeks to mirror by its structure the turbulent overlapping and clashing of events, their unfolding at once simultaneous and sequential, parallel and intersecting. This profusion that is the essence of reality, the Spiralist text reproduces formally by means of stylistic effects based on polyphony and polyrhythm, on clashes and harmony, on opposition and fusion. Like the spiral, ubiquitous in nature from the conch shell to the Milky Way, the Spiralist narrative is a dynamic construction based on both stasis and movement, involving simultaneously ascent and descent, circularity and linearity, hence the repetitions and reiterations even as the story advances. At once abstract construct and a thing of nature, the spiral is, in Frankétienne's view, the most apt paradigm for accounting for the complex, profuse, living reality that solicits the Haitian writer:

> The spiral, by its unfolding movement, its to-and-fro movement, its palpitation in every direction, represents life's movement. Moreover, it moves forward. It is a progression forward and upward. Several theorists have said it before. Take the famous example of the barley grain in Anti-Dühring. It falls on fertile soil under weather conditions favorable to germination. This small barley seed becomes a plantule, which grows and becomes a plant, and the plant eventually produces thousands and thousands of barley grains. The point is we have a starting point, which is the barley grain. But the barley grain, moving like a spiral, returns to the barley grain, but exceeding itself in the process: we no longer have a single barley seed, but an infinity.[25]

Frankétienne perfected the techniques of the Spiralist narrative in several successive works of fiction. A sequential reading of *Mûr à crever, Ultravocal, Dézafi, Les affres d'un défi,* and *L'oiseau schizophone* readily brings into relief the elements of content and form that constitute the distinctive generic characteristics of the Spiralist novel. Thus, there is the spiral-like narrative structure, the unfolding of the story with many returns toward the starting point, repetitions, and reiterations, as the plot moves forward and upward toward its climax and dénouement. There are also the multiple narrative perspectives and voices, and the conflation of narrator or narrators and audience, that suggest the protean nature of reality and the notion that reality is collectively constructed and that its existence is both objective and subjective. Stylistically, there are the varying tempos and multiple rhythms, the combination of polyphony and polyrhythm that ultimately results in harmony. And to further convey the complexity and pluridimensionality of reality and experience, there is the ubiquitous presence of doubles and character pairs, metaphors and symbols of the fragmentation of consciousness. One finds as well in the Spiralist novel a juxtaposition and mixing of genres, whereby the story is told pell-mell through realistic narration, myth, folktale, *lodyans,* gnomic segments, and free verse. As if words were not enough to represent a chaotic world and complex human experience, Frankétienne resorts also to a visual code consisting of empty spaces, drawings, graphics, different typographical compositions for different segments of the narrative, a semantic system which Jean Jonassaint calls "a differential and signifying typo/topography."[26] Such formal abstractions, verbal constructions, are made concrete in Frankétienne's paintings, which by their composition, their bold color schemes, their characteristic mélange of stasis, fluid movement, and tension, their coded evocation of reality, and their Vodou esthetics may be considered visual actualizations of Spiralisme.[27]

In the Spiralist optic, words may not suffice for an accurate representation of the world and the human experience in and of the world, yet the Spiralist novel, like any other work of fiction, is a verbal construction. In fact, it is not only built with words, it is also very much about words, about language itself. In filigree in the Spiralist novel, in the recurring metaphorical and symbolic references to speech, to words, runs the notion that the world is willed into existence through speech, that language is both the instrument and the material with which the world comes into being. Frankétienne has suggested as much in a lapidary statement about the creative power of language, in which one hears a faint biblical echo: "Give me one single word, and I will re-create the universe."[28] His Spiralist novels, beginning with *Mûr à crever*, may be considered stages in his quest for the right formula by means of which he could conjure up the world in its boundless complexity. *Dézafi* signals the success of this quest inasmuch as this emblematic Kreyòl novel epitomizes the Spiralist worldview, re-creating the Haitian material and social reality in its essential chaotic complexity, in the very language in which that reality is constructed and experienced. To some extent, it even seems that the Spiralist novel could best have been written in Kreyòl, for the language itself is inherently Spiralist in its allusiveness and precision, circumlocution and directness, ellipsis and completeness, earthiness and abstractness. Thus through the Kreyòl language, with its discourse full of *dits* and *non-dits* and with its unique capacity to depict the visible and to allude to the invisible, Frankétienne's Spiralist novel taps directly into the Haitian imaginary and narrates the collective reality without translation, without mediation. It is precisely because his writings reproduce structurally and semantically the very Spiralist essence of Kreyòl, and the very Haitian way of seeing and narrating the world embodied in the language, that Frankétienne justly merits the status of national writer.

Frankétienne first wrote in the national language at a rather advanced stage in his career, however. He had already published seven works in French before he penned *Dézafi*. This is quite understandable, for even today, notwithstanding a spike in Kreyòl publications in the 1970s and 1980s, French is the preferred literary language of Haitian authors. Subject like everyone else to the effects of the colonial experience, most aspiring Haitian writers consider French a more prestigious language, one moreover that would deliver their writings to a wider national and international readership than could the language of the Haitian masses. Another reason for most writers' preference for French is that they have internalized the French literary models, to which education and reading habits had conditioned them. They are therefore more conversant with French literary esthetics than with Kreyòl poetics. One further reason for the relative dearth of Kreyòl authors may well be that writing in the Haitian vernacular is a daunting technical challenge for most. For the French-educated middle-class writer, creating in Kreyòl would involve overcoming ingrained linguistic habits and switching from a Kreyòl characterized by a Frenchified diction and a French syntax to a deep Kreyòl with its sui generis lexicon, syntax, and image-making techniques. It is a step which most are unable to take because they have not mastered the language of the masses sufficiently to use it for literary expression. As the poet Georges Castera, a self-described bilingual writer very much conscious of the difficulties of literary creation in the language, asserts, "Kreyòl writing is still a work in progress; one writes in a written language that is yet to be fully constructed."[29] Nevertheless, there does exist a Kreyòl literary corpus going back to colonial Saint-Domingue as well as a vibrant and robust oral tradition from which writers determined to create in the vernacular can draw inspiration in order to construct a full-fledged literary language.

A number of anthologists and literary scholars, notably Jean-Claude Bajeux in his *Anthologie de la littérature créole haïtienne* (Anthology of Haitian Creole literature) and Maximilien Laroche in his *L'avènement de la littérature haïtienne* (The advent of Haitian literature) have chronicled the historical development of Haitian Kreyòl literature, showcased its productions, identified the representative works in the two-centuries-old corpus, and researched its defining characteristics.[30] Between the earliest written text in Kreyòl, the poem "La chanson de Lisette," also known as "Lisette quitté la plaine" (1757), attributed to the Saint-Domingue French planter Duvivier de la Mahautière, and Frankétienne's *Dézafi* and Kreyòl plays, there has been a constant if sporadic flow of writings in the vernacular, with production spiking in response to the political and cultural zeitgeist, as it did during the 1940s and during the 1970s and 1980s, decades of popular struggle for democracy and social justice.

Short of an exhaustive inventory, it is worthwhile to highlight the signpost writings that punctuate the development of Kreyòl literature. Such notable works include the nineteenth-century poet Oswald Durand's famous poem "Choucoune" (1883); Georges

Sylvain's collection of fables, *Cric? Crac! Fables de La Fontaine racontées par un montagnard haïtien et transcrites en vers créoles* (1901), Haitian versions of the French fabulist La Fontaine's works; translations and adaptations of classic European dramatic works such as Franck Fouché's *Oedipe-Roi* (1955) and *Yerma* (1956); Félix Morisseau-Leroy's collection of poems *Diacoute* (1953), and his Kreyòl version of *Antigone* (1954); Emile Roumer's French-inflected Kreyòl series of sonnets, *Rosaire Couronne Sonnets* (1964); and a number of creative works, amid the political tracts and the explosion of Kreyòl in the mass media in the 1970s and 1980s, including Émile Célestin-Mégie's *Lanmou pa gin baryè* (1975). Also usually included in the Kreyòl canon are literary creations, such as the radio plays of the comedian Théodore Beaubrun, also known as Languichatte, who delighted listeners for a half century, from the 1940s to the early 1990s, and the *lodyans* tales of the storyteller Maurice Sixto in the 1980s. These works of popular theater and traditional *lodyans* reached a vast public thanks to their dissemination in audio forms as recordings or as radio broadcasts. Some scholars, among them Maximilien Laroche, consider the corpus of oral tradition, from the Bouki and Malis folktales to the myths, proverbs, aphorisms, Vodou songs, and secular songs, an integral part of the literature as well.[31] They aver that this rich oraliture embodies an indigenous literary esthetics and exemplifies Kreyòl poetics in its living, authentic form, in addition to providing Haitian writers with a semantic frame of reference, symbolic code, and linguistic instrument for modulating the French language. When all is said and done, however, as the poet Saint-John Kauss has pointed out at the end of a survey of Haitian literature in the vernacular, the Kreyòl literary corpus, compared to the number of works in French produced in two centuries, is relatively small, evidence that "Kreyòl was always, and still is, a language treated with contempt and neglected by Haitian intellectuals."[32]

Ultimately, neither the number of authors writing in the language nor the size of the existing corpus should matter much. What is of greater critical and historical interest, rather, is the evolution of the literature, the process by which it grew until it reached its mature expression in Frankétienne's *Dézafi*. At the heart of this process have been the efforts of successive generations of writers to define and master a distinctive Kreyòl poetics consistent with the genius of the language as practiced by its speakers, the "deep Creole" of the masses, in George Lang's phrase.[33] This is a language which, in its folk register, is unmoored from its original French roots phonetically, syntactically, and lexically, with its distinctive rhythm and lilt, and its sui generis social and cultural referent. Kreyòl literature evolved as a result of writers' application of creative strategies and rhetorical techniques that would distance their texts from French literary models and bring them closer to, and more in harmony with, the esthetics of deep Kreyòl. It is rather interesting to note that this process of crafting the language into a performing instrument of literary creation is parallel to the historic evolution of the orthography of Kreyòl from a virtually French spelling, through a system consciously signaling the French etymology, to the pragmatic phonetic spelling that has been current since 1980. Maximilien Laroche, in *L'avènement de la littérature haïtienne;* George Lang, in "A Primer of Haitian Literature in Kreyòl"; and Rafael Lucas, in "La littérarisation de la langue haïtienne" have analyzed at great length this process of harmonization of literary Kreyòl with deep Kreyòl through the gradual distancing of Kreyòl texts away from French poetics, a process that can readily be mapped through a critical reading of representative texts from "Lisette quitté la plaine" down to the works of twenty-first-century authors.

Frankétienne himself has been quite aware of what it takes to produce literary texts in Kreyòl that are respectful of its poetics and that exploit the immanent connection between the language and Haitian reality. In an interview with Ulrich Fleischman, a scholar of Haitian literature, the author explains that only a mastery of the specificities of Kreyòl and a thorough appropriation of the very spirit of the language will enable the writer to create a work with any degree of authenticity in content and form, with any literary esthetic value: "Kreyòl is the language where Haitians find their roots. The masks drop; reality reveals itself, surges, naked. And if you wish to embrace this reality, you too must be stark naked, but with what I would call a concern for esthetics. And it is in this regard that Haitian writers who create in Kreyòl have much to do. As Haitians writing in Kreyòl, we must not open ourselves up to the facile critiques, to the destructive critiques of those who say that Kreyòl does not lend itself to an elevated esthetic expression."[34]

Dézafi is the product of its author's profound awareness of the autonomy of Kreyòl and of the obligation incumbent upon the writer to create within the parameters of its sui generis esthetics to be found in the language as spoken by the masses. As Franketienne emphasizes, he "wrote *Dézafi* from the perspective of a reading of Haitian reality by the Haitian people, the peasant masses."[35] Thus, building upon the achievements of a long line of predecessors, especially of such craftsmen of Kreyòl as Franck Fouché and Félix Morisseau-Leroy, and in dialogue with the masses in their own idiom, with *Dézafi* Franketienne completed the process of what critic Rafael Lucas calls the *"littérarisation"* of the Haitian vernacular,[36] the consecration of Kreyòl as a mature literary language, an achievement as significant as Dante's transformation of Italian into a nimble instrument of literary creation.

DÉZAFI, OR THE NATURALIZATION OF HAITIAN LITERATURE

Upon the publication of *Dézafi*, Franketienne's peers and literary critics saluted the novel as a signal achievement and spotlighted its implications for the development of Haitian literature and, in a larger context, for the literatures of the Americas. Thus, for George Lang, *"Dézafi* . . . is the unrivaled masterpiece in the language and certainly among the great literary achievements in any Creole."[37] Martinican authors Patrick Chamoiseau and Raphaël Confiant, the two major figures of the *créolité* movement,[38] opined that with Franketienne's novel, "Creolophone literature is going to find its *lettres de noblesse*."[39] In Jean Jonassaint's view, Franketienne is, as "a poet, novelist, playwright, one of the rare authors to write with both strength and felicity in two great Caribbean languages, French and Haitian [Kreyòl]."[40] For Maximilien Laroche,

"Franketienne's work will transcend his time."[41] An avant-garde text with great disruptive power, *Dézafi* stands at the intersection of the past and the future of Haitian literature. It would not be an exaggeration to say that the timeline of the formation of Haitian literature, in both French and Kreyòl, may be divided into two major segments, a pre-*Dézafi* period and a post-*Dézafi* period.

A magical blend of myth, poetry, allegory, and social realism, *Dézafi* is, by critical consensus, a unique work in the canon of Haitian literature, indeed of Caribbean letters. Interweaving realistic narrative, poetic interludes, Vodou iconography, typographical coding, calligraphy, and other Spiralist markers, the novel tells a story that revolves around the phenomenon of zombification. It chronicles the struggle of the inhabitants of the village of Bouanèf to liberate themselves from the murderous oppression of the *oungan*[42] Sintil and dramatizes the return to life and freedom of Sintil's band of *zonbi*, who rebel under the leadership of Klodonis, one of the *oungan*'s prized *zonbi*. This core plot unfolds in short cuts punctuated by dramatic scenes of the *dézafi,* the cockfight tournament that takes place in the village over several days. The action moves at intervals from the rural setting of Bouanèf and Ravin Sèch to the city of Port-au-Prince in the house of Jédéyon and his little housemaid Rita and in the seaport neighborhood where Bouanèf native son Gaston tries to earn a living. Eschewing the twin traps of folklorization and idealization, the novel evokes realistically yet with great economy the works and days of both peasant and urban masses, their trials and tribulations, and their efforts to overcome the constraints imposed upon them by both an unequal society and an often unkind nature that visits upon them hurricanes, droughts, and floods. Generally informed by an intimate familiarity with the social realities, myths, belief systems, social rituals and practices, symbolic code, historical narratives, and landscapes that form the rich Haitian semantic tapestry, *Dézafi* conflates two significant elements of Haitian popular culture, the *zonbi* and cockfighting, to tell a story about oppression, struggle, and liberation in a novel that is both a work of political and social commentary and a philosophical reflection on life and death, on oppression and freedom, on love and death, on language and the liberating power of speech, and on man's struggle with nature and with his fellow humans. A storyteller sans pareil, a keen observer and deft recorder of the collective experience, the author of *Dézafi* is, among all contemporary Haitian writers, as T. S. Eliot calls Ezra Pound in his dedication of *The Waste Land,* "il miglior fabbro." As students of his Kreyòl oeuvre know, Franketienne is a master craftsman of the word from whose prolific pen flow with deceptive ease imaginative neologisms, transporting alliterations, arresting puns, and vertigo-inducing magical-realist images. In *Dézafi,* as he does later in such plays as *Pèlin-tèt* and *Bobomasouri* (1986), he mines with dizzying virtuosity all the unique qualities of Kreyòl, putting into play the allusiveness, circumlocution, pithiness, musicality, and rhythmic syncopation inherent in the language to create a polyphonic text of inebriating poetry. With its polysemous *andaki* language,[43] its overlapping and yet separate multiple narrative voices, its panoptical plural points of view, its spiral-like structure built around repetitions and reiterations, its varying rhythms and moods, *Dézafi* is the Spiralist novel par excellence in its imaginative representation of the complex chaos that is the world, the site of man's ceaseless struggle for the triumph of life over death.

TRANSLATING *DÉZAFI*

As suggested earlier, language as the principle of creation and the power of language to represent reality form the conceptual foundation of *Dézafi.*[44] The distinctive mark of the *zonbi,* what sets him apart from living humanity, being his inability to speak, the novel may be seen as a chronicle of the recapture and reconstruction of language. In Franketienne's perspective, the very language in which he pens the novel, Kreyòl, by its very nature, would be the most fit instrument for representing the Spiralist view of the world as the site where chaos contends with order and life with death, that informs the narrative. This premise posits a significant challenge for the translator in view of the essential differences between English and Kreyòl. To highlight the most obvious, the two languages differ in terms of their respective syntax, rhythm, sonority, word formation, and image-making techniques. And of course the two tongues have different symbolic codes and semantic reference frames, which are welded to the respective history and culture of their speakers. The poetics of English, particularly modern English with its insistence on precision and conciseness, on denotation over connotation, on directness over circumlocution, are sufficiently familiar to speakers of the language, so it is not necessary to expatiate at length on its defining traits. Before I initiated the translation of *Dézafi,* however, I found it imperative to reflect on the characteristics of the Haitian vernacular.

Kreyòl is the vernacular of a high-context culture, a speech characterized by willful indirectness, intentional polysemy, and crafted imprecision. It is an essentially poetic language whose speakers and listeners are forever engaged in parsing and interpreting. This characteristic of the language is evidently rooted in its origin in the colonial plantation, where its creators, the enslaved Africans of Saint-Domingue, forged it into a superb instrument of marronage, perfecting the art of naming and not naming, of saying and not saying. Imprecision and polysemy are not the only traits that differentiate Kreyòl from English, however. Thus, the euphonious sounds and rolling rhythms of the Haitian tongue, with its lilt and musicality harking to its West African roots, distance Kreyòl from English, with its often staccato-like delivery. Finally, as is the case for all languages, the semantics of Kreyòl are rooted in the culture, the history, and the material environment of its speakers. Consequently, the text of *Dézafi,* which refers to the works and days of the Haitian rural and urban masses, to the Vodou religion, to Haitian secular and sacred myths, and to the folk tradition, should pose no comprehension problem for the culturally literate Haitian reader. For someone unfamiliar with Haiti, however, or without the requisite cultural literacy, the meaning of certain phrases or images might not be evident, and some allusions might be undecipherable altogether.

In addition to these concerns arising from the very nature of Kreyòl, as a translator I had to consider the idiosyncrasies of Frankétienne's style. His already rich vocabulary, mined from the vast lexicon of deep Kreyòl, is further enriched with neologisms, which a native speaker might intuitively grasp but which a non-native speaker might find puzzling. In addition to his propensity for coining neologisms, Franketienne is extremely fond of word-plays, alliterations, assonances, and unusual metaphors, which would be rather difficult to render in English. With these considerations in mind, I found it necessary to think up strategies and techniques for making the English language do elegantly what Kreyòl does naturally, consistent with Walter Benjamin's description of the task of the translator as "finding the particular intention toward the target language which produces in that language the echo of the original."[45] Keeping in mind what Benjamin calls "the kinship between languages,"[46] with an eye on possible overlaps, parallels, and convergences between the two tongues, I sought then to produce an English version of *Dézafi* that, without sounding stilted or exotic, would echo the deep Kreyòl of the original. Such a strategic approach obviously precludes slavish fidelity to the Kreyòl text, for, to evoke Jorge Luis Borges's ironic observation on the inverted nature of translation, "The original is not faithful to the translation."[47]

While the views of Benjamin and Borges on translation served me as a reliable guide throughout the entire process of translating *Dézafi,* on three specific occasions I found them most invaluable in resolving a particularly thorny translation problem. Here is a first instance in which I found it best to betray Franketienne's text in a Borgesian manner. Among the many leitmotivs in the novel there is the recurring alliterative and symbolic juxtaposition of the two words *lanmou* and *lanmò.* This is a powerful pairing in Kreyòl, which dramatizes the archetypal connection between love and death, *eros* and *thanatos,* thanks to the closeness in sound of the two quasi-homonyms. Finding a similar pairing in English, one with the same coincidence or near overlap of sound and sense capable of evoking the same archetypal connection between these two concepts, proved impossible. No synonyms of these two words could be found in English that could achieve the same effect as the two original Kreyòl words. In the end I had to settle for the two simple words "love" and "death," which meet the criterion of sense but not that of sound and sense at the same time. There is a slight stylistic loss, even though the pairing of love and death does express conceptually the Freudian linkage between the two. Compromises of this sort are sometimes forced on the translator by the structural (both semantic and formal) limits inherent in the different natures of the source and target languages.

The different natures of Kreyòl and English could not be reconciled in one significant aspect of *Dézafi*. As pointed out earlier, one of the defining elements of the novel is its use of multiple narrators and diverse narrative points of view. Events and settings are narrated and viewed not only by the usual omniscient narrator but also by a multitude of anonymous actors and witnesses whose fragmented reports cohere into a single story. It takes a village to tell a story, and among the multitude of village voices, the most audible throughout the novel is the first-person-plural narrator. This first-person-plural narrator in Kreyòl is "*nou*," which in the language stands variously for "we," "you," "I," or "they," depending on the context. The use of this plural pronoun as the principal narrator reinforces one essential notion underpinning the narrative, which is that as experience is collective, the relation of experience is also collective. While the Kreyòl pronoun "*nou*" semantically fuses the voices of narrator, actors, witnesses, and audience, the English pronoun "we" does not achieve such a fusion of persons and perspectives. Yet, I had to settle for "we" as the only possible translation of the polysemous Kreyòl "*nou*," an unfortunate loss.

But there are times when a problem arising from differences between the two languages calls for a creative solution that respects the genius of the original tongue while being consistent with the esthetics of the language of translation. Here is another occasion when I had to betray the original and find a creative solution to a translation quandary. The many wordplays in *Dézafi* are always evocative of a theme, making a semantic and symbolic point in the unfolding narrative. While some wordplays can be replicated successfully, with the sound and sense preserved in translation, others less so. Such is the case with the tongue twister, a category of wordplay that relies for its effect and effectiveness on sound, pronunciation, rhythm, a slightly absurd or humorous sense, and cultural context. In one of those key passages in the novel where Frankétienne indicates a shift in the plot and in the scale and tonality of the narrative, a shift signaled typographically as well, appears a Kreyòl tongue twister. Probably harking back to the 1940s, when yaws, or pian, as the disease is more rarely called, was endemic in Haiti's countryside, the phrase has been the delight of Haitian children for generations: "Anba plapié frè Piè plin pian."[48] The literal translation, the rather flat sentence, "The soles of brother Peter's feet are full of yaws," is obviously unsatisfactory; the meaning is true, but it is not a tongue twister. At the spot where it occurs in the novel, this tongue twister has a structural function, marking a turning point in the narrative. It also serves as a thematic and symbolic signaling device, as it is built around the foot motif scattered throughout the novel in the form of expressions such as *pié poudré* (dusty feet), or embodied in the wandering characters Gaston and the inseparable pair Filo-jèn and Kamélo. A literal translation of the tongue twister sans alliteration and assonance would still keep its structural role as well as semantic function intact, but it would not be stylistically true to the original. After having looked in vain for an appropriate substitute in a half-dozen collections of English tongue twisters and browsed with increasing frustration through hundreds of tongue twisters built around "foot," searching for some that might contain the word "yaws," I resolved to betray the Kreyòl text and to produce an entirely new English tongue twister with the poetic truth of the original. Translation is both *prise de possession* and *crise de possession*. At some point the translator must own the text, and at the same time, while not replacing the author, he must allow himself to become possessed by the author's spirit as the Vodouist is possessed by a *lwa* and then speaks and behaves as the *lwa*. I asked myself then what sort of tongue twister would Frankétienne have written at this particular spot in *Dézafi* had he been writing in English. The tongue-twisting sentence would have to be composed of monosyllabic words, have the same cadence as the original, approximate its sounds, and resonate culturally. I grant that my tongue twister, "Bro Piè's pian plagued flat feet bleed blood," is not a literal translation of the original

"Anba plapié frè Piè plin pian," but it is an invention in the style of Franketienne and in the spirit of the Kreyòl language, a most apt re-creation that works. It works because it is mildly nonsensical as tongue twisters are; it is built around the recurring foot leitmotiv, managing to keep the reference to yaws, too; the name "Bro Piè" is culturally resonant, "brother" being a common mode of address and Piè (or Pierre) a good Haitian name; it reproduces a very Kreyòl expression, *senyen san*, "to bleed blood"; it combines alliteration and assonance; it keeps its structural function, marking a twist in the plot; and it serves as a thematic signaling device.

In addition to these decisions bearing directly on the language of the text, I made a number of choices that are somewhat ancillary but still very germane to the translation. First, I should like to point out that for this English translation I worked with the historic first edition of *Dézafi* published in Port-au-Prince by Dieudonné Fardin in 1975 rather than with the updated 2002 *Dezafi* published in France, which differs from the Fardin edition notably in the modified typographical architecture, the spatial distribution of the text, a number of textual additions, and the elision of the graphic in the last part of the novel that combines text and a cross evocative of a Vodou *vèvè* and of the esoteric significance of the crossroads. The first edition follows the Kreyòl spelling system current at the time, one that was closer to French orthography, whereas the text of the 2002 edition uses the standardized phonetic spelling in place since 1980. I have maintained the orthography of the 1975 text for the Kreyòl words kept in the English translation out of a concern for historical consistency. I have also chosen to keep the original Kreyòl title for a similar reason, especially as its literal translation as "cockfight" or "cockfight tournament" lacks the cultural resonance of the Kreyòl term.

Besides the title *Dézafi*, I have also kept a number of words in their original Kreyòl form because they have no English equivalent or because they are so bound up with the narrative and have such sociocultural resonance that translating them would do a disservice to the story. Such words as *potomitan, oungan, ason, péréstil,* and others are not translated; they are defined or explained in the glossary. In any case, their meaning can be deduced or intuited from the story. In one particular case, I have used French words because they might be more recognizable to readers than their Kreyòl equivalents. Thus, I refer to iconic place-names or landmarks with which both Kreyòl speakers and foreigners are familiar by their customary historic French designation. For example, I felt no need to Creolize Port-au-Prince, l'Hôpital Mountain, Croix-Bossales market, Sacré-Coeur church, Saint-Marc, or La Gonave Island. In contrast, I have retained in the original Kreyòl the settings of the novel—Bouanèf, Ravin Sèch, real but obscure locales, unknown outside the novel but such an integral part of the narrative. Similarly, the novel's characters and mythological or folk figures (Lasirèn, Grinn Pronminnin, Tèt-san-kò) have retained their Kreyòl names. Sometimes the latter are used as metaphors or semantic shorthand, as they often are in everyday speech; in such cases I have translated them literally or used the Kreyòl original and provided the English equivalent in apposition. One such case is the folk figure known as Grinn Pronminnin, literally "wandering seed." When the two characters Kamélo and Filojèn are referred to as "grinn pronminnin,"[49] obviously the name of the folk figure is being used as a metaphor meaning "wanderers," "vagabonds," that is, "wandering seeds." In one other instance, though, the reference is clearly to the folk personage, and so he is given his customary Kreyòl appellation.[50]

It is not superfluous, at this point, to specify that the novel translated here is not *Les affres d'un défi*, Frankétienne's French recreation of *Dézafi*. This *mise au point* is necessary because the two works are sometimes confused, and the assumption that the French text is but a translation of the Kreyòl work is not uncommon. Notwithstanding the identical plot, settings, and cast of characters, and the French title that vaguely recalls that of the Kreyòl novel, the two works are distinct. Besides the fact that different poetics inform the composition of each, *Les affres d'un défi* contains textual additions, elisions, and typographical arrangements that define it as an autonomous creation rather than a mere translation. In this regard, in a two-sentence preface to *Les affres d'un défi*, Frankétienne insists that his French novel be received as a wholly original work, a stand-alone text: "Issued from the fertile and burning matrix of *Dézafi*, this work must not be approached as a translation of that Kreyòl novel. *Les affres d'un défi* represents an authentic creation in the author's adventurous literary journey, a new experience in his unending quest through the vast forests of poetry and art."[51]

My personal resources alone would not have sufficed to meet all the challenges in completing this translation of *Dézafi*, and my wisdom and experience would not have been enough to guide me in all my choices. In a translation project, collaboration is always to be preferred to working in isolation, as the translators of the Greek classics during the golden age of Islam and the scholars responsible for the King James English version of the Bible remind us. In translating *Dézafi*, therefore, I actively sought the counsel of several people conversant with Frankétienne's oeuvre, with the Kreyòl language, and with Haitian culture. Thus, I frequently consulted Frankétienne himself and his wife, Marie-Andrée, who always made themselves available to clarify particularly difficult or obscure words or phrases. I also relied on the insights of the Haitian scholars Jean Jonassaint and Maximilien Laroche, *de regrettée mémoire,* unequaled exegetes of Frankétienne's writings. Finally, I received invaluable help from such speakers of deep Kreyòl as my late mother, Anneceé Guillaume, and the passionate promoter of the language Baba Yaw. Ultimately, though, the translator like the author is responsible for his text, so I assume whatever defects may be found in this translation and absolve all my generous collaborators and consultants. For the possibility that "the original is unfaithful to the translation," Frankétienne cannot of course be faulted. Yet, I assure both the author and the readers of the Kreyòl masterpiece out of Haiti that, like the poet to Cynara,[52] I have been faithful to *Dézafi,* in my fashion. Given that "all translation is only a somewhat provisional way of coming to terms with the foreignness of language,"[53] and that each generation deserves its own version of a great work, my hope is that this first published translation of *Dézafi* will be followed by many other betrayals into

English as well as other languages, thus ensuring the perennity of this Haitian and Caribbean classic novel.

Asselin Charles
Toronto, 26 October 2017

NOTES

1. Linguists and foreigners refer to the Haitian vernacular as Creole or Haitian Creole, and nationalist promoters of the language call it Haitian. Native speakers customarily call their mother tongue Kreyòl.

2. "Haiti's most innovative writer": *Dixit* the Haitian poet Rodney Saint-Eloi, qtd. in Peras, "Frankétienne," par. 12; "most innovative writer in the world": ibid.; "one of those giants": Jonassaint, ed., "Frankétienne, écrivain haïtien," 7.

3. The dictatorial regime of the Duvaliers, father and son, lasted from 1957 to 1986.

4. See Jean Jonassaint's comprehensive study of the most representative of these émigré writers, *Le pouvoir des mots, les maux du pouvoir* (Paris: Éditions de l'Arcantère, 1986).

5. Jonassaint, ed., "Frankétienne, écrivain haïtien."

6. Frankétienne was designated a UNESCO Artist for Peace in March 2010 and made a Commander of the Ordre des Arts et Lettres by the French government in 2010.

7. Frankétienne, *The Noose (Pèlin-tèt)*, trans. Asselin Charles, in *Metamorphoses* 11, no. 1 (Spring 2003): 141–70.

8. Frankétienne, *Ready to Burst,* trans. Kaiama L. Glover. According to Archipelago Books, the release of the translation of *Ultravocal* is slated for 2018 (see the publisher's website: https://archipelagobooks.org/book/ultravocal/).

9. *Dézafi* was the first Kreyòl novel published apparently because the publication of Émile Célestin-Mégie's novel *Lanmou pa gin baryè,* written earlier, was delayed. *Dézafi* was brought out in August 1975, whereas *Lanmou pa gin baryè* was released by Fardin in October 1975 (see Marc-Yves Volcy, "De Franck à Frankétienne: Fragments de mémoire fraternelle," in *Typo/Topo/Poéthique sur Frankétienne,* ed. Jean Jonassaint [Paris: L'Harmattan, 2008], 181).

10. Jonassaint, ed., special issue on Frankétienne, *Journal of Haitian Studies*; Douglas, *Frankétienne and Rewriting; Glover, Haiti Unbound.*

11. A *lwa* is a Vodou spirit or deity.

12. Dieudonné Fardin, "Prezantasion," in Frankétienne, *Dézafi* (1975), 8.

13. Lang, "A Primer of Haitian Literature in 'Kreyòl,'" 137.

14. "une fluidité atavique de la langue" (my translation). Edouard Glissant qtd. in Gauvin, "L'imaginaire des langues," 16.

15. "[J]e suis profondément, et ce n'est pas de la démagogie, un Nègre haïtien. . . . Eh bien moi, quand je dis qu'Haïti m'a tout donné, cela signifie que l'écrivain a été moulé, formé, modelé par cette terre, par la vie quotidienne faite de douleurs, de joies, de mythes, de mensonges, de mythomanies, de tout" (my translation). Frankétienne qtd. in Tegomo, "Je me suis toujours défini comme un nègre avec la peau à l'envers," 211.

16. Thumboo, ed., *The Second Tongue*; Peras, "Frankétienne," par. 18.

17. "J'ai découvert la musicalité de cette langue: il y avait des mots tendres, des mots doux, des mots violents, des mots acides, sucrés . . . C'est pourquoi mon contact avec les mots—qui peut étonner les gens, ceux qui croient que je suis au septième ciel—est un contact physique, concret et sensuel" (my translation). Frankétienne qtd. in Peras, "Frankétienne," par. 18.

18. "[J]e me suis rendu compte que j'allais adopter cette même attitude, ce même rapport avec ma propre langue, parce que les textes créoles présentent autant de difficultés que le français. Avec L'oiseau schizophone, je me suis rendu compte que je ne pouvais pas me permettre de traiter ma langue maternelle comme si c'était un champ libre où j'aurais la possibilité de pondre des débilités. Non, il faut avoir le respect de sa langue" (my translation). Frankétienne qtd. ibid., par. 22.

19. Frankétienne qtd. ibid., par. 24.

20. Thumboo, ed., *The Second Tongue,* ix.

21. Laroche, "*Dézafi* après Duvalier."

22. For a concise history of Haïti Littéraire, see Phelps, "Haïti Littéraire."

23. For a summary of the group's views on literature, see Anthony Phelps, "Haïti Littéraire." For analyses of the works of Davertige, Philoctète, and Phelps, see Gouraige et al., *Littérature et société en Haïti.*

24. Phelps, "Haïti Littéraire," pt. 3.

25. "Donc, la spirale par son mouvement d'ouverture, de va-et-vient, de palpitation dans tous les sens, représente le mouvement de la vie. De plus, elle avance. Il y a une progression dans le sens de la largeur autant que dans le sens de la hauteur. Plusieurs théoriciens l'ont déjà dit: si on prend le fameux exemple du grain d'orge, dans l'Anti-Dühring, qui tombe dans un sol fertile, réunissant les conditions climatologiques pour la germination. Ce grain d'orge donne une petite plante, qui grandit, devient un arbuste, devient un arbre et l'arbre à son tour donne des milliers et des milliers de grains d'orge. Le point central c'est qu'on est parti d'un point qui est le grain d'orge. Mais le grain d'orge qui dans un mouvement spiraloide revient au grain d'orge, avec un dépassement: ce n'est pas un seul grain d'orge, mais une infinité" (my translation). Frankétienne qtd. in Fleischmann, "Entrevue avec Frankétienne sur son roman Dézafi," 23.

26. "une typo/topographie différentielle et signifiante" (my translation). Jonassaint, "Frankétienne: Une introduction," 14.

27. For a study of Frankétienne's art and the connection between Spiralisme and his paintings, see Jonassaint, "Beyond Painting or Writing."

28. "Donnez-moi un seul mot et je recrée l'univers" (my translation). Frankétienne qtd. in Tsunekawa, "Portrait d'un charmeur haïtien hors gabarit," 156.

29. "L'écrit créole est toujours un écrit en construction, dans une langue écrite à construire" (my translation). Castera, "De la difficulté d'écrire en créole," 6.

30. Bajeux, ed., Anthologie de la littérature créole haïtienne; Laroche, L'avènement de la littérature haïtienne.

31. Laroche, L'avènement de la littérature haïtienne, 59–62. Malis, a trickster character, and Bouki, his eternal victim, are the inseparable protagonists of a cycle of traditional folktales.

32. "Tout cela prouve que depuis toujours le créole fut et est une langue 'méprisée' et négligée par les intellectuels haïtiens" (my translation). Kauss, "La poésie haïtienne d'expression créole," 2.

33. Lang, "A Primer of Haitian Literature in 'Kreyòl,'" 137.

34. "Le créole est la langue où l'Haïtien retrouve ses racines. Les masques tombent, c'est la réalité toute nue qui apparaît, qui surgit, et vous aussi, pour accueillir cette réalité, il faut que vous soyez tout nu, mais avec ce que je pourrais appeler le souci esthétique. Et c'est là qu'il y a beaucoup à faire pour les écrivains qui écrivent en créole. Nous ne devons pas, nous Haïtiens qui écrivons en créole, prêter le flanc aux critiques faciles, aux critiques destructives qui disent que le créole ne se prête pas à une expression esthétique élevée" (my translation). Frankétienne qtd. in Fleischmann, "Entrevue avec Frankétienne sur son roman Dézafi," 20–21.

35. "écrit Dézafi dans la perspective d'une lecture de la réalité haïtienne par le peuple haïtien, les masses paysannes" (my translation). Frankétienne qtd. ibid., 22.

36. Lucas, "La littérarisation de la langue haïtienne."

37. Lang, "A Primer of Haitian Literature in 'Kreyòl,'" 137.

38. Créolité is a literary movement that held sway in the 1980s among Francophone writers from Martinique and Guadeloupe who sought to define and assert an identity grounded in the Caribbean, in opposition to the earlier Negritude conception of an identity rooted in Africa.

39. "La littérature créolophone . . . va trouver ses lettres de noblesse" (my translation). Chamoiseau and Confiant qtd. in Jonassaint, "Frankétienne: Une introduction," 16.

40. " . . . est un de ces géants qui ont marqué et marqueront les littératures américaines. Poète, romancier, dramaturge, l'un des rares à écrire avec force et bonheur dans deux grandes langues littéraires caraïbéennes: le français et l'haïtien" (my translation). Jonassaint, ed., "Frankétienne, écrivain Haïtien," 7.

41. "[L]'oeuvre de Frankétienne transcendera son époque" (my translation). Laroche, *"Dézafi* après Duvalier," 97.

42. An *oungan* is a priest of the Vodou religion. Some, like the novel's character, misuse their power and knowledge to do harm.

43. *Andaki* is a register of Kreyòl whereby the speaker makes use of circumlocutions, allusions, proverbs, and other discursive misdirections to craft a message to be understood by the person for whom it is intended and not by others, but with plausible deniability on the part of the speaker.

44. See Frankétienne's previously quoted statement, "Give me one single word, and I will re-create the universe," in Tsunekawa, "Portrait d'un charmeur haïtien hors gabarit," 156.

45. Benjamin, "The Task of the Translator," 258.

46. Ibid., 256.

47. "El original es infiel a la traducción" (my translation). Borges, "Sobre el Vathek de William Beckford" (1943).

48. *Dézafi* (1975), 218.

49. For example, the term is used metaphorically in the sentence, "Kamélo ak Filojèn pi rèd pasé grinn pronminnin," in *Dézafi* (1975), 28. It is appropriately translated thus: "Kamélo and Filojèn are worse than wandering seeds."

50. Such is the case in this sentence, "Nou gin dizon ak grinn pronminnin," in *Dézafi* (1975), 270. It is appropriately rendered as, "We have an understanding with Grinn Pronminnin."

51. "Issue de la matrice féconde et toute brûlante de 'Dézafi,' cette oeuvre ne doit pourtant pas être abordée comme une traduction de ce roman créole. Les Affres d'un défi représente une authentique creation dans l'aventure littéraire de l'auteur, une nouvelle experience dans son interminable quête à travers les vastes forêts de la poésie et de l'art" (my translation). Frankétienne, *Les affres d'un défi,* i.

52. The allusion here is to the well-known refrain, "I have been faithful to thee, Cynara! in my fashion," of Ernest Dowson's poem, "Non sum qualis eram bonae sub regno Cynarae."

53. Benjamin, "The Task of the Translator," 257.

BIBLIOGRAPHY

Bajeux, Jean-Claude, ed. *Anthologie de la littérature créole haïtienne.* Port-au-Prince: Éditions Antilla, 1999.

Benjamin, Walter. "The Task of the Translator." In *Selected Writings,* vol. 1, *1913–1926,* edited by Marcus Bullock and Michael W. Jennings, 253–63. Cambridge: Harvard University Press, 2002.

Berrou, Raphaël, and Pradel Pompilus. *Histoire de la littérature haïtienne illustrée par les textes.* Vol. 1. Port-au-Prince: Éditions Caraïbes, 1975.

————. *Histoire de la littérature haïtienne illustrée par les textes.* Vol. 2. Port-au-Prince: Éditions Caraïbes, 1976.

————. *Histoire de la littérature haïtienne illustrée par les textes.* Vol. 3. Port-au-Prince: Éditions Caraïbes, 1977.

Borges, Jorge Luis. "Sobre el Vathek de William Beckford" (1943). *Arte y Literatura Fantástica,* 24 May 2013. http://arteyliteraturafantastica.blogspot.ca/2013/05/sobre-el-vathek-de-william-beckford.html.

Castera, Georges. "De la difficulté d'écrire en créole." *Notre Librairie,* no. 143 (January–March 2001): 6–13.

Célestin-Mégie, Emile. *Lanmou pa gin baryè.* Port-au-Prince: Éditions Fardin, 1975.

Chalifour, Annik. "Frankétienne: 'Le monde est en panne de l'imaginaire.'" *L'Express,* 31 July 2012. http://l-express.ca/franketienne-le-monde-est-en-panne-de-limaginaire//

Chalmers, Mehdi, et al., eds. *Anthologie bilingue de la poésie créole haïtienne de 1986 à nos jours.* Brussels: Actes Sud/Atelier Jeudi Soir, 2015.

Courlander, Harold. *The Bordeaux Narrative.* Albuquerque: University of New Mexico Press, 1990.

Douglas, Rachel. *Frankétienne and Rewriting: A Work in Progress.* New York: Lexington, 2009.

Fleischmann, Ulrich. "Entrevue avec Frankétienne sur son roman Dézafi." *Dérives,* no. 7 (1977): 17–25.

Frankétienne. *Les affres d'un défi.* Port-au-Prince: Imprimerie Henri Deschamps, 1984.

————. *Bobomasouri.* Port-au-Prince: Kolèksyon Espiral, 1986.

————. *Dézafi.* Port-au-Prince: Éditions Fardin, 1975.

————. *Kaselezo* (Kreyòl version, 1985). In special issue on Frankétienne, *Journal of Haitian Studies* 14, no. 1 (2008): 171–230.

————. *Mûr à crever.* Port-au-Prince: Presses port-au-princiennes, 1968.

————. *The Noose.* Translated by Asselin Charles. In *Metamorphoses* 1, no. 1 (2003): 141–70.

————. *L'oiseau schizophone.* 1st ed. Port-au-Prince: Éditions des Antilles, 1993.

————. *Pèlin-tèt.* Port-au-Prince: Éditions du Soleil, 1978.

————. *Ready to Burst.* Translated by Kaiama L. Glover. New York: Archipelago, 2014.

————. *Ultravocal.* Port-au-Prince: Imprimerie Serge L. Gaston, 1972.

Gauvin, Lise. "L'imaginaire des langues: Entretien avec Edouard Glissant." *Etudes françaises,* nos. 282–83 (1992): 11–22.

Glover, Kaiama L. *Haiti Unbound: A Spiralist Challenge to the Postcolonial Canon.* Liverpool: Liverpool University Press, 2010.

Gouraige, Ghislain, Maximilien Laroche, Maurice Lubin, and Claude Souffrant. *Littérature et société en Haïti: Davertige, Philoctète, Phelps.* Montréal: Éditions du CIDIHCA, 1987.

Jean, Eddy Arnold. *Pour une littérature haïtienne nationale et militante.* Lille, France: Éditions Jacques Soleil, 1975.

Jonassaint, Jean. "Beyond Painting or Writing: Franketienne's Poetic Quest." *Research in African Literatures* 35, no. 2 (2004): 141–56.

———. "Franketienne, écrivain haïtien." Special issue, *Dérives,* nos. 53–54 (1986/87): 5–12.

———. "Franketienne: Une introduction." In *Typo/Topo/Poéthique sur Franketienne,* edited by Jonassaint, 11–21. Paris: L'Harmattan, 2008.

———, ed. Special issue on Franketienne, *Journal of Haitian Studies* 14, no. 1 (2008).

Kauss, Saint-John. "La poésie haïtienne d'expression créole." *Potomitan.* PDF. 24 April 2014. www.potomitan.info/kauss/kauss_poesie.pdf

Lang, George. "A Primer of Haitian Literature in 'Kreyòl.'" *Research in African Literatures* 35, no. 2 (2004): 128–40.

Laroche, Maximilien. *L'avènement de la littérature haïtienne.* Québec: GRELCA No. 3, 1987.

———. "*Dézafi* après Duvalier." *Dérives,* nos. 53–54 (1986/87): 97–109.

Lucas, Rafael. "La littérarisation de la langue haïtienne." In *Typo/Topo/Poéthique sur Franketienne,* edited by Jean Jonassaint, 123–46. Paris: L'Harmattan, 2008.

Métraux, Alfred. *Voodoo in Haiti.* Translated by Hugo Charteris. New York: Schocken, 1972.

Morisseau-Leroy, Félix. "La littérature haïtienne d'expression créole—Son avenir." *Présence Africaine,* n.s., no. 17 (December 1957–January 1958): 46–59.

Paul, Emmanuel C. *Panorama du folklore haïtien.* Port-au-Prince: Imprimerie de l'Etat, 1962.

Peras, Delphine. "Franketienne: 'Je suis un survivant de la misère, des Duvalier, de l'alcool.'" *L'Express,* 16 July 2010. www.lexpress.fr/culture/livre /franketienne-je-suis-un-survivant-de-la-misere-des-duvalier-de-l-alcool _905765.html.

Phelps, Anthony. "Haïti Littéraire: Rupture et nouvel espace." *Île en île* (September 2006). http://ile-en-ile.org/anthony-phelps-haiti-litteraire/.

Planson, Claude. *Vaudou—Un initié parle.* Paris: Éditions J'ai Lu, 1974.

Romain, Jean-Baptiste. *Quelques mœurs et coutumes des paysans haïtiens.* Port-au-Prince: Imprimerie de l'Etat, 1959.

Tegomo, Guy. "Je me suis toujours défini comme un nègre avec la peau à l'envers: Une entrevue de Franketienne." In *Typo/Topo/Poéthique sur Franketienne,* edited by Jean Jonassaint, 201–17. Paris: L'Harmattan, 2008.

Thumboo, Edwin, ed. *The Second Tongue.* Singapore: Heinemann Educational, 1976.

Tsunekawa, Kunio. "Portrait d'un charmeur haïtien hors gabarit." In *Typo/Topo/Poéthique sur Frankétienne,* edited by Jean Jonassaint, 149–60. Paris: L'Harmattan, 2008.

FOREWORD TO THE FIRST EDITION

Ever since Christian Beaulieu sounded the rallying trumpet for the defense and illustration of the Kreyòl language, much has been said and written and many an initiative has been taken in order to reconcile the lives of the Haitian people with their reality.

Fifty years have gone by, and it is time to bring to a close the endless debates about the orthography of Kreyòl and about the very existence of a language spoken by ten million people. Such matters as the proper spelling of Kreyòl will be settled in due time.

When a small nation frees itself from the domination of more powerful states, its people come to realize there can be no political and economic liberation without cultural liberation. A people's language is intertwined with their life.

We must mine the riches of the Haitian language, show its potential as a written language, take it beyond its oral stage, and create an authentic written literature. Such is the mission to be assumed by those who support the Kreyòl language.

In writing *Dézafi*, the first novel composed in Kreyòl, Frankétienne has invented a brand-new language, and a vibrant, vigorous tongue is now abroad in the world.

Éditions Fardin is very proud to have midwifed this novel and considers it a great honor to publish *Dézafi*.

Frankétienne is a true son of Haiti, an authentic Haitian. This is his eighth book. Poet, storyteller, painter, singer, teacher, leader of the Spiralist literary movement, Frankétienne is a true *sanmba* in the Haitian tradition.

Dézafi is a rich novel. More insistently and more clearly than does *Ultravocal*, Frankétienne's earlier work of fiction *Dézafi* explores a panoply of social, economic, and esthetic issues through the story of Klodonis, a *zonbi* under the roof of the *oungan* Sintil, who lights the flame of love in Siltana's heart.

> *Dézafi* in Bouanèf village
> *Dézafi* for a people
> *Dézafi* for a language
> *Dézafi* is a landmark novel that portends all sorts of possibilities.
> > The dézafi is in full swing
> > The band strikes up a tune
> > We're wondering
> > On which foot
> > We should dance.

Dieudonné Fardin, Publisher
Fontamara, 23 August 1975

DÉZAFI

The dézafi is in full swing

The band strikes up a tune

We're wondering on which foot
we should dance

A clump of gnarled trees with tangled branches looms at the far end of an old yard where people rarely venture. A handful of salt is dissolving in a pot of boiling water. A battered pot, bruised all over, a smoke-blackened pot. Salt crystals fallen into the flames explode like firecrackers. Life and death endlessly wrestling.

Sleep rise look walk eat lick finger blow fall run spend the day hungry. Talk nonsense. Tongue heavy. Tongue shredded in a thousand pieces. Full belly. Twisted guts. Thirsty for water. Dress up like a dandy. Go to bed in a foul mood. Get up happy. Laugh. Walk around naked. Wrap ourselves up in rags. Make mad love. Lose ourselves in death. Who among us is truly alive? Who?

A variegated crowd lost eyes wide open in a senseless dream with no left side and no right side. A long dream without feet or head, a gallery of scarecrows and monsters. Chameleons. Snakes. Mabouya lizards. Scorpions. Centipedes. Owls. Malfini hawks. Lasigouav. Madanbrino. Chaloska. Lamayòt.

We lose our way at a crossroads. We mean to walk straight, but we take a crooked path. At times we turn in circles. We move crablike, ass backward. Where are we going? Where do we want to go?

We mumble ceaselessly. We speak to ourselves. Our words come out upside down; the times are blue. Who hears what we say? Who tries to understand what we want to say?

They would rather say we're short a few leaves; they hurry to shut us up. Days go by. Nights go by. A strange season. We remain befuddled in a dream full of bad omens. A dream punctuated by nightmares. Wind. Lightning. Thunder. We shake our bodies a little. Between sleep and wakefulness, we open one eye. We remem-

ber. We forget. We remember a little. But we forget a lot . . . in the dream.

A clump of gnarled trees with tangled branches looms at the far end of an old yard. Stones and grains of sand clog up the earth's veins. Guts all twisted up. Rita breaks her back working all day long without food. Jédéyon curses as he wanders around the house. In the depths of the night an ear-piercing scream for help stabs our brains. We shudder to our blood. Our stomachs rumble. Our hair stands up on our heads. We bolt up.

Sintil is sitting comfortably in an armchair. A gaggle of zonbis are on their knees in the péréstil. Siltana is seated on the right on a straw bottomed chair. On the left Zofè is standing straight, holding a bullwhip in his hands. Three large candles are burning near the potomitan. Sintil shakes the ason.
"Siltana, my child!"
"Yes, Papa."
"Listen carefully."
"Yes, Papa."
"It's your job to feed the zonbis. Don't you ever forget, salt is a poison. Never forget, my child."
"Yes, Papa."
Sintil shakes his ason and speaks in langay. He looks to his left.
"You, Zofè!"
"Yes, Master."
"Shave the zonbis' heads tomorrow morning before sunrise. Don't leave a single hair on their heads. Do that before they leave for work in the swamp."
"Yes, Master."
"If any one of those zonbis drags his feet or shows the least hint of resistance, fillet him, grind his flesh, pound his bones, smash his skull, until he turns into flour. Then drink his blood."
"Yes, Master. I'll keep them on a short leash."
Sintil stands up along with Siltana. Then he shakes the ason. He walks up to the potomitan. Then he takes a few steps back. He

grabs a bottle of rum, spills three drops on the ground, raises the bottle to his lips, and pours the rest down his throat.

"Hey, you all, zonbis!"

"Wee waan! Wee waan! Wee waan!"

"Bow your heads!"

"Wee waan! Wee waan! Wee waan!"

"You're here because you showed disrespect."

"Wee waan! Wee waan! Wee waan!"

"There's only one bull in this savanna, and that's me."

"Wee waan! Wee waan! Wee waan!"

"I never repeat myself for anyone."

"Wee waan! Wee waan! Wee waan!"

"Here you won't get to eat anything that has salt in it. You'll get your food only from Siltana's hands. You'll get a drink of water only from Siltana's hands."

"Wee waan! Wee waan! Wee waan!"

"And one more thing. The dead don't come back to life. Nothing will change for you. You'll starve. You'll be without. You'll get something only when I give you something, only when I feel like giving you something."

"Wee waan! Wee waan! Wee waan!"

Drum roll. A horse tethered to a pole paws the ground and champs at the bit. A wild cat jumps over a candelabra cactus fence. An avocado seed rolls down on the ground. From the rooftop a loud voice screams: I'm falling! From the ground a voice answers: Go ahead and fall! Just be careful; don't hurt yourself.

A bunch of dreams are clogging up our brains. Bundles of ideas are blinking inside our heads as we try to decide on which foot we should dance.

We don't clear the land	*the weeds grow.*
We turn the key	*the owl flies away.*

We stick our forefingers into the crack
of a lightning bolt; we get wounded to the bones.

We wager in our sleep.

They cheat us with our eyes wide open.

A clump of gnarled trees with tangled branches loom at the far
end of an old yard where people rarely venture. Arms stretched all
the way. Vigorous breaststrokes to keep us from drowning and to
keep us from being consumed by fire.

Still, life flays us alive; love wounds us
to the quick; death grimaces to our faces.

We must be wary of rats that bite and
blow on the wound to soothe it.
Our brains have turned into thunderstones throwing off blinding showers of sparks. Our confused minds stumble in the dark
looking in vain for a light to light our way.
We plumb the depths; we dive deep.

Not a soul answers.
No one speaks.

The tongue slices the tongue.
Our jaws are dislocated.

Banal words, venal words
Bloody words, windy words.

Words spread abroad
We stumble and we get a swollen groin.

They tease us.
We twist an ankle (our joints are dislocated).

We sit down, we stand up, we lie down, we crouch like frogs, we
curl up. No one has told us yet on which foot we should dance. We
talk to ourselves during the day. We talk to ourselves at night. We
talk nonsense. Then we shut our mouths.

Several days go by. We sit around haggard and passive, jaws
resting on hands.

Drum roll. The lougarou take flight. Naughty children dance a
pirouette at the crossroads. They jump, they twist, they grind and
bump. We look at them; we shake our heads. Sometimes we rock
our bodies in place. Lightning flashes. Thunder growls. Rain falls.
Flash flood. The rara bands come out anyway.

We half-heartedly stand up. But if we really want to start danc-
ing, on which foot shall we dance?

Our skins are raw.
We're wounded to our bones.

A clump of gnarled trees with tangled branches looms at the far
end of an old yard. To the left stands a fruiting mango tree. To the
right a mighty silk cotton tree is losing its leaves under the sun. A
skin-and-bones thin mutt is drooling by the fence. In the middle,
an ancient ill-tempered two-story house is showing its age. The
lightning rod on the roof pirouettes at the mere grunt of the hurricane wind. From time to time, the old ruin leans to the right then
to the left, twisting and stumbling like a drunk. The two-story house
twists, rocks, and nods each time the epileptic wind blows from the
direction of Port-au-Prince.

> A very strange game is on
> > The game is in full swing
> A mirror shatters
> > The game turns bloody
> Blocking
> > Unblocking
> Steamrolling
> > We're struggling

The Caribbean hurricane jumps champs at the bit gallops coughs neighs brays. The old two-story house dances, resolved never to kneel before some presumptuous wind.

Every year, from the beginning of August to the end of October, the hurricanes charge down the mountain slopes galloping and kicking right and left as they rush toward Port-au-Prince. The winds roar. The rain lashes down. The sea boils and foams. Up in the sky, the clouds wander, swell over the Sanfil neighborhood . . . lick the back of l'Hôpital Mountain . . . dive-bomb Mariani . . . zoom over the sea . . .

Drunken birds. Mad birds. Birds in shadowless flight. A direct cockspur hit. Tin roof sheets are dancing in the air. Flowers are up-rooted. People lain down wounded. People lain down dead. People lain down to sleep. People lain down hungry. People lain down to dream. A bedsheet for mardi gras masquerade. Congealed blood in our throats. A bitter taste in our mouths. We get up and spit.

> *We vomit our guts out in death's wake.*
> > *All speech turns rancid.*

The old two-story house does a balansé-yaya dance. Still it manages to stay upright. But then that two-story house is something of a mystery in the neighborhood. At night it is shrouded in darkness. A black darkness. Not once has a lamp ever shined in there.

Throughout the day, at dusk, throughout the night, all doors and windows are always closed. That house is a real mystery in the neighborhood.

We've been searching for a long time. When we make love, we shake like tree leaves.

One word uttered on the pillow in the dark and we tremble to our very marrow, we tremble to our very roots.

Grains of sand flow between our toes. Where is our life? The days come and go. The days speed ahead, sometimes in the right direction, sometimes backward. Torment. Trials and tribulations. Tolalito. We've been searching for a long time.

All roads cross in the woods / we rise up early / ass kissing flatterers go a long way / even with a single match you can light a big fire / a dandy at the cockfight / gamecocks fight / we break our backs working / we don't eat / we're feeling lethargic / wings dragging on the ground / a cockspur hit to the shoulder / a flow of words / a hungry belly will have you travel far / they hit us below the belt / never forget / cowards shouldn't bet / a hot stew should be lapped up with the tongue / who chopped up a patch of our garden? / the price of maize has gone up / no rain / the cow breaks her tether messing around / they've trashed our home / sitting around idle / nonsense talk with a nasal twang / illness brings down the strong / walking is better than sleeping / we pray for luck at the lottery / the feeble-minded lose / lackeys sniff around for scraps / they learn to scam / dummies lose their way / slutty women are standing stark naked/ we die of thirst in the midday sun / madness subverts memory / the curse of the truck porter / the children get beaten up / raging flood / the old folks mumble and

grumble / the savanna rooster flies away from the cockfight / cockers, gamblers, and spectators grumble no end / knives are pulled /
fighting sticks fly about / eyes are blinded / heads are split / fire
up everyone's ass / push and pull / panick and pile-up / wounded
bodies / words are whispered / they're looking for a fight / whispers and palaver under a tree / they snap food away from our
mouths / a dance under the shack's thatched roof / we sleep under
a bridge / we're fucked / no one gives us a handout / we help one
another / still not a bite to eat / twisted guts / twisted hands / a
vague taste in our mouths / a swindler promises more than he has /
we shuffle in place / the uninitiated doesn't know yet what goes on
inside the masonic lodge / fun and games no end / a ten-fingered
cat ripped off our yard / the harvest failed / they feed poisoned
grain to our cock in the first bout / the slob pays the oungan a visit
to learn the secret of dressing well / we're grooming our bruiser
of a rooster for a big wager / they're all tongue-wagging gossip-
mongers / they badmouth us / they want to upset us / the poor
go around begging / the dung beetle works hard rolling its ball of
shit / we dare them / eggs get broken / we can't sit still / our umbilical cord was buried in an anthill* / we can't lie still / the boat
capsizes / in Saint-Marc Channel the sea's all foam and spume /
the daredevils' corpses fertilize the earth / they set two cowardly
gamecocks up against each other / the needles get broken / work
ourselves to the bone / they rough us up for meat scraps / they
stab us / they harass us / they keep the heat on us / we explode /
we curse / we start a scene / we spill our guts out / we get it all
off our chests / the light of women draws us in like a magnet / the
eel darts under the lake's water / the blinded eye sees clearly / boll
weevils infest the cotton fields / a bit of tarp to shield us from the
rain / they better not set foot on our doorstep / their wings are
folded / the wind whisks gossip abroad / seven days at the cockfight and our bodies are crushed / each hit of those sharp spurs
gives us cold sweats / we dig for hidden secrets / a roll of the dice

---

* According to custom, a newborn's umbilical cord is to be buried under a
tree. If by some accident the burial site happens to be an anthill, it is believed
the child will grow into a restless adult.—Trans.

throws off the rank amateur gambler / we respond in kind / we
scrutinize the entrails of ants* / the laxative has cleared our blood /
we shoo away those importune idlers / year after year summer fever
mows the country kids down / they hurl pointed messages from
behind a veil of nonsense / clash over trivial things / fifty cents'
worth of street food / cheap food does stave off hunger / a millet
field left unguarded[†] / we shoot up like weeds everywhere / they
beat us up / the body bathes in its own water / we swallow a bitter herb laxative / a pile of charcoal / a pile of lime / one black /
one white / two stabs with a knife to the back of the neck / money
is a magnet / bad money has no roots / bad money doesn't reek
of sweat / we don't like this rooster's feathers / a crooked cocker
sneaks in a guinea fowl hybrid pintadin gamecock / all cockfighting stops / even killer gamecocks fly away / a rooster thief gets
his face slapped silly / we put the champion cock under care / we
were friends / now we're angry at each other / then we become
friends again / we bet on the same numbers / we field the same
rooster in the cockpit / we cry together at night / we're blood rela-
tives / ferocious caymans / voracious caymans / rotten-mouthed
caymans / our victory is uncertain / our child's been lying sick in
bed for three days / our child's slumped on a chair sick / hunger is
a disease that takes on many guises / we have no vice / we scurry
away fast / a snake has twisted itself around the roof beam / we
set some straw on fire / smoke spreads everywhere / we kick out
all harmful critters before lying down for the night / many children
sleep on the ground / we shoo away both flies and mosquitoes /
a fat and ungainly mannil gamecock loses in the first bout / we
save the carcass for later / we swallow a bitter herb laxative . . .

Kamélo and Filojèn are worse than wandering seeds. They've
walked everywhere; they've been to the four corners of the coun-

---

* An allusion to the proverb "With enough patience one gets to see an ant's
entrails with the naked eyes."—Trans.

† A translation of the Kreyòl expression *"pitimi san gadò,"* referring to a
millet field left unguarded and therefore liable to be looted by thieves.—Trans.

try. For twenty years they've been going to every dézafi. Their feet are caked with dust for having opened so many paths, for having pounded so many roads. Rain, mud, dust, good weather, bad weather, they would not ride a horse nor travel in a truck. Day or night they prefer to walk. They attend every dézafi, always staying until the last bout of the last fight. Yet they are neither gamecock trainers nor cockfight enthusiasts nor gamblers. They're simply there. They're always there. To watch. To look around. To enjoy the hustle and bustle. For the fun of it. For the beauty of it. And their mouths are never closed. They talk louder than corn kernels popping in a hot pan.

"Filojèn!"

"I'm listening."

"Day before yesterday we bought some fried food to eat on credit. Did you remember to pay the vendor?"

"I don't understand you, Kamélo."

"The fried food vendor has her eyes glued on us. Is it to reproach us or to compliment us?"

"She seems to be in love with one of us."

"Her face is not exactly pretty."

"But her fried food tray is beautiful, and loaded, too. If we flirt with that vendor and charm her, we should be able to eat our belly full every day."

"Filojèn buddy, you ought to try to be right when you talk . . . If you want to scam the lady, do so alone; leave me out of it."

"Kamélo, you won't slip away from this one. We'll chat up the fried food lady together. We'll bamboozle her together. We'll eat her up together. Trying to survive is no sin. Taking a shortcut is no crime. If one of us gets to have a bite, the other too will eat."

"Count me out, I said. I won't get involved in any scam."

He splits to get away from an altercation / just three piastres / we're dead broke / nothing to eat in the house these last two days / a ruthless country policeman rules the village with an iron grip / a wing-dragging cock always lets its opponent strike first / I bet twenty piastres on the red rooster / wait for the coming earth-

quake / big bets are placed left and right under the shack's roof /
no two-bit oungan will ever eat my child / a stubborn fever heats
our blood to a boil / a tornado is about to carry us away / a baka
spirit is sitting on top of a buried clay jar full of gold / our stomachs rumble / we break out in a cold sweat / we feel dizzy / we're
done, cooked in squalid misery / a fight breaks out over fifty cents'
worth of tafia rum / dead bodies litter the ground / the zonbis in
Sintil's yard are like ants in an anthill / the woman tempts Bouanèf's manhood / amateurs don't dare come near / their magic is
more powerful than everyone else's / Sintil casts spells for the big
guys / Sintil is deep into witchcraft / the cowardly rooster flies
away from the cockfight pit / it drags its wings on the ground / it
collapses / we lose our bets on a worthless cock / turn right turn
left, we still bump into each other / cracked ankles / he twists and
turns until he splits / we work till we break our backs / it rains
rocks and pebbles / dogs yapping at suspicious characters / the
sky's water breaks before the sun sets / spur thrusts / red splatters
from bloodied crests / eyes blinded by spurs / koumatiboulout! /
some big bastard shoves a pregnant woman / a rural policeman
beats up a chicken thief / breastbone caved in / tailbone shattered / broken bottles are wielded / a mean spur hit sends a gamecock reeling like a drunk / the brawling spreads / cockfight over /
we pour gum over congealed blood . . .

A clump of gnarled trees with tangled branches looms at the far
end of an old yard.

One evening, after the rain, the doors and windows of the old
decrepit two-story house in the Sacré-Coeur neighborhood finally
open. A dim light joins the soft sea breeze to caress a silk cotton
tree branch, massage the mango tree leaves, tickle the curtains behind the jalousies. A burning candle throws its light over the blue
walls of a room. From time to time the candle blinks. Lying prone
on his back, Uncle Jédéyon stares at the ceiling. Eyes wide open,
he is lost deep in a dream.

Under the ashes, in the swirling dust, on the other side of the smoke, behind the clouds, in holes dug in the sand, we open our eyes wide, we dip our fingers deep. We are searching.

So many secrets, too heavy to bear, slash our stomachs, stab our tongues, burn our mouths.

We stare until our eyelashes itch and burn. We grit our teeth. We keep staring. We get antsy. We want to talk.

Congealed blood on the rocks and pebbles.

Tangled knots of ideas marinating in our brains. Words are stuck in our throats. The words will out. A sinister drumbeat in the distance makes every hair on our heads stand. An evil wind is blowing trying to smother our voices. Before dipping our feet in the water, we must cleanse our souls, chase the evil spirit from our heads, remove the funky hairs from our armpits.

The journey may last several harvests and many returns. We must purge our guts, vomit the last particle of phlegm, fill our calabash with clean water, steel our wrists to defend ourselves against any ferocious beast who might want to slash and spill our guts on the high road.

We're living in a time with no in side and no out side.

Remember, we must talk to ourselves at each crossroads before moving on.

Pull the rope hard
Pull the rope far
Pull the rope and it'll break

Beware!

Early in the morning, Uncle Jédéyon sticks his batlike face through a crack in the window. His eyes scan the fallen silk cotton tree leaves and the mango peels scattered all over the yard of the old two-story house. Jédéyon mutters to himself. May lightning strike me! Rita's out of control. She neglected to sweep the yard on purpose.

"Rita!"

"Yes, Uncle."

"Get rid of the dirt in the courtyard."

"Yes, Uncle."

"I'm tired of telling you the same thing every morning. If you're trying to drive me nuts, I'll kick you back in a jiffy to your Bouanèf backwoods so you can eat dirt in Ravin Sèch."

"Yes, Uncle."

"I want you to sweep the yard spotlessly clean."

"The broom's handle is broken, Uncle."

"What do I care? You get rid of every single leaf and every mango peel littering the ground, or else I'll whip your ass red hot."

"Yes, Uncle."

A layer of dust covers the mirror's surface. We can barely see. Our eyelids are swollen for lack of sleep. Our eyes strain to see as if through a spider's web.

We're wounded. Blood flows. The earth drinks water as if there were no tomorrow. From under the burning ashes explosions as of corn popping and rock salt bursting.

Love and death share the same bed: all lovey-dovey at first . . . out for blood later.

What's past is so far.

What's past is so near.

Roads crisscross in all directions.
                    Thankless backbreaking work at a nameless cross-
roads.

Some horses get tethered to a pole.
                    Some horses roam free on the savanna.

The sky's water breaks
                    Our child's being born.

We force ourselves to grin.
                    But we just grin and bear it.

Every morning, as soon as Jédéyon gets out of bed, he sticks his gargoyle-like face through the window. He looks around, mumbles, grinds his teeth, coughs, yawns. He scratches his throat, shoots out two thick gobs of spit, then twists his jaws into a grimace to call out the little housemaid.

"Rita!"

"Yes, Uncle."

"Bring me coffee."

"Yes, Uncle."

"Put two teaspoons of sugar in the cup."

"Yes, Uncle."

"And don't forget my tisane."

"Yes, Uncle."

"Two pinches of tobacco snuff."

"Yes, Uncle."

"And heat up some water for me."

"Yes, Uncle."

"A handful of salt."

"Yes, Uncle."

"A bunch of orange leaves and some tar soap."

"Yes, Uncle."

"Check and see if the glazed face bowl doesn't have holes in it."

"Yes, Uncle."
"Goddamn it! Stop calling me uncle."
"Yessah, Massa Jédéyon."
"Girl, it's time. Hurry up. Move your ass."
"I'll get everything ready right away, Massa Jédéyon."

Stumble
              Sprain

Swollen ankle
                    Grit our teeth

Sweat pours from our foreheads, down our noses, over our lips, under our chins. Sweat drips over our bellies. Sweat pours from our armpits, runs down our backs, slides over our rib bones and down to our waists. Sweat pours from under our breasts, fills our belly-button holes, slithers underneath our groins, crosses over to our pelvises, flows down our thighs, runs all the way down to the spaces between our toes.
    Sweat spreads everywhere
                    Sweat curdles in every cavity.

A salt-strewn path. A bitter-as-bile path. Life is not easy. We go to sleep. We wake up in the morning and leave our dreams behind. But our hopes lie hidden under the ashes. Hens build their nests. They sit on their eggs. At dusk both angels and demons come out, both benevolent masks and evil masks.

Words blow colorlessly
                Yet blood flows

Tomorrow the horse gets saddled

                    The voice travels

Words are always longer than the tongue
Look and listen

Learn to forget
      Learn to remember

The hungry wait so long their appetite grows teeth. On every road dangers and traps aplenty await. If dizzy spells don't do away with you, if colic doesn't twist your guts, it must be because you wear an initiate's armor.

The hungry wait so long their appetite grows wisdom teeth.

Jèròm is angry . . . tired of hiding and feeling cooped up. Thoughts and visions clash inside his head like an unruly herd. Sometimes he takes a quick glance outside, peering with one eye through a hole in the roof. Most times, though, Jèròm can only imagine things. His dreams make no sense. What is it that's churning inside me, that's driving me crazy like this? For a long time now the sun and I have been at odds. Misfortune surrounds me, worse than the pain that overwhelms a body broken head to toe. Sometimes I feel really down. I want to be in the sun. From the depths of the serpent's eyes lightning flashes deadly. Fire spews forth. Words spread. Anyone running after life gets his legs caught in a trap. Hunger is hunger even for a Tèt-san-kò searching for his own shadow.

Curled up in a corner all day long, Jèròm glues one eye to a hole in the wall. Life has become heavy, painful to bear like a rough-hewn casket. Mosquitos scratch a maddeningly discordant banjo tune into his eardrums. Blackflies do acrobatics on his face. Rats dance the kalinda around his legs. Mice strut in his beard.

Treacherous road
>> *We fall down and we get up.*

In Ravin Sèch, in Bouanèf, life is hard for the villagers. Thick tangled underbrush, thorns, dense shrubs, whitethorn acacia, sisal. In the midst of the collection of decrepit huts that make up the village a few strangely elegant houses with corrugated iron roofs stand out. Under a rusty bridge a few children are sitting around, arms crossed. A chatty river the color of horse piss flows caressingly over rocks and pebbles. The MacDonald Company* railway tracks unfurl straight ahead flanked by two battalions of banana trees. Farther in the distance the sky and the sea are quarreling over whose blue mantle is prettier.

Backward
>> *Upside down*
> *Standing up to danger*
>> *Sleepless*

Enough talk, no more dithering. Time for our wrath to roll down from the mountaintop, gallop through the plains, break down the city's gate, and slay Death.

There's no wasting time.
>> *Break's over.*
So pull open your eyelids. Roll up your beds. Plant your feet in the ground. Flush the sleeping disease out of your bloodstream. Excise the disease that makes your wings tremble.

---

* An American corporation that operated a railroad and banana plantations in Haiti in the first half of the twentieth century. The company's operations disrupted the rural economy and caused widespread land dispossessions.—Trans.

The cock crowed long ago . . .
The drums have been rumbling, the bamboo
horns growling, and the conch shells honking for quite a while.
Don't keep hanging on to a rotten branch.
Don't rush to speak while the wind is blowing. Learn to listen
so you don't mistake the sound of rain falling for the rumbling of
the storm. You just open your mouth and the swirling dust changes
direction and the smoke somersaults. Let's learn to observe! Let's
learn to listen.

Leaning against a busted-up old boat wrecked years ago on the
sands of the river's mouth, Gaston is warming himself in the sun. A
bone-skinny donkey limps by. Its back is covered with suppurating
wounds. A rotten rope hangs from its neck down between its legs,
sweeping the ground and raising a trail of dust behind it. A barely
alive critter. It looks like some zombified beast. A short while later,
the donkey's owner appears on the path.

"Gaston, you lazy bum! You just can't lift a finger to help anyone, can you. All day long all you do is lie about, play dice, swill
liquor. You got out of bed this morning and you couldn't even manage to say good morning to me."

"Auntie Louizina, I've already greeted you. You must have been
distracted and didn't hear me."

"Don't you dare argue with me. About time you face up to your
biggest fault."

"And what fault would that be, Auntie Louizina?"

"You got a swift mouth for eating but leaden feet when it comes
to helping others. I'm old, and I'm still working hard to fill your
ingrate's belly. Weeding, planting, watering, that's me. You'll eat
me out of the farm with that appetite of yours. Just as bad as your
father who messed up my dear sister Anita before he flew the coop
and left behind a bad seed in the family. You just won't lend a hand
to anyone. Eating, that's all you're good at. You scum! Pig! Race
spoiler! Pea brains! Stinker! Useless bum!"

We hit hard. Our feet are on fire.

We say, let the light through! The path is steep. The stones are sharp. But we don't hold back. We are fearless, for our bones are immune to fatigue.

The sun and the earth are joined at the hip. Two shadows clasp each other tight on the high road.

We are fated to love each other
for twenty centuries.

Mumbling nonstop to herself, Louizina follows the tracks left on the ground by the donkey's rope. Gaston says not a word in response. He simply starts talking to himself. Nothing's holding me down here. Everyday life in Ravin Sèch is like trying to fill up the sea with rocks. The peasants here eat dirt; they're more miserable than a dried-up cowhide. They're born poor; they live poor; they die poor. My only salvation is to find my way to Port-au-Prince. I've been hustling for twelve years now to escape from this crushing squalor. Nothing doing. I've tried farming, I've tried fishing, it's like blowing air into a length of bamboo. Last year I busted my ass weaving straw baskets and hats to sell at the Saint-Marc market, but I didn't make one red cent. I'm sick and tired of walking barefoot on these thorny paths. I'm getting older. Go to bed, sleep, get up, walk about, drink liquor, chow down Auntie Louizina's food, I'm really sick and tired of it all. Ravin Sèch is worse than hell. I'm not gonna stay here and die in this hellhole. May lightning burn me to ashes! One of these days I'll just up and get out of here.

Secrets of the stars in a motley sky. We've been breaking our backs carrying bad dreams to a dump hole. Our shoulders are almost crushed. We're dueling with death. We're looking at love's light in a mirror.

Just a grain of salt under the tongue . . . to stave off hunger's pangs. No choice but to keep squeezing life's tits.

You run after a better future only to get your feet torn up by nails, broken glass shards, sharp rocks.

From under the bale of hay
          A sound escapes
The wind suckles it
          It turns into a clamor.

Herds of thoughts and dreams are jumping rope inside their skulls. They want a drink of vinegar for the road. Vinegar is the traveler's fuel. Confusion . . . On what foot shall we dance? The thunder rumbles angrily. No one gets scared.

The sanmba sings a biting song
          All voices respond
To avoid losing face
          The sun grins.

The sun lays a variegated egg. It rolls over the savanna without cracking. It dives into a muddy pond, slides through a gate, pirouettes on the sidewalk, bounces on the hard pavement, metamorphoses into a huge red-and-green balloon that spawns a litter of smaller ones and then rises and falls, somersaults over an open fire, dances on the point of a dagger, hopscotches over glass shards, whirls through a minefield, barges through doors, roams around, and still doesn't blow up.

Every day there is nothing but endless chores for Rita to do. Like a draft animal, like a rock in the burning sun, with Uncle Jédéyon she knows not a minute of rest. Up and down the stairs she goes. Cleaning up the bedroom. Dusting the furniture. Washing the floor. On her knees. Bending down. Standing up. Twisting her waist. Without catching her breath. And what is worse, she must cook Jédéyon's food just the way he likes it, which is like trying to climb up a greasy pole.

"Rita!"

"Yes, Uncle!"

"The Sacré-Coeur church bell rang twelve noon a long time ago."

"Yes, Uncle."

"Hurry up with the food."

"Yes, Uncle."

Without wasting time Rita sets the plate with the spoon, knife, fork, each in its proper place, then puts the food on the table. Jédéyon shoves his feet into a pair of slippers and drags himself to the table. Just as he is taking his seat the bell of Sacré-Coeur church starts ringing. It rings twelve times. Jédéyon is irritated. He looks disapprovingly at the way the table is set. Then he looks again, all upset, before he starts eating his food. He mumbles under his breath. He clicks his tongue. He curses.

"Rita!"

"Yes, Uncle."

"The food's no good."

"Yes, Uncle."

"The food's ugly."

"Yes, Uncle."

"Where's your head at? Take your time to cook a dish well. Don't rush it. Don't make such a shitty mess of it."

"Yes, Uncle."

"The plantain's hard like a piece of wood."

"Yes, Uncle."

"The sweet potato looks like lumber."

"Yes, Uncle."

"The meat is chewy and ugly like a monkey's ass."

"Yes, Uncle."

Jédéyon works his jaws with a cracking sound as he chews on the plantain. And as he chews, he keeps on mumbling and cursing.

"Girl, you didn't soften the beans enough."

"Yes, Uncle."

"The gravy is watery."

"Yes, Uncle."

"And where's the bottom crust of the rice?"

"It's still in the pot, Uncle."

"Go scrape it off and bring it to me."

"Yes, Uncle."

"After that bring me a glass of iced water."

"Yes, Uncle."

"God darn it! I'll slap that word uncle out of your snout. Retard!"

"Yessah, Massa Jédéyon."

The moon is pregnant
A star lies
prone on a female's navel in the intimacy of home.

Deep inside the heart of the yam's root
So many secrets are hidden.

The stone in the stream and the stone in the shade know noth-ing of the pain of the stone in the sun . . . of the suffering of the stone in the burning flame.

Remember
Remember smoke
and a bouquet of flowers are not kin.
Smoke rises in the air, twists, twirls, somersaults unconcerned with the fate of the bird feathers in the burning fire.
Smoke's signature
The vèvè symbol of death.

Swarms of voracious flies stab deep into our brains
Our ears ring

Our hairs stand on end
    The night owl brings bad news
The nomads with restless feet have picked up their machetes
    There is danger in the air. Disaster threatens.

The night prowler has met his match. He's in trouble. But he
folds up his pants legs, tightens his belt, and jumps into the fray to
fight to the end.
As the sun nods in assent, the moment horns are locked in battle
on the great savanna, the earth bleeds, light shines. We tremble.
Day breaks
    The gate is opened.

The game has been on since noon in Fabi's backyard shack in Bouanèf. From the start Gaston has made himself comfortable on an old straw-seat chair. He has a pint of klérin rum sticking out of his back pocket. He is wearing a washed-out red cap jauntily askew over his right ear.

On this particular Saturday Gaston is throwing dice like there's no tomorrow, his face hard like that of a demon on the prowl. Klérin rum laced with assorossi coursing through his veins, his head possessed by a thousand demons, lightning flashing from his eyes, he is full of repressed rage. No quarters for anyone. He is throwing dice right and left.

Money piles up on the gaming table. Both the MacDonald Company workers and the SHADA Company* workers have just gotten their Saturday pay. The bets are high. Fabi, the croupier, lets out a fat laugh as he picks up his percentage on each wager.

---

* SHADA, the French acronym for the Haitian American Agricultural Development Company, is a corporation that produced rubber and sisal for manufacturing ropes, strategic materials needed by the U.S. military during World War II. The company's operations from 1941 to 1945 disrupted the rural economy and caused widespread land dispossessions.—Trans.

Sometimes a fight almost breaks out. Curses and insults fly. Fighting sticks are drawn. Cheap rum flows nonstop. Gamblers sit at the table, get up, come again. Gamblers leave. Gamblers return. Only Gaston, solid as a rock, stays put at the dice table.

At dusk Fabi lights up two lanterns. A short while later Antonin shows up at the game in the shack.

"I want to throw some dice."

All the players look up. No one answers.

All around town Antonin is known as a good-for-nothing idler and a gambler with just too much luck. From Montrouis Junction to Hornets Gate he goes from game to game and never loses once. In the end no gambler wants to play with him. Every time he ends up pocketing the jackpot. Every time he ends up breaking the bank. Each throw of the dice brings the house down. All the other gamblers are just scared of him. Moreover, the rumor around town is that Antonin had given away his firstborn son to the bòkò in exchange for endless luck at dice. Antonin is the king of games of chance, the pope of gamblers.

"I want to throw some dice."

No one answers. Everyone gets up and leaves the gaming table. Everyone except Gaston. Antonin turns a chair around. He straddles it. He stares Gaston straight in the eyes.

"Ain't you the brave one! How much money have you got? How long is your fighting stick?"

Gaston counts a pile of change and a lot of bills. He swallows a shot of tafia rum and makes a face. Then he answers brusquely:

"A dice throw for fifty goud. No more, no less. I roll first."

"Go ahead, fool. I'll show you your mamma's loua, I'll show you your papa's loua, then I'll show you your dead grandma's bones."*

Gaston grabs the dice cup. He slams it angrily on the table. One die skids to the left and comes to rest with the top face showing four. The other die rolls to the right and stops, showing three.

---

* A phrase meaning "I'll teach you a painful lesson you'll never forget."
—Trans.

"I've scored seven for sure."

Antonin picks up the dice cup. As soon as he starts shaking it his eyes turn red and his face hardens. He slams the cup hard on the table. The two dice roll out, spin around like a pair of crazy dogs, then skirt the table's rim and slow down before each one stops with its top face showing six.

"And I score twelve, sweetheart."

Spreading his ten fingers open, Antonin dives on the wager. He looks at everyone around. He cracks his two thumbs.

"I challenge some other player to a dice roll. One single dice roll."

No one answers. Fabi, the croupier, scratches his head. The other players turn their backs. Gaston stands up stunned. He fingers a twenty-cent coin at the bottom of his pocket. Looking stunned like a rooster reeling from too many cockspur hits, he dusts off the seat of his pants and starts walking toward Louizina's house.

Banana tree trunks lain flat to dam the water on the mountain slope
A place where cooking fires burn relentlessly, where the sun is piti-less.

>   *The evil season lasts long in the veins.*
>   *The blood courses under the skin.*
>   *The blood rushes to the head*
>   *The blood flows down to the feet*
>   *The blood flows back up*
>   *The blood seeps through the joints*
>   *We shudder to our very marrow*
>   *We lie spread-eagled on an ants' nest*
>   *Our memory is in our heart*
>   *We remember*
>   *Open and close*
>   *Fall and rise*
>   *Kill and wound*
>   *Kill and die*
>   *Our memory is in our heart.*

The rib bones let loose an accordion tune to bitter misery.
A dagger of a season.
            An endless season
    Many birds have flown away to hide
            But our memory stays in our heart.

Every Saturday morning Rita makes her way to Croix-Bossales to run errands for Jédéyon. It's always the same shopping list: long grain rice, yellow corn flour from Saint-Marc, red kidney beans, meat, and vegetables for soup. No wasting time. Sometimes Rita would stop to watch kids like her play on the street. Her heart would beat faster. But when she remembered the beatings Jédéyon would give her, her heart would close up, her heart would swell up, her heart turn sour. Then she would feel like bawling her eyes out.

Sometimes Rita looks at some wall poster. She understands nothing; she doesn't know how to read. The letters look to her like flies, ants, mosquitos, butterflies, snakes, lizards, hummingbirds, sugarcane flowers, palm tree leaves, bird feathers, all doing a crazy dizzying dance. Rita has never understood any of it. But every time she looks at these kinds of vèvè symbols, she feels a sort of frisson from her feet to the tips of her hair braids that transports her to some faraway country. She soars all the way up to the sky. Then she dives into the depths of the sea, down in the castle of the Mistress of the Waters:
"O beautiful Lasirèn, please carry me on your back."
"The blind are not allowed into my palace."
"And what if I looked until I found your comb, Lasirèn?"
"Then you'd stop looking into a black bottle; then you'd know on what foot you should dance."
"I want to see clearly. Please take me with you, Lasirèn. Drag me along with you, Lasirèn."
"Learn to draw vèvè on paper. Then I'll put you on my back and bring you into my palace."

Rital feels dizzy, as though a windmill were turning inside her brain. A truck honks its horn; she hops onto the sidewalk. When she becomes herself again she is very close to the Croix-Bossales market. She hurriedly buys her groceries and rushes back to Jédéyon's two-story house to continue her calvary: up and down the stairs, cook the meals, roast the coffee beans, swallow insults, curl up all day in a corner.

All in all, Rita's life is a ladder with several steps missing, a greasy pole with a receding top.

A noisy ruckus erupts around a big wager as a fighting cock flies away from the cockpit to escape its opponent's spur hits.

Discarded meat has been left rotting on the ground, spawning worms and drawing flies. Some skinny dogs are grubbing on a pile of garbage.

At the drop of a hat death hurries back to the world of the living. The dandy pays a visit to the bòkò to buy a talisman.

Daggers are pulled out of their scabbards. The guts of the horse of misfortune lie in the dust in congealed blood. The long-famished man will not refuse rotten meat. War and death are inseparable comrades.

Between sleep and wakefulness we're confused.
            We hear a voice calling us from inside the govi; we don't answer.

All the animals are securely tethered, except for one being blown around by a feral wind.

Under a tamarind tree two shadows clasp each other discreetly in the dark.

All night long the dogs keep barking: love senses the closeness of death. Cats jump over fences. Owls fly over rooftops. Children slide deeper under their raggedy bedsheets. Before daybreak open your eyes so you can see what's out there.

The wind blows without cease all over Bouanèf, storming through every single farm plot, forcing its way through every single house, somersaulting over the railway tracks, bolting for the sea, whistling like a flute and honking like a vaksin bamboo horn over the mountains. The trees shake in epileptic fits under the blows of the merciless wind. The wind blows hard and fast in Bouanèf. The branches and leaves of the trees moan and groan as they undulate in a yanvalou dance. Dry grasses and green shoots whisper and murmur. It is one heck of a concert.

Looking through a small gap between the wooden slats in the attic, Jéròm can barely see outside with all the swirling trash and dust raised by the wind. He gets to thinking. A host of ideas and visions start crowding inside his head. For quite a while now the desire to scream has been scraping my throat, stabbing my guts, prodding my lower abdomen. For quite a while now my mind's been twisting and turning at a vertiginous speed. I open my mouth wide; no sound comes out of it. In the end I swallow my spit to avoid choking on my anger.

We are looking
> *We've found nothing yet*
We get antsy
> *Our brain's all muddled*
We talk in our sleep
> *We talk nonsense eyes wide open.*

This habit of brawling in our dreams sets our heads on fire. A night of fighting and our memory is messed up, our memory gets lost.

Bit by bit all anger is drowned; yet the fire is not dead. Our hopes are alive beneath the ashes.

We are walking in the midst of flames. The smoke from the burning fire overwhelms us. The dogs have their entrails ripped.

We talk. We talk nonsense. But when someday our hearts finally utter beautiful words, the sun will never set again.

Louizina has been working all day pounding millet. From time to time she pauses to wipe her face with a corner of her dress, a short break to catch her breath. She gazes at the sea. Two sailboats are crossing the La Gonave Channel. She raises her head to look at the sky. A flock of black boustabak birds are flying up toward the mountain's top. She looks inside the house. Gaston is lying on a straw sleeping mat, snoring.

"Dammit! My blood boils every time I see this good-for-nothing bum lying there sleeping in the old house."

Louizina lays the pestle down. She starts banging on the door. Gaston rolls over on the mat. With one eye closed and the other half-open, he curls up, pulling his knees up under his belly. Louizina bangs harder on the door.

"Drunken bum! You've been sleeping since last night. You came home quite late. Time to get up. You let booze make you forget your home. You've got no conscience! Even a dog would tire of your bones!"

"But Aunt Louizina, I don't disturb you if I sleep in a little bit longer. My whole body is bushed."

"Shut the hell up! I'm talking. You spend your time either getting drunk on cheap booze or lying around idle. You're always lazing around. I've been pounding millet since daybreak. All that time

you've been snoring away. Yesterday you spent the whole day playing dice at Fabi's. Ten piastres disappeared from the suitcase yesterday morning. You just stole those people's money. That money
doesn't even belong to me. It's money people asked me to hold in
trust for them. Aren't you ashamed to have stolen ten piastres so
you can go play dice? You ten-fingered cat! You're no use to any-
body."

Gaston sits up in a corner of the room, head down, both hands
on his cheeks. Louizina keeps on cursing. Pestle blows. Streams of
words. Her anger grows as she pounds the millet while lobbing biting curses at Gaston, who doesn't dare answer back.

The sun has set.
Looks like it's about to rain.

The storm has caught us in the bush. Evil air surrounds us.
We've been cornered on a narrow path. We're about to be over-
whelmed.

Do not allow the shaking disease to get under
your skin and suck the life out of you.
Slow down.
Calm down.

How long have we been searching? We flirt with life in our
dreams. We lick life's body when we're awake. It bites us. It shoves
us around.
*As we try to pick bones out of gumbo soup**
As we try to count hens' teeth†

---

* A riff on the expression "to look for bones in gumbo soup"—to show a
dogged if sometimes futile curiosity.—Trans.

† To engage in a futile action.—Trans.

We almost lose a few leaves
The darkness almost swallows us.

We hear a woman's voice in the distance. We move a bit closer to her. When we try to touch her body, she wooshes away, slippery as an eel, and escapes from our hands. Then we hear a woman's voice again in the distance. We forge ahead on a thorny path.

How long have we been searching? Our memory and our hearts are being consumed in a furnace.

To find ourselves again tomorrow we shall walk on fire to cross over the pit of misfortune.

Up in the attic Jéròm is straining hard to catch a few words of the conversations being carried on outside. A few country folks, squat on their haunches by a tree stump, are gossiping. A little while later Alibé walks into the house.

"Brother Jéròm, how's your day been up in the attic?"

"Not too bad, Alibé, my brother. How about you? How did it go with you with that wild wind blowing out there?"

"The wind blew all over the plains. It hit everywhere. I was crushed when I saw all those banana and plantain trees lying on the ground. In some places the wind just flattened the crops to the ground."

"Over here the wind stomped like a mule tethered to a pole. It shook up the houses' roofs like crazy."

"Brother Jéròm, you can come down now. It's all dark outside now. I'm gonna get you the ladder."

Every day it's the same old dull routine for Jéròm: get up early in the morning; climb up the ladder; spend the day curled up in the attic; climb down the ladder in the evening when Alibé comes home from the farm.

Climbing up and down that ladder is a painful calvary that brings Jéròm close to tears sometimes. He can't even remember how long he's been tripping up and down those ladder's steps. All he knows is going up and coming down. At night if he hears the slightest scratch on the door in his sleep, he jumps off the bed and hurries up the ladder. Sometimes it is all for nothing.

If a goat rubs its horns against a wooden pole, he rushes up the ladder. If a pig rubs its ear against the door, he rushes up the ladder. If a cow breaks its rope and escapes, he rushes up the ladder. If a donkey brays, he rushes up the ladder. If a dog barks, he rushes up the ladder. With all that climbing up and down like some acrobat Jéròm feels depressed sometimes. Whenever he startles up from his sleep, he has a nervous breakdown. He stomps his feet, pulls out his hair, tears his skin with his fingernails, rolls on the ground, screams. Then he holds his belly. Like two madmen, he and Alibé start laughing together until he calms down, regains his strength, and comes to his senses.

"Alibé, my brother, it's not my fault. The attic tires me out; the ladder wears me down. Some days I'm just emptied out. I'm about to go nuts. Without you I would have collapsed a long time ago. Thank you very much, my friend and comrade. Thank you very much."

"Jéròm, my friend, say no more. I understand your situation, old brother. Today or tomorrow, we help each other. That's the way life is. And that's the right thing to do, too. No need to talk about it. I understand."

From the start the cock takes three hits / watch out for low blows / slipping on a banana peel / the henpecked husband bends under the weight of a cuckold's many horns / he limps on splayed feet / a big-mouthed calabash will spread gossip everywhere / we're wounded / those dumb asses mock him / they hit us right on the festering wound / the cock is reeling drunk from spur hits / we don't take nonsense from anyone / we're big and we're bad / they're so eager to get into our business / what is it they want? / they want to be the first to jump on the dance floor / we jump over cliffs / you can grin and smirk as much as you want / you'll get rich that way / they get their hands dirty / Sintil ties up the zonbis' hands behind their backs / seasonal flowers / poisonous flowers / rotten fish ropes / jail ropes / hunger ropes / they slap our child a jawbreaking slap / behold our misery / the neighbor's cock got hit hard / if the child hadn't died we would be grandparents now / they killed him by accident just playing / the pelican moans and groans / the snipe pecks her own chick blind / getting around wearing a single sandal on one foot / why do they want to throw a gagit rooster against a pintadin gamecock in the pit? / they're not in the same class / we hate unscrupulous cockers / the greedy ones pull out their daggers to fight / cockfights attract criminals / we're tired of ceding to others / bad players lose early / mischievous kids who stick a finger in burning hot corn mush get it scalded / hot sauce burns the tongue / they catch us with our beaks in the water / we stay speechless for a long while / they always want our carcasses / though we stumble about we're not drunk / in the push and shove of a kerfuffle our clothes get torn up / iron picks are drawn / a ferocious dog-eat-dog fight breaks out every day / we get disoriented in the dark / we strain our eyes wide open / the times are strange and their meaning obscure / only the midnight truck roams the streets / the infernal machine grinds down the wanderer's knee bones / when a star falls we go mad / a flood of unpleasant thoughts overwhelms our brains / gossipmongers collect buckets full of nonsense / the rumor machine revs up / on which foot shall we dance? / we haven't given up yet / the winds have blown away our roof / the door is broken down / chairs are broken / we decline to bear witness / fighting sticks come down over and over / the weak fall dead at the criminals' ball in the shack / which foot shall we raise to jump over misfortune? / our ship is wrecked / how far do we have to swim to reach land? / our throats are on fire / the zinga rooster has awakened / the public switches sides / they're in hot pursuit of the rebellious player . . .

Kamélo lights up a cigarette. Filojèn is asleep on his feet. A fight breaks out. Bottles fly. Tables crash. Chairs break. The shack collapses. Filojèn wakes up with a start.

"Kamélo, looks like lightning has struck in broad daylight!"

"Open your eyes, Filojèn. Death is yawning right by our side. Death follows in life's wake. Get a move on."
"Right. Death's mouth is rotten."

The bridge has collapsed
> *We ford the river*

The sky has lost its ceiling
> *We fly to the four corners*

Doors and windows are shut
> *We know what color it is outside.*

Our leg bones aren't broken; our wings haven't been clipped; our eyes haven't been blinded. We'll be plodding along bad roads for a long while yet.

A bird flies by
> *It takes pity and lends us a wing.*

The wind blows
> *We hitch a ride on it.*

The smoke rises
> *We start dancing.*

The rain showers down
> *We wet the tips of our tongues.*

We've been trudging through brush, so our clothes have become mere rags. Our bodies are ripped apart by thorns. Still we keep walking, even though we're bleeding, even though we're limping, even though we're fainting from hunger, even though we're twisting from pain.

Whenever we get to a crossroads, we draw a vèvè on the ground with a piece of charcoal so that those who follow us will know on which foot they should dance.

The head travels faster than the body.

A thought that doesn't lie supine and doesn't limp as if bent on a walking stick shall never be suppressed.
                    An ear-piercing scream:
In which direction does the voice bend?
                    In which direction does the voice swell?

If the head travels faster than the body, which will arrive first?

Jédéyon is filled to the gills with tafia rum. He starts singing. He throws out andaki words: "Marasa, I've come to get you; we've got to go, I'm taking you to Guinea; I'm taking you to the island; we've got to go; I've come to get you, marasa."

Jédéyon drinks; he sings; he talks. As for Rita, she is restless in the house, breathless as she goes up and down the stairs, almost on the verge of losing her mind.

"Rita!"

"Yes, Uncle."

"Make me a spicy hot smoked herring dish with lots of onions."

"Yes, Uncle."

"Buy fifty cents' worth of sourdough bread at the store across the street."

"Yes, Uncle."

"Ten cents' worth of ice."

"Yes, Uncle."

"Four cigarettes."

"Yes, Uncle."
"Goddamn it, girl! Get moving."
"Yes, Massa Jédéyon."

Sunflowers are magnets for bees, butterflies, and wasps. Knives are drawn and wielded for a hint of sugared water. The drums unfurl their voices.

Will it be a koudjay dance or a massacre?

A hungry mouth wilts. Don't sit on your tail as if it were a walking stick. Get your body out there to see what's going on in town.

To keep from coming back to lie about in the house, bust up every chair, break up the bed before you leave.

Jédéyon is all liquored up. When he's done stuffing his face with smoked herring and sourdough bread, he drinks up and then he starts singing again: "A higher degree and I answer present. A higher degree and the evil spirit vomits blood. A higher degree for the beasts deep in the woods. A higher degree and it's death at the slaughterhouse." *

When the neighbors hear that song, mothers and fathers holler to the children to get inside the house. The children lie on their stomachs under their bedsheets and cover themselves up from head to toe. As for the grown-ups, they sharpen their spurs and stand ready to gut Jédéyon. Swearing on one side of the street. Singing from the decrepit two-story house on the other side.

"Lougarou! Give it a rest, Jédéyon!"
"A higher degree and I answer present."
"Baka without a conscience!"

---

* A degree is a level of initiation in an occult society. The power and esoteric knowledge of a member increase with each degree attained by said member.—Trans.

"A higher degree and the evil spirit vomits blood."
"Chòché! You relish kids' meat, don't you."
"A higher degree for the beasts deep in the woods."
"Zobòp! There are mountains beyond mountains."
"A higher degree and it's death at the slaughterhouse."
"Zoklimo! Shut your trap. Go lie quiet somewhere."

They give Jédéyon a verbal drubbing. They burn asafetida and incense all over the neighborhood. But all that is like water on a duck's feathers. Jédéyon keeps singing like there's no tomorrow. Then they rain stones on the two-story house. But that is like the wind blowing through a bamboo thicket. Jédéyon keeps shouting and singing late into the night. When every door and every window of every house has been pulled shut, he finally stops making a racket.

Jédéyon lights up a cigarette. He blows a cloud of smoke. He stumbles down and sits on the edge of the bed.

"Rita!"

"Yes, Uncle."

"Fill up the wash basin with clean water."

"Yes, Uncle."

Jédéyon blows another puff of smoke. He watches the smoke twirl in the air. Aye! My head is all scrambled up. They think they can torture me and drive me nuts. But they've lost the battle. I got the neighborhood to surrender. I would have made a racket all night long if they hadn't shut their doors. Still I feel my body all battered up with pain. I've been struggling by myself in this two-story house for ten years now. All my children have left and gone to foreign countries. My wife went to New York and never came back. Nobody asks about me. Nobody sends news or greetings. Nobody writes to me. And to think I broke my back so for children and a woman! For this and for that money poured out of the money sack. And here I am today, all alone in an old crumbling two-story house.

Jédéyon complains and complains. Tears pour out of his eyes. He smokes three cigarettes in a row. Nostalgia weighs him down and tires him out. He lies down on the bed.

"Rita!"

"Yes, Uncle."

"Sing me a song. My body's all beat up. I'm sleepy, girl. Sing for me, girl."

Rita moves a little bit closer to the bed. She starts singing: "My brother is far away. My brother is jealous. A beast in the woods cured my father. He gave me to the doctor as payment. But this doctor eats children. I'll scream and weep until daybreak . . . "

As she sings two streams of tears pour out of Rita's eyes. Her voice starts to shake and to weaken in a sad sort of way. But meanwhile Jédéyon has fallen asleep. His neck bends backward; drool streams out of the side of his mouth. Rita slips a pillow under his head. Then she walks away quietly and goes downstairs to lie down to sleep.

We want to pull our dreams alive and kicking out of the sun's womb.
One kick of the foot
And both door leafs open wide.

Dust
Rain
Mud
A chorus of voices rise

The teats of a cow
The spear of a bull sugarcane
The tail of a champion rooster
A billy goat roaming the savanna

Watch out

Jumping over a fence in the middle of the night to top a mare, the horny foal almost broke his neck. He swears it wasn't him, though.
                    Whom should we believe?

We want to pull our dreams alive and kicking out of the sun's womb.

Masked monsters
                    Masks over our faces
Our lips pulled down in a frozen grimace
                    The irresistible urge to wear a mask is in our
blood
An unexpected blow
                    We open our eyes right away
Our hearts sink
                    Why are we panicking?
We imagine the other shore of sleep
                    The other shore of life.
Light explodes
                    Heat plays hide and seek in our veins
A flash of lightning
                    We hurriedly throw a cover over the mirror
                    before lightning strikes.

In the darkness we fear even the sound of scurrying rats. Yet it is inside our heads that the buku demon is sitting cross-legged. The only way to save ourselves is to force him out with plenty of curses lest he crushes us.

Eat the meat
                    Leave the bone.

As soon as we've sawed off the greedy aloufa's teeth, trees, flowers, leaves, rivers, beasts, human beings, their features change; their colors change; they all become beautiful. The earth opens her legs wide for us. Her life-giving womb blossoms all red. Her belly is swollen. The birthing is for tomorrow. A girl child or a boy child we already hear its voice. We ready baby powder, soap, lotion, swaddling clothes, crystal water. We bathe together in the same bathtub; there's no need to hide our navels. We wash our hands clean at the fountainhead.

We want to pull our dreams alive and kicking out of the sun's womb.

Saturday has arrived. Over at Fabi's shack the dice game is in full swing. The gaming table is almost on fire under the repeated blows of the dice-rolling cup. The dice scamper all over the place. Tafia rum, cigarettes, foods and drinks galore. Players follow one another on the chair across from Gaston. He beats them all. His pockets are swollen with bills. Cans under his chair overflow with coins. A cigarette hangs with elegant nonchalance from the corner of his mouth. He is still smoking when Antonin appears at the curve of the road . . . Every single gambler withdraws without a word. Fabi rushes to stand by the table. Antonin pulls up a chair. He twists it on one leg like a top. He stops it with his knees. He sticks it backward between his thighs. Then he seats himself across from Gaston.

"How big is your pot this Saturday, you impertinent little cockerel?"

"Bottomless."

"In this here place there's no tree my axe doesn't fell. Wager as big as you want. Insolent little boy! I, Antonin Montilis, I thump my chest three times, I never back away from a wager. Damn impertinent boy!"

Gaston counts his money as fast as machine-gun fire. He pushes his cap slightly toward his right ear before he answers:

"We're up to our necks in money! One roll of the dice for two hundred piastres. You go first."

Everyone is shocked. Fabi's eyes open wide. Antonin bites his lips. Such a shock. He grinds his teeth. His jaws move like a mill. He spits out a gob of blood-filled saliva.

Antonin jumps up and runs inside the house. He returns to his seat three minutes later. He plunks a pile of money down on the table, cracks his thumbs, then picks up the dice-rolling cup. His eyes turn red as if they were on fire. He rolls the dice; one die stops on six as the other pirouettes and hits it before showing five. Fabi shouts out, "A total of eleven points for Antonin!"

Gaston now shakes the cup. He shakes. He sweats. He shakes. His face becomes shiny like a thunderstorm lizard's skin. He shakes the cup for quite a while, shakes it to his heart's content, then slaps it down on the table with a shout that makes the shack tremble. Two dice roll out stumbling to the edge of the table; they slide to the center; they dance; they twist. They collide in the midst of all that fancy high-stepping, stumble, and come to rest both showing six. Yells explode inside Fabi's shack. The game comes to an end right then.

Gaston picks up his winnings. After paying the house's share, he offers to treat all players to a drink. Antonin declines the offer. He gets up and leaves without a word. Gaston doesn't linger either. He makes a beeline to Louizina's house. Halfway there, he raises his head to look at the sky. Dark clouds, portending unpleasant weather, hang like ominous masks. The rain starts coming down over the sea. Gaston quickens his steps. When he arrives under the bridge, his head is already wet. The MacDonald Company train is running at full speed on its way from Port-au-Prince. He raises his head to watch. The metal-on-metal clanging sounds like a ditty: the trip costs six goudon; fork it over; I'll take you far, the trip costs six gouden . . .

Gaston watches. He watches until the train disappears at the end of the tracks.

Night surprises us in the haunted house.
              A sliver of memory pulls the hanging stars down
inside our heads.
                      We up and go walk about roam around bum all
over.

At each crossroads

        we sprinkle salt on the ground

                so those who follow us can find their way.

*Light blinds the eyes of the assassin lying in ambush in the
woods. We tiptoe around, our lips sewn up, our eyelids wide open.
We ought not to disturb sleeping danger as long as the hole to bury
misfortune hasn't been dug yet. One ought not to flap one's lips too
loud either if one's heavy arm is to follow one's head.*

Traps everywhere
                We're about to doze off
Nightmares disturb our sleep
                Watch out.

*A doped-up rooster blows its trumpet in the neighborhood at
the wrong hour. Two love-making mad dogs stuck to each other
are barking nonstop. To stay awake we pinch one another from
time to time. We're holding a bouapini hardwood club in our
hands, so the lougarou are afraid to come close. We're waiting for
daybreak.*

Gaston wakes up early. He packs up his suitcase, dresses up
in his fancy clothes, then shakes a sleeping Aunt Louizina awake.

"I'm leaving, Aunt Louizina."

"Leaving to go where?"

"Port-au-Prince."

Louizina gets out of bed. She pulls up a chair and sits down. She pours water and washes her face to get rid of the sleep still in her eyes.

"Gaston, where are you going?"

"Port-au-Prince."

"My boy, what do you want in the big city?"

"I'm sick and tired of eating dirt in Bouanèf. I'm going to look for work in Port-au-Prince. When things get better for me I'll come back here."

Tears pour out of Louizina's eyes. She talks; she paces around; she sits down; she stands up. Gaston simply won't listen to reason. Yet his heart is being torn apart. Feeling his eyes welling up, he rushes to Aunt Louizina's side, picks up his suitcase without a word, and rushes out onto the road. As he gets to the curve of the road by Fabi's house, an old passenger truck arrives at full speed with a clanging noise. Gaston's heart sinks. As he boards the truck he turns his head to look around. Thorny acacia trees, weeds and bushes, fishing nets, straw-roofed houses, wild birds, they're all doing a wild dance in his head. His throat tightens up. The truck starts with an infernal roar. Dust rises up in the air. Gaston takes one last look at Bouanèf. The sun is timidly showing its young horns from behind an old bare mountain.

Gossipmongers get their tongues cut out.
            Words are nailed fast to our throats.
    While we're lost in deep sleep an army of rats bite and blow on our toes, on our ears, on our fingers, on our lips. Grinning skulls peek from behind doors.
    They smash our bones into a thousand pieces
            they spit in our hands.
    How many reasons can one hold in one's hands?
            Think of tomorrow.

In the close quarters of a shared yard one hears all sorts of sounds. Good sounds and bad sounds clash. When the music starts we forget to separate the good from the bad.

The brownnoser rises from his seat. He looks up; he looks down. He's scratched himself so much that his whole body is covered with bumps. A millet field without a watchman doesn't always fall prey to thieves. You won't discover life's secrets simply by talking. Should our thoughts and our dreams be about to die, should our courage be flagging, we will learn to swim under the sea.

We'll catch our breath farther ahead.

There's food stewing on the stove. They look at us askance. The seed of hunger germinates in the guts, shakes up the stomach, and goes on to dance in the brain. A garden as wide as a hand's span flowers in our dreams.

A flood will wash away the worms infecting rotting navels.

We're spooked by our very shadows. Our memory falters under the weight of crosses.

Our memory has been nailed over and over. Our memory has been crucified.

Jéròm spends the whole night talking with Alibé. Such talk calls for comfortable chairs, so they get out of bed.

"Alibé, tell me all about that big fracas in the village earlier today."

"Jéròm, I have no mouth to tell you everything that went on in Bouanèf today."

"Talk to me. I'm listening."

"Sintil, that shark who's sworn to have you dead, killed two people in one fell swoop this very afternoon."

"What?"

"Just as you've heard. Sintil lay Boss Odilon down on the ground with one blow to the temple with his walking stick. The poor man splashed about like a dying chicken. Just by happenstance, Oktilis the madman came by the péréstil at that very moment. Sintil went at him with his stick like a blind man. Oktilis fell unconscious on the ground. Sintil kept beating him with his stick until he sent the poor innocent man to the land where everyone goes hatless."*

Jéròm starts chewing on his lower lip in anger. His blood is boiling in his veins. He keeps shouting at Alibé. They almost come to blows. Jéròm paces around the room. He chain-smokes half a pack of cigarettes.

"Alibé, I just can't believe it. Everyone in the village just lies down and swallows such a crime without a word of protest!"

"With lots of spit too. We all just lie low to keep from getting our arms caught between the mill's wheels."

"Really! And no one said a word? No one made a move against Sintil? No one went inside the péréstil to ask what's what? Folks, you're all such cowards!"

"What would you like us to say? What would you like us to do? Sintil swims in deep waters."

"A raging stream may uproot a tree, that's true. But no flood can carry away a whole forest. No flood can sweep away a whole population."

"Jéròm, you don't know how long Sintil's tentacles are. He's stolen land. He's stolen cattle. He's stolen water. He's stolen women. He's stolen souls. He's wreaked havoc in Bouanèf. Country folks shake when they hear Sintil's voice. Dead people are scattered all over his farmland. Corpses lie in the four corners of his backyard. Children get buried alive under his péréstil's floor. His ounfò is adorned with skulls. The rooms in his house are crowded with zonbis. Human intestines hang on his property's fence. So then, you tell me, what can we do?"

"Start by wiping the wax off your eyes. Get rid of the shaking

---

* The land of the dead.—Trans.

disease in your blood. Pluck the dank dead feathers weighing your wings down. Cut out those corns that hurt you when you walk on rocky ground. Only then, our hands joined and pulling together, we'll find out on what foot we should dance. Corn-plagued feet are too painful to walk on."

Our blood rises; the sun drinks it up to give out light. Sometimes we're sad, we're depressed, we're down. Sometimes we're gay, we're hot as pepper, we're raring to go. Other times we hear a woman's voice from far away. We look and we look in vain. Love is tumbling around in our hearts. A cornucopia of words echo deep inside our guts.

We stand up
   We are fearless

Sintil has been sharing his house with his only child for a long time now. He loves this child, who is more precious to him than his very eyes. Siltana never sets foot outside the péréstil. She always obeys her father without ever talking back or looking surly.

"Siltana, my child, you've been responsible for feeding the zonbis since you were fifteen years old."

"Yes, Papa."

"You're about to turn twenty, aren't you?"

"Yes, Papa."

"You've been helping me with my work without a fault for five years now."

"Yes, Papa."

"You've never given me cause to complain. You've never done anything to anger me. I've never had any reason to stomp my foot at you."

"Yes, Papa."

"I say thanks a lot."

"Yes, Papa."

Sintil moves close to Siltana. He caresses her hair. He sticks his finger in her ears. He takes her face in his hands. Then he kisses her on the lips. A long kiss. A tremblingly passionate kiss. He presses her body against his, his breath coming out in short spurts. Siltana feels dizzy. Sintil seats her on a mahogany divan.

"Siltana, don't you ever forget to taste the zonbis' food before you serve it to them."

"Yes, Papa."

"Remember salt is poison to zonbis. Make sure you remember that."

"Yes, Papa."

"The moment they get to taste salt, we lose them."

"Yes, Papa."

Sintil goes inside the bedroom. He comes out with a white head-scarf. He wraps it around Siltana's head. He looks outside. The sun, its color a blend of orange and apricot, is diving into the sea in slow motion. In the yard, a clump of coconut trees are swaying, their leaves waving in the Lent wind like a woman's uncombed hair.

"Siltana, my child."

"Yes, Papa."

"There's no moon tonight."

"Yes, Papa."

"Get the whip ready for me."

"Yes, Papa."

"Tonight I'll be going to the graveyard early. I'll be coming back with a young colt."

"Yes, Papa."

"He was one impertinent colt when he was healthy and alive. He was a grandstanding young man, a loudmouth who spoke salon-grade French."

"Yes, Papa."

"I'll tame him. I'll take his soul out. I'll take his spine out in one single night."

"Yes, Papa."

"And don't you ever forget salt is poison to zonbis. Never forget, my child."

"Yes, Papa."

The river has flooded and its raging waters have been rushing over the parched land. We're in dire straits. The mud has curdled near the river mouth. Over in Bouanèf the wind is blowing, the mountains are showing their teeth, and the rocks are sticking their bones out. A toad starts croaking just to show off; he swallows so much dust he chokes. Countless birds have suffocated, dying on the tree branches where they perched. They got caught in bad weather. Thorns got stuck in their throats. Excruciating pain bound their voices.

You, who've been walking for such a long time without food or water, learn how to press on your belly so you can be more fleet of foot.

Gaston arrives in Port-au-Prince in the morning. In one single day he manages to explore every nook and cranny of the downtown district. He walks around the Bicentenaire neighborhood. He watches three large ships at anchor in the port. He looks inside a few shops across from City Hall. Bolts of fabric, shoeboxes, dishes, wristwatches, gold necklaces, shiny earrings, gallons of paint, crystal glasses, porcelain plates, silver utensils, perfume bottles, soaps, powders, shirts, neckties, metal roof shingles, iron bars, cement bags, all sorts of furniture, a cornucopia of goods on display.

Gaston suddenly gets dizzy. He misses Bouanèf and Ravin Sèch. His head starts spinning. A sensation of nausea grips his stomach. A violent hiccup punches his diaphragm, and he feels his lungs almost bursting and his throat tearing up. Out of breath, he leans against one of the pillars along the shopping gallery.

Tangled bushes, thorny burrs, fish fins, cow's hooves, banana bunches, avocado seeds, millet flowers, straw-roofed shacks, the SHADA Company's sisal hemp fields, the MacDonald Company's railroad tracks, boat oars, all these images are playing hide-and-seek in his brain. Car horns are blaring up and down the street. His ears start ringing. He opens his eyes. The masses crowding Port-au-Prince's seashore district look like crazy ants.

A moment later Gaston starts walking toward the Croix-Bossales market. He's so hungry he gobbles down two plates of chow crouched by a muddy puddle. Right in front of him he sees the police arrest a plantain thief and beat him bloody with their sticks.

Gaston spends his first day in Port-au-Prince looking around. He takes his time to observe. He looks at all the poor devils like himself, country folks like himself. The poor porters with their heavy loads; the poor shoeshine boys with their shoeshine boxes; the poor shaved-ice vendors; the poor truck loaders; the poor with their dirty clothes; the poor with their smelly bodies; the poor pulling their two-wheel carts; the plantain-stealing poor; the blood-covered poor under their heavy burdens. Gaston takes it all in. He starts thinking. He feels a sharp pain in his guts.

A shadow scampers away into hiding.
In the back of an old yard a shrunken shape is lurking.
An evil air is hanging over the back side of the neighbors' house.
> *We stand up and mumble and grumble and curse*
nonstop.

In the middle of the night an owl perches on a roof. A bright red eye glares through a hole in the wall. A window rattles; a door creaks; a bed squeaks; the floor shakes.
In the middle of the night, someone throws a handful of salt and sesame seeds on the roof. The owl flies away. Flames flare up. Sparks fly. Lightning flashes. A wild cat jumps up. A bottle of klérin rum falls to the ground. A bucket full of water is overturned.

Go ahead and fall.
> *Don't you dare touch me!*
> *Don't you dare burn me!*
> *Don't you dare get me wet!*

The children are wilting on stick-thin bony legs while the starving dogs lean on brittle tails as they drag their skinny bodies around. Amazon women are out to geld all tomcats. It's been like this since time immemorial: masked bands invade the streets; they go wild on the city's pavement. A week later, stormy winds flatten the plantain and banana trees in the flatlands, break the millet plants in the neglected fields, and whack all pregnant donkeys. The ill winds are pitiless.

We walk through a room chock-full of razor blades
> *Our bodies get sliced to the bones.*
We lie down to sleep and wake up on a bed that spells danger
> *We won't get caught in some rusty trap.*

Even though we're starving
we don't crave other people's food.
Even though we're thirsty
we don't covet other people's drinking cups.

We've learned to pause and think if we're handed a goose egg, stringy meat, day-old leftovers, stale bread, or moldy cassava bread. Yet, our stomach could grind iron or wood. When things really get tough, not even sour spoiled food repels us.

> *In the end, what is it we're afraid of?*

If we grumble, the enemy gets the better of us, conmen fool us. Small kids have overrun Bouanèf. They trot around on stick-thin bony legs. The children are wilting like plants. We struggle and work to sustain life.

Djipopo troublemakers all around us are dancing a jig. We glance at them from time to time. A siren tries to tempt us; we say nothing. We fluff our pillows, we spread our bedsheets, we make our beds for tomorrow. We're real men; we've been in love for a long time; we'll be in love for twenty centuries; we have enough love and then some for our children. Our arms will get stronger to protect our grandchildren against the rapacity of hawks. We must be on guard against the cowards and the sneaks who lie low in some corner. As for us, we will never run away from our homes or from ourselves.

When our horse weakens under the midday sun, we take heart and continue the journey on foot on the long rocky road. We pay no mind to the salesman's spiel nor to the conman's beautiful words. A scammer's face is painted all sorts of colors.

Karang   *Ocean fish*
Karang   *Prison pest*

We didn't do any cooking. Which family member has been suck-ing on bones in secret?

A stab with a dagger
            to puncture the two-headed drum
A flash of lightning
            to reveal the double-edged knife
A loaded word
            to unmask the fifth-column traitor
A shedding of skin
            to undress the mardi gras figure
A handful of salt
            to knock out the lougarou's teeth

A stroke of the whip
        to knock off the rotting navel
A cup of water
        to kill the death vèvè
A single rock thrown
        to blind the eye of the devil peering through the
peephole
A single word uttered
        to open up the road to the sun
A single cry for help
        to clear the path to the light.

Louizina is asleep on a rough-hewn four-poster wooden bed. In the middle of the night she suddenly wakes up scratching herself as she blindly pops bedbugs with her fingers and crushes mosquitos with the palm of her hand. Damn blood-sucking critters! I need some avé root to get rid of those bedbugs. The smoke of burning orange peel will keep those mosquitos away. I don't eat well, I don't drink well, I don't live well, I don't sleep well. I'm just about to go crazy. I'm at the end of my tether. For three months now I've been hustling on my own, I've been paddling my boat on a stormy sea. Nothing tastes good in my mouth; even water has a bitter taste. Gaston is gone; he's lost in Port-au-Prince. He hasn't sent news of himself. I really miss him though.

We look far ahead. Our temples throb, warning of impending misfortune; our neck veins swell, warning of coming death. We look closer; the children's bodies have ballooned after they've been fed bitter cassava roots. Cow-shit-shaped green slime is floating on the lagoon's surface. We taste the water from the pond; our tongues are raw and bitter. They've plotted it so that the river flows through our backyards foul and dirty. The sindik, the irrigation officer, has managed to steer the canal's water away from our fields. It won't even rain. We struggle and resist the temptation of the old begging habit. We've gotten rid of the old vice of laziness. We've ridden our voices of the least hint of self-pity. No water for our fields; we hang on and suck on our thumbs. When it hurts on one side, we bite our fingers on the other side so that we don't faint on the road.

The smell of food makes our mouths water. But we're good at repressing hunger. We tie up our guts for days. We have so many secrets for waging this battle: we chew on green leaves; we pop a small chunk of salt under our tongues.

Life put its stamp on us early
              We aren't angry
We aren't happy
                    We're trying to find out on which foot to dance.
To take heart we laugh in the midst of our misery. We look at ourselves in the mirror and we grin to keep ourselves from getting older. We laugh at ourselves to our heart's content.
We have plenty of battle secrets.

The tide has carried so much junk, trash, and debris to the river mouth. A violent wind starts blowing in the middle of the day, filling the air with sand. The sun pours vitriol on the festering wounds on our backs. The sun trashes us. The sun strafes our bodies.

Jédéyon drank a distillery's worth of klérin rum. He woke up late. He's a mess. He has one hell of a hangover. He woke up riding a bucking bull.

"Rita! Rita, goddamn it!"

"Yes, Uncle."

"Go to the shop across the street and buy me twenty kòbs' worth of baking soda."

"Yes, Uncle."

"Two goudens' worth of sugar cane syrup."

"Yes, Uncle."

"Make me a cup of punch."

"Yes, Uncle."

*We're tired of gnawing on dry corncobs to relieve our belly-
ache, to stave off our hunger. A sudden colic pain in her womb sets
the pregnant woman panting . . . She's lying down, legs spread,
mouth open. An ear-splitting scream rattles the house's roof. We
see a shooting star. We see the child's light. Let them get angry, let
them grumble, we've stopped grooming their fighting roosters for
them. They raise their hands to hit us; our skin is covered with
welts. Anxious thoughts depress us. Memories obsess us. The skin
of our thin necks hangs loose. We knock on doors until our wrists
hurt; no one opens. Trouble. Dire straits. Our situation is grave.
Colic pain takes our breath away.*

Hard to get a handle on it / hard for us to get a grip / the
work is a killer / they make us sick / hurts like a painful wisdom tooth / we've become hardened long-distance trekkers / how
can we stay calm with itching-pea powder on our skin? / they've
turned us into distracted fools / they've driven us mad / they'd
like to finish us up / pull our guts out and fill our insides with
straw / we haven't found an escape shortcut yet / deadly love /
plenty of trouble / they've got us on a short leash / they've sicced
the sindik on us / no matter what you do the water in a drinking
hole for horses is never clear / Sintil is the village's unchallenged
big man / Zofè keeps all the zonbis in line with his whip / how
could we possibly sneak away? / they deprive us of sleep / blows
lay us zonbis down / blows pull us zonbis up / we break our backs
hauling heavy loads / at night our bodies ache so / season in season out they work us to exhaustion even on off days / our armpits collect dust under the burning sun mud in the pouring rain /
bad luck stalks us / our blood burns like fire in our veins / they
guffaw loud / they talk loud / the milling crowd doesn't know
which way the wind is blowing / when calamity strikes the hurricane's whirlwinds change direction / the poor maids own only
one dress / curled up in a corner / our dreams are stewing in our
heads / misery engulfs us / we say nothing and hang on tight /

they conspire against us / inseparable chums one day / quarreling foes the next day / love and death go hand in hand / well-shod feet walk swiftly on one side of the street / bare bloodied feet tread on the other side / who will get the dégi with his purchase? / the band plays loud / roads cross / we arrive suddenly at an ominous crossroads / to save face we keep cool / but our insides are rumbling with fear / they just can't get the better of us / our tires are all patched up / the ride is rough for the road is rocky and potholed / but we stumble ahead / unfortunately our wheels shimmy badly / we keep struggling / when we get tired we lean on our tails to rest / when we roll downhill at breakneck speed we strengthen our hearts with hope / we prudently stay far away from ravines / we look for shortcuts / after each rush we pause to catch our breath / they send thugs to lean on us / our ears are stopped up with cotton / we don't listen to sweet-talking women advertising mardi gras junk / the news spreads through the town / we have no quarrel with anyone / Sintil takes on the Bouanèf zonbis / clashes in Ravin Sèch / teeth chewing on flesh / shattered bones / disjointed wrists / broken jaws / dislocated shoulders / clubs hitting buttocks / caved-in chests / slashed-open bellies / guts hanging on candelabra cacti / skins turned inside out on fences / thighs stuck on barbed wire / blood spilled on stones / corpses littering the ground . . .

Kamélo crushes a cigarette butt on a branch of an elm tree. He pulls out a handkerchief. He wears a frown on his face. He wipes his face with an angry gesture. Filojèn bursts out laughing.

"Kamélo, why are you so angry?"

"They've sprinkled black pepper all over the cockpit."

"That's none of your business."

"Lots of people went into a dead faint in the last forty-five minutes."

"That happens every day."

"But Filojèn, there's no doctor in the village."

"We know that."

"It was Sintil who sent Zofè to sprinkle ground pepper all over the cockpit. Nobody's said anything. Nobody's done anything about it. Even you said it doesn't concern us! Aren't you ashamed?"

"I'm telling you, Kamélo, it's none of our business."

"You've got a heart of iron, Filojèn."

"You're very wrong, my old brother. I'm suffering just like you. My heart's bleeding just like yours. The only difference is that I've learned to repress my anger when things get tough; I've learned to smile in the face of misery. I want you to understand me, Kamélo. As long as the villagers don't rise up to defend themselves, Sintil will keep on breaking everyone's balls. Try and keep that in mind. Take your time too, my dear friend and comrade! The ground is more slippery than gumbo soup."

One hell of a commotion at midnight's crossroads. We taste with the tips of our tongues. It tastes bitter like bile. We make a face.

Our dreams hang upside down. We catch our breath. We breathe in deep. We hang on come hell or high water.

The engine of death is rumbling on the high road. Before disaster strikes we hurry and take shelter.

The sun was on its way, but it ran into trouble and went back. Swish! Dusk falls. The sky is turned inside out.

This out-of-whack season has been upon us for quite a while now. The season of troubles started a long time ago.

One hell of a commotion at midnight's crossroads. The engine of death is careening down the road at full speed.

"Get moving! I say, get moving! I've come to get you for your insolence. Willy-nilly, we're going. I'll drag you all the way to hell's pit."

Sintil cracks his whip in the middle of the graveyard and slaps Klodonis's face time and time again.

"Get moving! I say, get moving! Remember how you disrespected me last year. I did warn you. Today you're paying the price for your insolent tongue. Get moving! You boasted you were a philosopher. You said you were an intellectual. You went to school in Port-au-Prince City. You did all your lycée studies in Port-au-Prince. You spoke a refined French like some Parisian salon rat. Show me how big a man you are tonight. I took your soul and turned you into a zonbi because of your impertinence, because of your pride, because of your big mouth. Get moving! I warned you, you loud-mouthed philosopher! Speaking fluent French doesn't mean you're smart. I'm going to send you to grow rice in the swamps so you can show me what a big man you are. I warned you too many times. Tonight I say, get moving!"

The whip cracks and falls again and again in Bouanèf. The night is all black. There's not even a sliver of a moon. In the sky a few stars are winking. Here and there a few ragged clouds change shape from time to time. Sintil shouts, "Get moving! I say, get moving!" The tree leaves shake in the wind. Crickets chirp. A donkey brays. In the distance, the sea washes over the sand with a moan. Slaps lay Klodonis down, slaps raise him up.

"Get moving! I say, get moving!"

Sintil walks Klodonis down all sorts of paths. They walk on dusty roads, they walk on muddy roads. They go through thorny bush. They cross a river. They walk in a circle. Klodonis is drunk; he is gaga. He falls on his face several times, splitting his lips. Blood drips on his abdomen. Thorns slash his body. His clothes are all tattered.

"Get moving! I say, get moving!"

When they arrive at the Ravin Sèch crossroads, Sintil brings his whip down harder and faster. He rains a volley of slaps on Klodonis's face.

"I'll slice you up. I'll slash your legs. I'll spill your brain out. No zonbi can resist my will. I'll take you all the way to hell's pit, all the way to the ball-breaking dungeon. Get moving! I say, get moving. Zofè is going to fillet you. Zofè is going to grind your bones into flour. Get moving! I say, get moving!"

Sintil does a pirouette at the crossroads. He cracks his bullwhip three times. Klodonis hits his foot against a tree stump; he stumbles; his legs collapse under him akimbo; he almost falls on his mouth. He moans softly in a raspy voice, in a twangy voice. Wee waan! Sintil smacks Klodonis hard on the nape of the neck with the back of his hand.

"Shut your trap, you pigheaded zonbi! Stop that grumbling! You talk only when I want you to. You answer only when I ask you to. You take only when I give. Get moving! I say, get moving!"

Blows, knuckle raps to the head, karate chops, double-handed slaps across the face rock and roll Klodonis now to the right then to the left. His clothes are all stained with blood and mud. He limps, his two arms tied behind his back with sisal rope. Sintil shoves him across a field of thorny bushes.

"Now we're going to walk on the main road until we get home. On the way I want you to shout out loud, 'This is Klodonis passing through! This is Bouanèf's philosopher passing through! This is Bouanèf's insolent boy passing through!'"

Klodonis mumbles. He speaks through clenched teeth. His voice sounds strained, muffled, shaky: "Wee! Waan! Wee! Waan! This is Klodonis passing through! Wake up to watch Klodonis passing through! It's me Klodonis passing through!"

No one gets out of bed. No one opens a door. No one speaks. Everyone crawls under their bedsheets. Everyone stops up their ears to keep from hearing. Everyone shuts their eyes to keep from seeing. When by chance the people in a house notice a window is slightly opened, they rush to pull it closed and hook it tight, then they blow on the lamp to kill its flame.

When Sintil arrives in front of Klodonis's family home, he whips him and slaps him hard and fast again and again.

"Stop and talk to your mama. Stop and talk to your papa. Tell them you're passing through. Tell them you're on your way to hell's pit. Tell them you're on your way to the ball-breaking dungeon. Call your mama. Call your papa. Tell them you're passing through. You insolent zonbi!"

"Wee! Waan! Mama! Wee! Waan! Papa! Wee! Waan! This is Klodonis passing through! It's me, Klodonis, passing through! Wake up to see your child passing through."

No one gets out of bed. The wind is blowing. The tree leaves are shaking. The dogs are barking. The stars are winking in the sky. Inside Klodonis's family home one hears the sad muffled sound of a woman weeping and sniffling and hiccupping. Sintil stomps his foot angrily and shouts at the top of his voice:

"Get moving! I say, get moving! It's time we got home. I did tell you, didn't I. Remember, I warned you. Today you're paying the price for your impertinent tongue. Today you're paying the price for your insolence. It's time you met General Zofè, the commander, the iron-handed master of all the zonbis in my péréstil. With him no one dares to rebel. I say, get moving!"

Caterpillars hang down from the tree branches in thick tight bundles.

We haven't had the slightest glimpse yet of a single butterfly perched on a flower. From time to time we stumble in the dark against a tree stump. The night is thick; the night is raw. But we keep our hopes hidden deep inside our hearts.

A bright yellow moon is waxing from behind the mountain. Its light catches a flock of wandering clouds.

Every night we look longingly at the stars.

Gaston has been looking for work since the day he landed in Port-au-Prince. It's been a long while since his money ran out. He hasn't found a job. At night he sleeps on the shops' porches. When it rains, he gets soaking wet. Every day he wakes up and goes wandering aimlessly through the streets by the seaport. His pockets are filled with nothing but air.

Sometimes he feels like going back to Bouanèf. He misses Ravin Sèch, the dice games at Fabi's, Aunt Louizina. But he feels ashamed at the thought of going home penniless.

Once he spent a whole day standing in front of a factory on Delmas Road waiting for a chance to get a job. Around noontime his guts were all twisted up with hunger. He was tired of waiting. He started talking with a woman taking a break from work in the shade of an acacia tree.

"How much do you get paid here?"

"I can't answer that."

"What?"

"Wouldn't you like to know!"

"What kind of work do you do in there?"

"Harder than lighting and feeding a fire in hell."

"And why do you stay?"

"Why have you come?"

"I'm not from around here."

"Me neither. I'm from out of town, from the provinces. I'm really sorry I left Jacmel. I've been working like a donkey for nine months now. I make just enough money to buy lunch. Nothing left after that. Can't make ends meet on that kind of money. Two kids on my hands, and no father to support them. I'm tempted to sell my body sometimes, but I won't do that. Walking the sidewalks of Port-au-Prince at night all rouged and powdered up doesn't pay either. And then food is so expensive. Costs more than a Negro head at the slave market. The cost of food is higher than the tide back in Jacmel."

"Damn! Why the hell did I leave Bouanèf in such a rush?"

"Well, you'll find out soon enough."

"I, Gaston, really thought Port-au-Prince was a paradise. You look for trouble, you find trouble. I'm tired of twiddling my thumbs. What can I do to earn a living?"

"Grit your teeth, tighten your belt, get ready to light and feed a fire in hell."

A dinky shack. A ramshackle shack. A shack with a leaky roof. A shack made of matchsticks. A shack made of smoked herring cases. A bunch of little runts screaming and crying all day long. No room to lay our bodies down comfortably. Impossible to get a good night's sleep. If by chance we get to doze off, we're beset by nightmares. When we wake up, we're startled, we feel dizzy, we feel as if we had come from afar. Our sleep is full of nightmares. We fight in our sleep for a few grains of rice.

The river has left its bed
We're confused through and through.

Sunday is the day Jédéyon hates the most in his life. This is when he thinks about his wife and his children who are living in a foreign country and who haven't bothered to write in a long while. They send a little money every three months, but they never send news of themselves nor ask him to send news of himself.

Jédéyon grumbles and cusses. A bunch of ideas crowd his mind. All day long he speaks to himself. I'm searching. What am I looking for? Why am I looking for anything at all? It's too late for me. My life has almost run its course. My codpiece is cursed. Misfortune has chased away my luck. A velvet curtain and a woolen coat to warm up ingrates. Wonder of wonders! A hole in the wall is grinning at me. A dog is about to dunk cassava bread for me. What seed did I swallow to have such hexed fruits grow out of me? Women cut like a scalpel. Risky games, madmen's games in my youth. My actions have come back to haunt me today. In life sometimes you're saved by the skin of your teeth; sometimes too death overtakes you by an inch. If only I had known! A ball has no feet; it rolls all over the place. Misfortune hits hard. I gambled on a number and a color and lost on both. The mardi gras masks are out. The children are wearing masks. The grown-ups are wearing masks. The skin on everyone's face has been turned inside out. Weird disguises are driving me mad. Stumble after stumble, how can I block a wrestling throw? I'm tired of taking hits. I'm cursed and haunted. My tail's been cut off. The grass has been cut under my feet. My old body is shuffling about in a stupor. I used to be so gung ho. It's all as meaningless as the sound of sandals on the floor. Every joint in my body hurts. Being married has been like dragging a ball chained to my ankle. It would have been better to spend my life pulling a heavy handcart. Seven kids and what did I gain from it? My mouth feels pasty. I look like a rooster with the flu. I'm nervous and tense. Panic. Marasa double cross. Death cross. I fell in love with the woman when I saw her on her knees before the Calvary cross on a Friday in Lent. I couldn't take my eyes off her. The sun was burning hot. She looked me up and down. Cowards don't gamble. Look at those flies on the table! Look at all that dust!

"Rita!"

"Yes, Uncle."

"Today's Sunday. Why don't you try and clean the house."

"Yes, Uncle."

"Make the house smell fresh and clean. Sprinkle water on the bedroom floor."

"Yes, Uncle."

Jédéyon stands up. He pulls out a stack of moldy newspapers from under a mahogany table. Then he starts rummaging through them.

We gather on the street and stand up in a crowd for no reason. We don't even know what we're looking at. We don't even know what we're looking for. The road isn't smooth; we don't travel in comfort. We don't live well. We'd like to take another road, but our memory is like a sieve. We wrap our heads in a big scarf to keep our thoughts from escaping. We roll a piece of cloth into a head cushion so we can haul heavy loads without breaking our necks.

We're anxious and fearful. A tied-up woman starts screaming. We run away barefoot through the bush. Over thorns. Over broken glass shards. We breathlessly climb the mountain. We drag ourselves up the trees. Trials and tribulations for our children. We run in vain after the wind.

Tie the knot tight and you miscarry. Tie the knot tight and the rope breaks. What's worse, several times we just let them take advantage of us. They drag us far; we simply have to roll with the punches.

Low blows. Head blows. A serpent's spawn. A foe's offspring. A pimp's child. The kid's not ours. Enough to kill us dead. Enough to bring our hearts to a sudden stop. No matter, we persevere and keep looking for the child of our blood.

Even though we're writhing in pain, we're not broken. Even though we're bent under a heavy load, we keep plodding along. Hot and tired as we are we sprint after the clever filly bolting away. We start testing life again, still looking for the child of our blood.

Camouflaged love
We won't get trapped
            We catch a skittish horse only by trapping him on
a narrow path.
            The day we catch a mare with a mule there will
be wild dancing from the mountaintops to the lowlands.

When Sintil arrives at the péréstil's gate he brings down his whip on Klodonis's back again and again. Get moving! I say, get moving! Sintil wields his whip like a blind man. Klodonis writhes in pain. He stumbles. He mumbles nonstop: "Wee waan! Wee waan! Wee wann! Wee waan!"

Zofè and Siltana rush out. They start singing a mystery song. Sintil starts speaking in langay. Then he shoves Klodonis inside the péréstil.

"Zofè! Commander!"

"Yes, Master."

"Gather all the zonbis in the yard."

"Yes, Master."

Faster than a cat could somersault, a platoon of zonbis are brought out to stand side by side in silence. Siltana moves closer to her father. Zofè is grasping a whip dipped in vinegar. Sintil grabs an ason and starts shaking it.

"Down on your knees, you bunch of soulless pétévi!"

All the zonbis kneel on the ground, heads down, arms behind their backs, lips sealed. Zofè undresses Klodonis, who is standing haggard next to the potomitan. Sintil wraps shirt, pants, undershirt, underpants in a length of Siam cloth. He pours a bottle of klérin on the bundle, then he strikes a match. The flame goes up, whoosh! The pile of clothes burns in a heartbeat. Sintil collects the ashes and pours them into a calabash bowl. Klodonis is standing up stark naked, head down, both arms hanging by his sides. As soon as Siltana takes a look at that hunk of a man her heart starts beating fast. She keeps staring. She gets dizzy. But she cannot take her eyes off Klodonis.

Sintil shakes the ason louder, deep wrinkles on his frowning forehead. He draws three vèvè crosses on the ground in front the ounfò's door. He turns toward the potomitan and makes a sign with his shoulders. At that moment Zofè takes a few steps toward Klodonis and hits him hard with two loud slaps on the face. Siltana recoils in shock. Her heart starts galloping. Her stomach starts rumbling. Her insides churn and feel about to turn topsy-turvy. She struggles to keep from throwing up. She looks at the bunch of zonbis on their knees. She gets a hold of herself and comes back to her senses.

Sintil grabs a bottle of tafia with a special mixture of herbs. He takes three quick swallows. He comes out into the yard, walks around the house, then comes back inside the péréstil, his face a hideous mask.

"Zofè!"

"Yes, Master."

"Shave off Klodonis's hair. Sprinkle bouziyèt sap on his bare skull. Rub it in."

"Yes, Master."

"When you're done, baptize him with the ashes in the calabash bowl."

"Yes, Master."

Sintil downs three more swallows of tafia. He shakes his ason. He walks up to Siltana who is still feeling faint and nauseous.

"Siltana, my child."

"Yes, Papa."

"Prepare Klodonis's shabrack so he can join the family of démanbré all saddled up tonight."

"Yes, Papa."

"Put him up in the last shack at the end of the yard."

"Yes, Papa."

"He's not allowed to eat or drink anything tomorrow."

"Yes, Papa."

"Day after tomorrow serve him a watery soup without spices, without salt."

"Yes, Papa."

"My child, never forget salt is poison. Never forget that, my child."

"Yes, Papa."

The sun rises. The sun sets. Many days go by. Sintil's reign over Ravin Sèch is absolute. The fearful peasants toe the line. Hunger spreads through the land; starvation twists people's guts and blasts their gizzards. Zofè has become a master bonebreaker. Klodonis and the other zonbis are taken every day to the swampy fields to plant rice, silent, passive, soulless creatures. But Siltana, for her part, has become a different person. She falls ill from time to time; she's become thinner; she's lost her colors; her face looks faded; she's lost her appetite; she's always sad. Some sort of blood disease is sucking the life out of her. Sintil caresses her, to no avail. Her mind is in some faraway place. No one understands why Siltana is fading away so. No one understands anything.

In Alibé's house Jéròm spends the day hidden in the attic. Every morning he hurriedly climbs up the ladder. Every evening, he carefully climbs down each step of the ladder.

In Jédéyon's house Rita spends her days going up and down the stairs. The old two-story house twists to the right then to the left every time the wind blows. It has been buffeted by countless hurricanes, but it remains standing like a rock in the neighborhood. Jédéyon, for his part, lies in bed crippled with joint pain.

In Port-au-Prince Gaston has been wandering through the streets, hustling and grabbing whatever crumbs he finds. He's done all sorts of honest little jobs, but he's never managed to put together enough money to travel back to Bouanèf. Worst of all, he's had no news of Louizina, no news of Ravin Sèch. He has become a bum without roots, a loose leaf blown around by the wind, floating on still water, covered with dust, soaked by pouring rain, coated with mud. Life carries him hither and thither. Like a boat he rolls now to starboard then to port. One day he sleeps in La Saline. Another day he wakes up up in Bel-Air. The next day he's lost in Lakou Bréya. The day after he's stuck in quicksand in Lakou Kodjo. He's become a wandering seed rolling through every nook and cranny of Port-au-Prince. He hangs on to one idea, to one hope: that he will return home someday with lots of money to live like a big man. But, as much as he's been hustling, nothing seems to want to change for Gaston.

The sun rises. The sun sets. Many days go by. Siltana is still in charge of cooking the zonbis' meals. But when Sintil talks to her, she still has that faraway look in her eyes. She takes time before she responds. At night she is sleepless. Every time Sintil comes to her bed to touch her and caress her, it is always a struggle. She moans. She complains about a stomachache. Her body goes stiff. Sintil groans in anger. Sintil simply cannot understand.

Yet, Siltana has been doing a lot of thinking ever since that night Klodonis arrived at the house. So much thinking has worn her down. She used to be so beautiful. She used to be so plump. Her face used to be so radiant. She used to be so full of pep. Now she's forgotten how to laugh. She's wilting away. She's about to lose her mind.

Like she's done several times in the past after Zofè has gone out to get himself drunk on tafia, Siltana tiptoes into the zonbis' quarters. She grabs Klodonis's hand and leads him away to another room.

"Klodonis, I love you. I love you so much. Can't you see I'm going stone crazy? I've lost my mind. I've become mad because of you. I lost my bearings the first night you came into this house."

Klodonis remains mute, a haggard look on his face like a soulless pétévi. He understands not a word. Siltana talks to him. Siltana caresses him. Nothing changes. Neither words nor caresses move him.

"Klodonis, I love you more than the apple of my eyes. I'm in pain. I'm tired of Sintil. I'm tired of Zofè. But you, you don't seem to be tired of it all at all. Don't you have any blood in your veins?"

Klodonis remains silent, both arms hanging down, lifeless. His shaven head shines in the light of a burning candle. His body is wrapped in an old faded shabrack that covers him from his neck down to his feet. His lowered eyes stare unblinkingly at his toes.

One of his shoulders hangs lopsided. His tongue protrudes loosely out of his mouth. A stream of viscous saliva flows from his lips down to the ground.

"Klodonis, please answer me."

"Wee waan! Wee waan! Wee waan!"

"Klodonis, I want to run away with you. Let's escape together. Let's get away from this house. Let's go hide in the bush together."

Klodonis doesn't say a word. Siltana starts weeping. The tears roll from her eyes down to her chin. She kneels down at Klodonis's feet, crying tears of blood. She stands up, walks in circles, rolls on the ground. She feels like pulling her hair out. Her flaring nostrils open wide. She jumps up and hugs Klodonis. Then she kisses him . . . puts a hand on his belly . . . runs her hands all over his body . . . caresses his crotch . . . Nothing. The engine won't start.

"Take me! Take me, Klodonis! Lie down on top of me! Ravish me! Manhandle me! Fuck me silly!"

Nothing works. Klodonis just stands there passive, soft and flaccid as a hanging liana. Siltana leaps up like a madwoman who's inhaled ground pepper. She grabs Klodonis by his collar. She slaps him, scratches him, bites him, shoves him and drags him all the way back to the zonbi's room. Then she goes back to sit and cry alone in a corner.

One hell of a dézafi

Words thrown to the wind

Andaki words

The roosters' spurs are sharp / the cockfight is on / cockers gamblers spectators are packed in tight / bets are made / Kamélo and Filojèn start talking / wing slaps and spur thrusts and hits nonstop / the first round is on / we're going to pitch roosters in the pit / watch out or some smart-ass gambler will field a doped-up pintadin cock in the cockpit / noises / shouting and fighting / who has the upper hand? who's allowed to talk? / harsh words are uttered / thirsty for water / haggling / we've been sold a light-as-the-wind chicken / the hen is weightless / the bunch of plantains is light as a feather / money is tight / jaws . . . tight . . . blows / stick blows between the legs / Sintil is enjoying himself at the cockfight / the dézafi is on . . .

True love doesn't play tricks
True love never walks on twisting paths

In those twisting alleys that are like a women's prison, in those twisting alleys that are like seven blows of a dagger, in those twisting alleys that are like anthills, in those twisting alleys that are like ball-breakers, a gaggle of starving children are drawing graffiti with bits of charcoal on the corrugated metal fences. Lots of weird signs and magic symbols on the sidewalks . . . then they go wilding through the streets.

The parched land looks like a head with a few widely spaced reluctant hairs.
Nothing grows or bears fruit.
In the country trees need rain
Tèktègèdèk!

Just a drop of water on the tips of our tongues so we don't die of thirst, so we can walk farther. In the blink of an eye the face of the earth changes. They stick their noses into our affairs, they want to upend us; we fly over the stony ground, we hit the streets, we gather stones, we rain stones on the enemy. Pain. Suffering. Deep thoughts. To keep from weakening we tear our hearts out and dump them on the ground. They bounce and rise all the way up to the sky.

Still water

> *Rotten water*
Pigs wallow in the muddy mess
> *The stench of the mud rises*

Come to think of it, why did we take a vow to wear nothing but clothes made of old burlap sacks? Nothing but a masquerade in front of the Calvary cross. The knives are sharpened before the sentence is passed. The water is set to boil even before the rooster crows at the wrong hour. We wash our bed rags in the river; we've stopped shitting around with shitty pant shitters.

Gaston is always on the hustle. He was just sniffing around one night when all of a sudden his eyes caught a running Pastor Pin Kris jumping over the neighbor's fence, nearly naked, his shirt open on his chest, his pants halfway down to his thighs, holding his shoes in his hands. What the hell! Gaston shouted. Pastor Pin Kris stumbles to a halt. Ever since that night, between the two of them it's been a rat-knows-cat-knows game.* They've become friends, like a pair of loaded dice. Pin

---

* An allusion to the proverb "When both the cat and the rat know where the bag of maize is stored, the maize is safe." I have changed the Kreyòl spelling of the pastor's name, Pi-n, to Pin so that it may be pronounced in English as it is in Kreyòl.—Trans.

Kris preaches the Gospel on the right while fucking women on the left. Gaston meanwhile has become his soubréka, his errand boy.

Who is messing with our blood under our skin? The sun has shut its eyes; the chickens fly up to roost in the middle of the day.

The hurricane has flattened the crops, pounded the straw roofs. Many people are at the ends of their tethers; many people have lost their marbles; many people have swallowed the wind; they're pawing the muddy ground. We'll never forget the clowning of the baton twirler.

Children play mayanba, kick balls made of a stuffed sock, balls made of rolled-up strips of rubber. Children kick cans, avocado seeds. Children play marbles, fly big kites, play lago. Children fight, run around in the sun, jump ropes. All that is out of fashion now. The moon waxes and wanes. But how high can we hang our rucksack? Hunger surrounds us. Misery squats in our houses, our enemies speak ill of us, they insult us and call us ne'er-do-wells. They don't understand how we manage to walk all day long under such a burning sun. We have lots of battle secrets. We learned to smile even though we're hungry. We're trying to decide which foot to lift first to join the dance.

But who is messing with our blood under our skin?

Pastor Pin Kris has his eyes on every sister in his Protestant church. He never tires of frigging the wives and girlfriends of friends and acquaintances. Every night he goes jumping over some fence or other.

Gaston swears he'll discover a buried jar full of gold doubloons on La Gonave Island someday. And he'll hit the jackpot at the lottery, too.

Gaston has been freeloading under Pin Kris's roof. Maize, flour, powdered milk, used clothes, second-hand shoes, leftover foods. Gaston has become Pin Kris's boy.

Who is responsible for this noisy fracas? The sound of a clash is a magnet to us. The light of a fight draws us. We hear a woman calling us from the other side of the tracks. We rush headlong toward her; we find a rape in progress. The perpetrator is some mad baka. He turns around, head down. He's angry. We pound his belly good and hard; he can't stop talking.

It's the curse of the dung beetle to keep rolling a ball of dung. The yard stinks of rotting carcass. The latrine is filled to the brim. The bayakou latrine cleaners to the rescue. The pallbearers are all smiles in the graveyard. The casket breaks open. We stop up our noses fast.

The ràbòday band is rumbling.
        If we're hesitating it's because we're trying to decide which foot to lift first to join the dance.

They let gamecock owners field doped-up pintadin roosters in the cockpit / too much laissez-faire / Kamélo and Filojèn are lying low / the hateful neighbor takes a loss / they harass us / the rooster with the drooping wing has the upper hand / the savanna rooster flies away from the pit / all hell breaks loose / a fracas in the middle of the night / our hearts are anxious / Sintil is in the cemetery speaking in langay / Zofè is getting his whip ready / the zonbis all have their tongues hanging out / they bully us / gossip-mongers point their fingers at us / they incriminate us / unrelenting bad luck / we whack all slanderous tongue waggers / we mete out blows all around / they lay the entire burden on our backs /

more bad luck / we're shacked up with a sterile woman / if our firstborn didn't die we'd be a grandmother now / there's a plot afoot to destroy us / they're planning to castrate us / we get up on our feet quick / they take notice / they look / they touch / we talk / no one answers / no one takes pity on us / an old man bursts out laughing / his mouth is full of rotten teeth and decayed teeth / hanging bellies / we're in trouble / we hear a woman's voice / cheeky children are impatient / they get up in a hurry / danger is lurking / we don't budge / we're not ready to face misfortune / we're not ready to walk on fire / we're waiting for daybreak / we stumble against a stone / we fall down on our knees / the stones are like snarling teeth / we fall face down on the ground / we're wounded / we're bleeding / we're in pain . . . in pain / we crawl off the ground like a crab sparring with its shadow . . .

Fire up our asses
        They want to drive us mad
Bad winter season
        Ill winds blow us hither and tither
Dirty floodwaters overwhelm us
        A commotion erupts
Cowards are mocked
        A fight breaks out before you know it
Blood flows
        We feel nauseous
We vomit phlegm
        But who will win in the end?

A damned curse. The sea is full. We make a quick exit. We give our buddy a break; we give our buddy time to talk.

Itching-bean powder on the crowd at the cockfight / we don't stick around because we don't want to get caught in the net / we don't stick around because we don't want to get caught with a fishhook / Zofè pulls food out of Klodonis's mouth / Sintil tantalizes the zonbis with food / Siltana is lying flat on her stomach / what's wrong with her? / Gaston's ankle is swollen / the second round has started / the midnight machine is grinding fresh meat / bums will get their legs chopped up with a hatchet / the hatchet cuts through the bones / smart gamblers lay big bets against one another / we tiptoe out of there early / those who wish to brave danger are on their own / wasp nest / ambush / lots of river crossings / lots of cliffs / we learn to parry blows in the dark / machetes are drawn / Alibé is wielding his stick / the sindik hasn't released the water / we haven't watered our fields / Jéròm is sucking his thumb in the attic / the wound is festering / the abscess has burst / the flies are swarming / the galipòt and the sòlòkòtò are in love . . . / the lasigouav monster is hiding under a rock / the neighbor's cock is punch-drunk from spur strikes / the greedy gamblers want both the money and the rooster's carcass / the fried food vendor's tray has fallen to the ground face down / the sorcerers are out / Klodonis gets a drumming with a club / not a single tear from his eyes / Siltana tenses up and tries to control herself / the Bouanèf cockfight arena is rumbling / Filojèn wants to talk / saliva rises up in his throat / the ground is slippery / the razor blades are sharp / the greedy beasts are up and about / drum beats and rattle sounds wake us up in the middle of the night / the corn hasn't budded yet / there's no trouble / with patience you get to see an ant's guts / the birthing is painful / a festering wound keeps us from walking straight / courage to resist hunger / what it takes to avoid losing face / there's a risk of gangrene / rashes and boils all over our skin / a daffy blowhard starts talking back / words like smoke / verbal fireworks / we look / we stare . . .

Our memory has become unreliable. To help us remember we tie three knots in our handkerchiefs.

One hell of a fracas blows up at the cockfight / they badmouth us / they insult us / what an incredible mess! / the woman . . .

walks funny / her kite is flying high and loose / chaos has taken over the village / Zofè wakes up angry as a crab / he rains whip strokes on Klodonis / welts and wounds on our backs / Filojèn speaks frankly to Kamélo / stoke the fire to keep it from dying / they don't see / they don't hear / they want to count the eggs in the hen's womb . . .

The house key can't be found.
We're sitting astride a fire anthill; we're restless.
We misspeak:
we say left to mean right, we say death to mean love.

Put the squeeze on them
Break their bones.

A bunch of people are bathing in the river. We scrub our backs with corncobs to get rid of the scabies.

Things blow up in the third round / a short and stocky gambler wants to start a fight / Sintil rains whip strokes on all the zonbis / Siltana looks very beautiful / she has a cute dimple on each cheek / we're walking on slippery ground / Klodonis twists his ankle / we pick up discarded entrails from a pile of garbage / we're being put through the wringer / we're going through great trials and tribulations / we're laying low / we're eating dust / we're swallowing air / our throats are dry / we take heart / we smell rain / seasonal fever / the lougarou fly low / we fear for our children / cowards shouldn't gamble / the lasigouav monster loves children's flesh / twin stars fall from the sky / the moundong loua want their due / give them iron / tighten the screw / break bones / to dance at the gate is to invite misfortune / they go after the restive horse / someone is stoking the fire to cause a blowup at the cockfight / the smell of fresh meat attracts vultures / doors and windows are shut

in broad daylight / dangerous beasts are hatched in darkness /
Bouanèf villagers are on a losing streak / the crops have failed /
their pants are torn at the knees / their shirts are rotten at the armpits / the whip slices Klodonis's skin / we're wounded / we lick
our blood / we take heart / we don't feel nauseous . . .

*We talk so much in our sleep that we disturb our dreams. Worst
of all, we get angry at ourselves. They twist our hands. To keep
from screaming we whisk ourselves away fast; our buddies take
our place.*

*Now we've learned to keep our mouths shut. We're trying to
decide which foot to lift first to join the dance, on which foot to
dance. They give a feast, but we eat nothing; we clench our teeth.
We don't talk; we say nothing because we don't want them to put
words in our mouths. We've learned to live inside ourselves. The
only thing is we open our eyes from time to time, and the light
pierces our bodies.*

What's the galipòt's nickname?
The enemy has gutted us to the bones
We give them a wordless answer
The vlingbinding are out in the streets
The children all hide under their bedsheets
The zobòp have taken over a dangerous crossroads

Insults don't scare anyone / we may lose / we'll keep betting
and egging our roosters on in the cockpit / a house built on a rock
doesn't collapse / the fried food vendor lost her moneybag ped-
dling her wares / deadly spur hits rain in the very first bout / the
criminal's path / bad trouble awaits us / he's come to the cockfight just to blow powdered black pepper over the crowd / he's
really out to get us / anyway Filojèn and Kamélo are watching out
for cheats and scammers / a cowardly rooster flies away as soon

as he's released in the cockpit / he'd lose in all sorts of ways / he would have lost anyway / most zonbis talk with a nasal twang / a fire is burning / all sorts of critters burn to a crisp / Pastor Pin Kris is shocked / Gaston lands on La Gonave Island to look for a buried jar of gold / don't knock on our doors at night / we disappear into thin air / moths are eating away the steps of that ladder in Alibé's shack / Jéròm is about to croak in that attic / with lots of patience we're about to master the game / we travel on rocky roads / they want to scare us / gotcha! / we remain steadfast / before we even blink they set after us / backbreaking work in the swamps for the zonbis / the corpses are piling up in Sintil's yard / a swarm of blackflies keep Jéròm from sleeping up in the attic / watch out! / our kids have stopped running around like hungry dogs / our kids have stopped begging for food at the neighbors' / we've become expert cockers / they've blocked the door to our house with a heavy beam / we open to let the sun in / they want to run / our heads / a tarp to keep us from seeing anything / to keep us from seeing at all / Zofè brings down the whip / many zonbis are injured / zonbis never show even a hint of anger / the cockfight is heating up / two-bit gamblers take a hit / Klodonis's shabrack is in tatters / watch out or the zonbis will infect you / watch out! . . .

We take shelter from the rain. We parry every low blow. We discover every trap placed in our path. We dodge relentlessly in the dark. What do we care about a rat's noise? We're looking for a way out farther ahead.

Jédéyon has gone to put in the old two-story house. He has recurring fainting spells. He suffers pain in his bones, his lower back, and his joints. He has no appetite; he feels weak in his whole body. And then he has heart troubles; his guts are sloshing about in liquor; he's been driven mad by his own anger. Sick as he is, though, he never puts down his saddlebag of insults and curses, he never stops grumbling. On the contrary, he is now spewing even more invectives over the neighborhood. These days, as she goes up and down the stairs to bring Jédéyon medicine and water, Rita resembles a revved-up mechanical doll, a puppet in a funny puppet show.

Water on Sintil's property / the zonbis are let loose in his fields / all the other Bouanèf villagers are eating dust / Siltana cries tears of blood at Klodonis's feet, but he still understands nothing / Zofè whips the zonbis on the legs just for fun / they pursue us relentlessly / they lay traps / we dodge the funnel fish traps / the rooster has an epileptic fit from all those spur hits / it's a damned devilment / misery has scarred our bodies all over / misery has gone to our heads / misery rides us / misery pounds us / clangs of a machete fight resound on the other side of the cockfight arena / cheap cheating players / let's not let scammers get the better of us / Zofè cuts Klodonis's skin with the whip / a stumble then a twisted ankle . . .

A zonbi sleeps on the edge of the yawning chasm of death.

The two-bit gambler . . . joins the dance / a dice game is in full swing under an acacia tree / temptation / we'll bring an end to this / a violent quarrel erupts / the fete is heating up / Sintil is in a bad mood in the village / the lash comes down on the backs of slow-footed zonbis / for the sake of the kids / our horse gets injured / our horse is limping / we've fallen in the mangrove / we haul loads that are too heavy / our arms are dead / our hands are limp / players with no skin in the game love to egg others on / zonbis with chigger-infested feet / they've prepared a poison to put our tongues to sleep / a zonbi steps on a sleeping snake / Siltana has fallen hard for Klodonis / love at first sight / the enemy has attacked us / they have overwhelmed us / our feet are badly injured / our toes are crushed / hope the wound doesn't get infected! / a stint in prison / several beatings with a stick / they keep us from moving around / we're shackled / prison fever seizes us / who went hiding in the bushes? / we'll hustle our asses to find out the truth / they pounce on us / since time immemorial they've been messing with our blood under our skin / beating clothes with a wooden bat at the river / a melee . . .

> Siltana grabs Klodonis by the collar; she shakes him up; she slaps him; she bites his lips.
> "Klodonis, get a grip and wake up. Answer me. Looks like you'll never understand anything."
> "Wee waan! Wee waan! Wee waan!"

We want to scream so much our throats burn.
We reel from the piercing pain through the night.

Woosh!
> *The chameleon changes colors.*

Highway assassins are plotting to cut our throats / cockers and gamblers are ashamed to return to the cockfight with a savanna rooster / they've emptied the fried food vendor's tray / they've left us only some crumbs / Zofè is bullish / the tafia flows / Sintil cuts off the tongue of a rebellious zonbi / a young zonbi tried to run away once; Zofè sawed off both his legs with a rusty saw / blood spilled all over the stones . . .

Lovers clasp under the silk cotton tree
> *An audacious dream is simmering in our heads.*
> *We kick in our sleep.*
We hear a woman's voice from far away. We beg her to stop and wait for us. She'd rather escape deep into the woods.
> *Why does love hint at death so?*

A zonbi dares to talk in Sintil's presence . . . Zofè pulls . . . his teeth out one by one / the neighbor releases his gamecock in the cockpit in the fifth round / it takes three dizzying spur hits one after another / a zonbi with a toothless mouth / scrofula causes some zonbis to walk crooked / they want to destroy us / they want to bust us up / there are worms in our garden / who has in mind to destroy hope? / But hope grows branches everywhere / hope grows roots deep in the earth / hope and life are clenched in a tight embrace . . .

When the sun rises and shines, open the doors of your houses wide to get rid of the bad air.

Jéròm spends his days confined and restless in the attic. When Alibé gets home from the fields in the evening, he sets up the ladder so Jéròm can come down.

"Alibé, my brother, that attic is hell. The ladder is like a cross being hauled up Mount Calvary. My life is heavy like a rough wooden coffin. Seems like I'm hopelessly cursed. It looks like I'm going to die without ever seeing the outside."

"Take heart, my friend and comrade! Hang in there! Don't give up! Who has ever witnessed the moment a caterpillar changes into a butterfly? The weather is dark and cloudy. Keep in mind too that lightning may strike in Ravin Sèch in broad daylight. My friend and comrade, take heart."

A rooster is crowing at the cockfight / another one in the throes of death is beating its wings on the ground / a greedy gambler is demanding both money and the rooster's carcass / life keeps on budding / too much of a hurry and you'll serve the food half-

cooked / one slip and we could have died / bad trade / we slip
away far from there / A merciless Zofè whips the zonbis with a
thick rope steeped in vinegar / acid spray / vitriol causes infected
wounds to foam up / they've cut off the mango tree's branches /
the silk cotton tree has been losing its leaves / Siltana's face is
covered with psoriasis patches / we learn to eat hot sweet corn
mush from the side of the bowl / we leave the middle alone / we
got badly burned several times / the shabrack hangs floppily on
Klodonis's body / a ceaseless comical spectacle / Jédéyon is getting to be hard of hearing / the rooster reels under its opponent's
wing slaps and spur hits / we straighten up the chair's crooked leg
so we can sit up straight / the hurricane wind has blown the roof
off our house / the thatch sheets got blown away / we're cracked /
they want to make us lay eggs / all the zonbis tread softly now /
the moon has drowned / a harmless madman is playing hide-and-
seek with his shadow / his mind's twisted / he's lying flat on his
face / Filojèn is lost at the cockfight / hunger is gnawing at Kamélo's stomach / sweat is pouring down our backs / who has a
back strong enough? / who devoured the tiger's cub? / the parrot's
tongue's been cut off . . .

*We try hard; we exert ourselves. We're misunderstood. Why
do old friends turn their backs on us? We should sleep light. Our
dreams are folded into many layers. Our dreams are bumpy. We
should pinch one another from time to time so that the sleep of
death doesn't overwhelm us. Let's find an ant's entrails! Let's search
for a star's navel! Let's put our heads together to decide which foot
we shall lift to dance.*

One morning, while planting rice shoots in the
swamps, a young zonbi named Mako walks up to the
fence. Zofè falls on him with his whip, grabs him by
the collar, and slashes his skin. In the evening, in front
of Sintil and Siltana and the assembled zonbis, Zofè
sharpens a long iron sword. He undresses Mako. He

burns the shabrack at the foot of the potomitan. He hands the ashes to Sintil. Then he castrates Mako. The iron sword is rusty and not very sharp. Mako screams: "Wee waan! Wee waan! Wee waan! Help!" For daring to utter this last word, Zofè cuts off his tongue. Mako is bathed in blood. He rolls in pain on the ground. He finally comes to his senses. His eyes are now open. He sees clearly. He looks at Sintil. He looks at the other zonbis. He wants to talk but he can't. From his throat comes only garbled sounds, a wordless tangle of noises. Sintil cracks the knuckle of his right thumb. Zofè stabs Mako in the temple.

The pickaxe uproots the tree stump
The head leads the body

Death may come to us anytime; our bodies will rot in the earth. But a solid idea does not simply melt away. An idea rooted in life's core will not fade into darkness. An idea that has a soul sparkles, jumps over walls, fords rivers, flies over flames.

We dream with our eyes closed.
We dream with our eyes wide open.
We're hunting a trove of secrets.

Things take a turn for the worse for the neighbor's cock / wing slaps loosen its feathers / spur hits blind its eyes / twenty goud on the red rooster / double or nothing / they look us up and down / they make a turn at the next crossroads / we hear a woman's voice / we open the door a crack / it's all dark outside / it's all dark inside / misfortune mushrooms / an army of thieves dig up the sweet potatoes in our fields at night / the fortune-teller's mouth is a machine gun / the earth boils / the sea foams / the sand heats

up / razor-sharp words / poisonous words / windy words / trea-
sonous words / they let a crooked two-bit player release that pintadin rooster in the cockpit / Zofè forbids anyone to come near
the ounfò / we've avoided the trap / be careful in the damp dusk
air! / we won't go outside / Jédéyon is gaga from binging on tafia / he won't get sober anytime soon / the zonbis' skin is raw and
scaly / Filojèn asks why anyone would bring a cowardly rooster to
the cockfight / they surrender without a fight / Zofè kills a rebellious zonbi / lots of wax in our eyes / nausea / we have a hard
time swallowing our food / a commotion near the fried food vendor's stand / the rural policeman rains blows with his stick / heads
get broken / wrists get twisted / panic in the crowd / people get
shoved around / wipe that grin off your face / a nuisance / we stay
out of the way / Siltana looks faded / Rita is tired of working for
no pay / Jédéyon's pants are thinning at the crotch / he'll be going
around crotchless / Gaston misses Bouanèf / Sintil separates two
zonbis who have been rebelling in the room they share / teeth get
knocked out / roosters start sparring in the darkening weather /
the cockfight is heating up / chairs get broken / shoulders get disjointed / horses are let loose on the savanna / one of Jédéyon's
shoes rolls down the stairs / a strange dream disturbs our sleep /
Klodonis's shabrack is faded / a patchwork shabrack / Zofè rains
blows with his stick / the zonbis' heads piss blood / Siltana rushes
into her room / Zofè starts getting suspicious / the weather hasn't
cleared yet / we're still having bad dreams / Sintil is still in the
dark about Siltana / Jéròm's head is crowded with thoughts up
there in the attic / the zonbis are all disfigured / Zofè punishes
zonbis even for talking in their sleep / a rooster crows / words are
unfurling / words are unfolding . . .

> *The moon is waning*
> *We hold our tongues*
> *Lightning strikes*
> *Fire breaks out in broad daylight*

The winds buffet the trees. The winds uncap the straw-roofed shacks. We remain vigilant and watch our backs. We've put our corn out to dry in the sun. We're watching. We mark out the course. We blaze a trail. We get ourselves out of trouble.

A fight breaks out / the gamecocks' crests stand erect / the fried food vendor looks Kamélo up and down as he stands between two candelabra cacti / voices in the night sounding like a country rara band wake us up / water carries / the wind pushes / we gird our loins / a cowardly cock flies away from the cockpit / a mother hen is clucking in the bushes / women get manhandled at those country dances . . .

The trip is grueling
             Darkness gums up our eyelids
Our tongues are tangled up
             We're clip-clopping our way in the dark.

We stumble against tree stumps. We slip on sharp stones. We're wounded. We bleed. We fall face down in the mud. We get back on our feet. We don't lie there crippled. We take heart. We won't give up!

One day Gaston bumps into a Bouanèf villager at the Croix-Bossales market. He is told a load of gut-wrenching, heartbreaking news. Aunt Louizina died from malaria fever four years ago. Antonin hanged himself the very week Gaston left the village. Sintil has been lording it over the villagers of Bouanèf and Ravin Sèch with an iron hand. Zofè has been pounding the zonbis like millet in a mortar. Fabi left for Nassau a long time ago. Bouanèf has completely lost its soul. Gaston raises his hands to his face and cries like a child.

We make our beds / we're sleepy / we lie on a bed of nails / a frisky colt will mount a mare with no holds barred / a knife to the throat / a rusty dagger / a bad draft is pulling us / the dézafi is in full swing on the other side of the tracks . . .

Dreams adrift
    Words thrown to the wind
Love and death walk hand in hand

    We've had to harden our hearts so that pain doesn't
drain us too much.

An electric jolt to our stomachs, to our guts, so we can have some relief from the gut-twisting pain of so much misery.

A blinding blow to the head / we look for a shortcut / a gutsy player doesn't surrender easily / as soon as the sun rises Gaston hits the road / we'll take care of things no matter what it takes / we've got guts / Zofè cuts a zonbi's finger off with one blow of his hatchet / this time we're able to follow the tracks of the madlèn snake / the darkening face of the sky keeps us from going out / a sickly colored sky / Jédéyon grumbles / Rita hasn't brewed the coffee yet / the rib bones of the Ravin Sèch children are sticking out / life is strange / they had to take up a collection in Bouanèf to get enough money to bury Antonin / sudden anger / looks of resentment / the ship got wrecked on a reef / our love is new / the rain disappointed us / all the flowers have wilted / a blowout in the county / we throw every piece of junk on the street / roosters preening about / broken-legged cocks / a pack of dogs on top of one another / the land has been plowed deep / a herd of goats wander into Sintil's garden / Zofè cuts off the head of every single one of them / they've scattered poisoned corn for our roosters throughout the cockfight arena / Jédéyon drank a whole barrel of tafia / he has trouble waking up / we bet on the wrong cock / we're mortified / a woman without dignity will return to the brothel / our wings are on backward / how could we ever fly? / a smoldering fire / the blowback will come later / Jéròm has a constipated look on his face from being so secretive / they want to take their revenge on our children / words have been weighing heavy on our chests for a long time / if the child hadn't died we'd be grandparents now / the crime weighs on our conscience / anger has spoiled Kamélo's blood / he's angrier than a conger eel / Siltana is in deep doo-doo / a pack of dogs are barking their hunger / party poopers / a fight breaks out in the shack / our fault that the plate full of food broke / we haven't suffered enough / our suffering has just begun / we ought to stop taking it easy / you get the ball of yarn all tangled up if you pull on it too much / the fighting and betting finally end / then the betting starts anew . . .

Two look-alike clouds up in the sky start fighting with each other. Which one will tear up the other? Down here on the ground we can only watch. There's no way we can get between them.

Our pain is more than we can bear
            We're dragging a strange cross draped in rags
They're running after us with their machetes drawn
            They've set our asses on fire
The moon is mottled like turkey feathers
            The moon's face is pockmarked from smallpox
The night is so long
            But where is our memory?
We're in trouble if we listen to our anger.

The sixth round opens / the neighbor's cock is a loser / don't bet on it / Gaston stays in his little corner / several checkers pieces are trapped / the slug crawls back into its hole / we fall on our backsides / we nearly break our tailbones / the game is dicey / the golden mouth smiles wide / tall cliffs stand in our way / hammerlock / scrofula / we take heart / we swallow our medicine /

we drink down our purgative / our collarbones show how skinny
we are / we don't stand up and dance on just any foot / we have
a clear mind / we ask for just a tiny bit / they spit in our hands /
they enjoy hassling us / Siltana can't sleep at night / her face is all
crumpled up / she looks like a mad dog / Zofè is suspicious / the
sound of feet on dry straw / Jéròm climbs up the ladder in a jiffy /
eating straw / drinking kerosene / supping on matches / little kids
don't go to cockfights / a machete fight breaks out / people shit in
their pants / people dash away / bones get disjointed / the shack
gets smashed up / they go around looking for trouble / loose
bowels / the horse gets saddled up / utter chaos / scattershots /
they're out to get us / they try to push our buttons / they can't get
to us / prowlers run away to the bush / Filojèn doesn't fall into
traps / Filojèn was born with a veil over his head / Filojèn sees the
dead / suspicious characters prowl around our house / they can't
get to us / days go by / they want to tie us up / Kamélo is chilling
under an acacia tree / we haven't entered the game yet / they're
putting the heat on us / the mad dogs are loose at the cockfight /
we'll never set foot here again / our bodies are itching / but we
hang on / we keep our mouths shut / we manage to walk down a
narrow path / we still hold on tight / we'll hold on come hell or
high water / we're cool / we haven't unpluggled / there's no end
to us / we're in the dézafi for the long run . . .

*Our house is about to collapse. The night birds fly away at sun-
rise. They've slipped a hook around our necks. We stall midway up
the mountain. Still we don't go and fall down a cliff. Blood curdles
into a ball in our throats. In a wrestling match we parry a goat's
throw. We go on, we continue our journey. But we whisper into a
calabash to keep them from stealing our voices.*

*Dusk has fallen. Fog surrounds us. We've been walking in shit
for quite a while. We're in trouble. At the drop of a hat they drop
a crushing load on our backs. The night is long. We rely on no one
but ourselves to build our dreams, to put our words together.*

The fried food vendor is making a killing at the cockfight / Kamélo screams / food is so expensive! / they call him a preemie /
they say he's a leaf short / a madman is lying flat on his stomach
caressing his shadow in the midday sun / lots of gossip boiling /
rumors spread throughout the village / Filojèn is eating a snack
in the shack / dark rituals in Sintil's yard / sharp thorns in the
zonbis' backsides / the sea's in a bad mood / boats overturn / the
sky's water breaks / Zofè brings his stick down right and left /
bumps shoot up on the zonbis' heads / with his stick / we get
blows on our ears / blood pours out of the stones / chameleons
shouldn't come near us / Sintil prepares a three-drops magic potion / Jédéyon is binging / we're thinking of getting into the cockfight / a bunch of loudmouths start talking nonsense / a hell of a
pileup / Filojèn looks crestfallen / some gamecock trainer is spewing curses and insults / the words foam / a savanna rooster goes
beak down / Kamélo and Filojèn are masters of the biting loaded
word / worms down in the trees' roots / we plunge in deep waters
where divers have to do the breaststroke / get yourselves together
on dry ground / the water reaches up to our chins / serious players
don't talk much / the game is in full swing / the beast of burden
is pregnant / Gaston is crossing swords with Pastor Pin Kris over
charity rice / the cat knows / the rat knows . . .

> We're famished
>> Much pushing and shoving
> A patch of sky of clashing colors
>> A patch of sky the color of parrot shit
> A sliver of light
>> Our memory is returning

The klérin rum flows like water in the shack / the zonbis are
limping over metal wires under the Spanish beard moss hanging

from the trees / shaven heads / both arms behind their backs /
tongues hanging / they start whining wee waan! wee waan! wee
waan! / they've been baptized into the family of the démanbré /
the family of the debrained / the family of the despirited / the family of the denerved / the key's under the door to Fabi's house / he's
scampered away to Nassau / a dice game has been set up on the
edge of the cockfight / a big fete in Sintil's yard / the dusty-footed
traveler gets a head start / Siltana's chewed off her thumb up to her
shoulder / a fruit dried up to pit and skin / Zofè is busy beating
up the zonbis / the hairs on Filojèn's back stand up / the ounzi
kanzo raise their voices in song / they clap their hands / the sixth
betting round is in full swing / gamecocks don't nap / the gabfest's
on / Zofè and Sintil are a molly and tom couple / they spit in each
other's mouths / Filojèn and Kamélo are two peas in a pod / they
tether their horses to the same post / Gaston and Pin Kris are thick
as thieves / they hatch plots together / Jéròm and Alibé are joined
at the hips / they sleep in the same bed / Siltana and Klodonis are
two blades of a mill / a troubled journey / Jédéyon and Rita are
like the drumstick to the drum / strike the skin get a sound / a mos-
quito swarm dance / a watch-out-for-zonbis dance / a what-do-I-
care dance / but on which foot should we dance? / several times
we've been done in for good / they found our soft spot / tit for
tat / they come down hard on us / the zonbis stutter / two gamecocks are crossing spurs / they go claws against claws / a nervous
gambler is mopping up his face / a straw sack full of junk goods /
mouth closed over a bridle's bit / who's given up? / the fried food
vendor has caught a cheater / the zonbis' skin is leathery / the
zonbis' skin is scarred / Klodonis's shabrack is torn open under the
sleeves / his head is smeared with greenpondmudpigshit / whatever it is / the rural police officer is shoving everyone around /
Klodonis is as clueless as a pétévi / the rain is rattattating on the
metal roof of Sintil's house / Klodonis blows a dry fart / Zofè
sets him straight with a slap / Siltana's heart rises to her throat / a
whole lot of people talk nonsense / stillborn monkeys / the roosters are punch-drunk from spur jabs / greedy caymans plow the
mud with their snouts / Jédéyon went daft a long time ago . . .

They've blinded our eyes. Mouths open, we spend the night counting the stars. Our eyes have turned squinty. We haven't eaten a thing. We haven't drunk a single drop. They're cheapskates. Still, we don't lose hope. A woman's voice attracts us. The mistress of our house is counting the days until she gives birth. Our baby is already in the birth canal; we swallow our saliva.

Klodonis's shabrack hangs loose over his body / a bunch of greedy gamblers have invaded the cockfight / they blow fire / they set things aflame / not a day goes by without us finding our lucky woman / no wind can disturb our horse tethered to the pole / at daybreak the zonbis are already hard at work in the swamps / jujus don't scare us one bit / Gaston's found a porter's job / Siltana got tired of cuddling Klodonis / love and death go hand in hand / we draw a vèvè cross on the ground / we make a cross on our lips / we bind the bad loua to keep our dreams from getting disturbed / we swear our dreams will not be chopped up / we rise up to keep our dreams from getting stabbed / expect the tremors of the thunderstorm / the cooking pots have been upended / the Ravin Sèch folks are roasting the wind / a killer cock has flown away / two-bit gamblers lose by a hair's breadth at the dice game in the shack / a bloody fight erupts / so many gamecocks at this cockfight! / today the fights will go on for a long time / the wick has been lit / they won't let us sleep / they won't let us breathe / we work / our hands are as rough as a grater / they've planned quite a rebuke for those dusty-footed ne'er-do-wells / we take just one look at those angry gamblers / our heads feel dizzy / the rooster reels under the spur hits / death spasms / the thuggish gamblers demand the cock's carcass / fool's gold fools no one / plop-drip-plop / we hear a woman's voice / we move closer / she slips away / she has the spirit of an eel / they've burned magic herbs on our backs / caribbean sun / bouziyèt sun / Jédéyon's trousers are flapping loose on him / they've prepared a sugarcane peel covered with ants for those shameless bums / a few words thrown to the wind / they want to pull us with a rope / we don't go along / the weather wears a frown / they're out to involve us in some messy trouble / a wasp's nest / we avoid clashes / bitter pain stabs a stomach that has been hungry too long / he's rasping / the road to a faraway country / the sun is sleeping off his drunkenness in the sea's navel / insolent kids mock shuffling zonbis / Jédéyon bought shark bones for his joint pains / a head cushion of words supports a load of ideas / we're courting the moon / a comet appears in the sky / our whippy snake has simply evaporated / many people are shocked and anxious / who eats beans? / who devours the tiger's cub? / a flock of massive clouds hang behind the mountains / we haven't eaten in three days . . . we're famished . . . we're hungry . . . that's true . . . but we don't have a whoring stomach . . . we don't take the bait and get ourselves caught in someone's fishing net . . .

> The wind is blowing
> > Trash scatters about
> We place two stories on the balance
> > One weighs more than the other
> The singing birds are hungry
> > The birds are so weak they faint
> Our bodies are tired and frail
> > We're feeling lethargic
> We fade in
> > We fade out
> We fall asleep
> > Misery blooms
> Rain drizzle
> > The devil's piss

The spittle in our hungry mouths is more bitter than gall. We just grit our teeth. Poisoned food tempts us. Day in. Day out. We refuse to eat zonbi cucumber.

Caymans flicker their tongues in and out of their rotten mouths. Then the worms swarm; the flies hum. Fresh meat is ripped. Guts are torn up.

The measure of our hands is the measure of our actions. When it rains, we grow leaves.
We grow buds
We hustle to live.

The seventh round opens with the mother of all fights / two mean cocks face off / two well-matched cocks / a bitter taste in our mouths / our tongues feel heavy / love lies in quiet wait for death / it's a tough fight / we bolster our hearts with hope / the music has started / we haven't started dancing yet / Filojèn asks the fried food vendor for a dégi / Sintil asks for vinegar to give to a restive horse . . .

They've driven us insane
We've learned to keep our ideas close to our chests
It looks like rain is coming
Our tongues are tied
Our tongues are raw
Stagnant water is brackish

The game's in full swing. We take our time. We think before we speak. We observe. Our ears ring. We hear a pregnant woman's scream. Her water has broken; she'll be dropping the baby anytime now.

The seventh round is heating up / a stupid referee allows someone to pit a mad dog against a wild cat in the middle of the cockfight / a fire burns our house down / bad luck pursues us / we've become misery's regular customers / the neighbor's rooster drops dead / one of the ladder's steps suddenly breaks / Jéròm twists his ankle / Zofè lays slaps on everyone / a brawl at the cockfight /

Kamélo gives as good as he gets / a zonbi has cold blood / a zonbi never sweats / the ugly ones are on their way / the fried food vendor rips a length of cloth / heavy acid spray / two cockers are egging their roosters on in the cockpit / we go through hell / they may hand us millions / we will not twist our tongues / the gamecocks reel from spur hits and wing slaps / they've hit the jackpot / we find nothing / avocado green snot drips from the zonbi's nostrils / we will finally tame that wild mule / disarray / bad call in a bad fight . . .

We frolic in the water. When we get tired of swimming we float around on our backs.

The weather's donned a mask. House doors are shut. We're looking for a passkey.

The killer cock is wounded / the killer cock dies / the killer cock lies dead flat on the ground / crest chopped up / feathers scattered / zonbis' teeth fallen / a crowded cockfight / at the blink of an eye / Zofè reaches for his bullwhip / Klodonis falls down on his face / he loses face / drumbeats up in the mountain / we measure the sun's height / we cannot throw a challenge yet / a heavy weight on our chests / we're spent / they persecute us / Gaston's gone all the way to La Gonave to look for buried jars of gold / the seas are rough / misfortune awaits . . .

A wee bit of hope
A sliver of memory
Where do our branches meet?
Where are our roots?

Our path is full of dangers. Poisoned food. Ravines. Cliffs. Jagged rocks. Tree stumps. Glass shards. Man-eating aloufa. Broken bottles. *Monstrous beasts. Mud ponds. We're thirsty. We're hungry. We're tired.*

We walk by death's side with our eyes shut. Our dreams aren't to the measure of our hands.

Our beds have been broken; our homes have been burned to the ground; our clothes are in tatters. We keep walking. We keep searching.

A flock of birds is flying in the distance
   Bunches of flowers are wilting on their branches
Questions erupt by the load.
   We mull things over; we mumble; we give a few answers. They ignore us. But, day in, day out, we get the better of the enemy at that hide-and-seek game.

   Seaweed is piled up in a messy tangle. Sweat has congealed on our bodies. Our mouths taste bitter. A protective oungévé necklace around our necks, a piece of sacrifice flesh on our tongues, our fight has just begun. We'll keep wielding our swords till kingdom come.

   They blow on the fire. Shock. Diarrhea. Fatigue.

Tarbaby bad luck / tenacious bad luck
  We flee from the coffin
Only to stumble against the corpse
  We drink verbena tea

A purplish sun spreads its arms over the sea. First turn we catch it. We slip. We fall. We quickly take a shortcut to the other side of love, to the other side of death.

Why do we change sides?
Our lips got burned sucking on a bamboo stick
    A pipe in our mouths wrong end in
We're swallowing smoke
        The okra slips from between our fingers
Sadness weighs heavy on our hearts.
        Neighbors
        Friends
        Family
        But why do we change sides?

The seventh round is at full throttle / we have a cock in the
fight / Man-eating aloufa have their eyes on our kids / some ne'er-
do-well fool grins mockingly / he gets his hand chopped off at
the wrist with a single machete blow / backbiter / no escape for
him / Jéròm is choking with anger in the attic / an aroused bull
is mounting a gazelle / hell's fire burns in broad daylight / cockfight fans pull out their iron swords / cockers and gamblers wield
their sticks / the earth bleeds / we jump into thorny bushes / our
bodies are limp with exhaustion / a fracas at the cockfight / we lie
low in a corner / Kamélo is in the thick of the stick fight / Filojèn
jumps up / he takes off like some cowardly rooster / the battle
heats up / a rural policeman is thrown to the ground / the sight
whips up our blood / Filojèn turns back / two gamecock owners
want to set pintadin roosters in the cockpit / a brawl erupts . . .

They prod us right and left. Our faces are drawn and gaunt. We
swallow our words. We walk to the end of the earth looking for
our shadows we still haven't found any trace of it . . .

A bunch of greedy scamming gamblers challenge us to a bet.
They offer double or nothing. We ignore their siren's song. We de-
cline their poisoned offer. They insist. They prod. They cajole. We
don't respond. We're not alone.

Our offspring are countless
        Our race is legion.

One rooster goes beak down / Zofè is suspicious / he keeps Siltana on a short leash / the cock wakes up / they want to wipe the blood on us / the sea foams / a smell rises from the graveyard / the smell of death spreads / Sintil is digging a grave / the night is ominous / Sintil's never found out where Jéròm has been hiding / the seventh round drags on / two well-matched cocks are sparring . . .

We've just come out of our mother's womb. Yet we've been on the way for a long time.

        Our work is not done yet
        Our work cannot be done
        Our work cannot be done yet
        Our work will never be done
        Our work has just begun

Several chain links have been broken
        Many daggers have been sharpened
Yes!
        Yessirree!!!

        We've just come out of our mother's womb.
We warm our blood by a fire
        That is yet to be lit.
We warm our blood in a fire
        That has been lit in our heads.

Whenever there's a fight among brawlers wielding iron swords, the undertaker is happy. Our eyes aren't closed. We sing songs with loaded lyrics. Death turns back. Death makes a turn. If we ever happen to lose our voices, who will take up the song in our stead?

The night is long, very long. We've gathered into a tight crowd at midnight's crossroads. Our heads are full of stars. Our memory has sunk in bottomless water. We suffer painful burns before a mirror. Our voices are torn to tatters. Who will take up the scream until daybreak in our stead?

A harsh light blinds our eyes. Our backs arch like humps under the heavy loads. There is still a long way to go before we find the roots of death. Flowers of evil. Cursed buds. Epileptic shade. Should the sun flee to the other side of the ocean, should it go into hiding for good, who will warm our children's blood?

Water covers the rooftops
        The dogs drink water through their nostrils
An ill wind is blowing
        We dance till we're drunk

A flock of birds in full flight
        never comes to ground.
A spitfire mouth
        never rests.

Brighter than lightning, the tongue is a two-edged sword.
Sharper than a dagger, the tongue pierces guts.
Nimbler than thunder, the tongue jumps over fences.
Lighter than a feather, the tongue floats hither and thither.

        Two gambling partners start cursing each other in the middle of the cockfight. They tear into each other. When you listen closely to their insults you hear quite a lot of nonsense.

We spend the whole night searching behind the looking glass.
We go through walls. We lose our shadows.

The sun has yet to rise.
>   *We don't see the least hint of a soul*
>   *We don't see any sign of a soul*
>   *We don't sniff out anyone*
>   *We don't smell anything*
>   *We don't hear any voice*

Words thrown to the wind
Andaki words
Flaming poison burns the tongue of the indiscreet speaker
>   *We dream*
>   *We rise*
>   *We walk*
>   *We seek.*

We haven't found out which foot to put forward to join the
dance. We try to find out again; our quest has barely begun.

Plop

>   *drip*

>   *plop!*

A slither of serpent words are unfurling their bodies
A herd of horse words are galloping on the savanna
A cacophony of hard-edged music spills through the streets

Words have branches
Words have knots
Words have curves

Even though we're not possessed by the loua, we say, Ayibobo!

We're in a mean and foul mood in our dreams; we wake up all
gung ho. We keep searching. When we get tired we lurk about, we
slink around, we skin our faces against the rough walls.

A tiny flake of corn under our fingernails, a grain of salt under
our tongues, no fight scares us, twenty centuries of labor do not
trouble us. Patience. Courage. Stoicism. It's all in our blood.

The moon is drinking water from the pond under the gum tree.
We delve into the darkness under the bushes.
We lie down on thorns, on an ant's nest.
We prick our ears, we hear many sounds.

Master Antouan Langonmié!
Which way is the wind blowing?

Conceited people are skilled liars
As for us, we'll just take in the scene.

Dry straw swells in our throats, blocks our uvulas, and chokes
us as it slides down our gullets. We stutter as we try to speak.

The seasonal fever is in our blood; our bare feet are splayed in
the sticky mud; our toes draw vèvè symbols that look like death
flowers; a curse gums up our eyelids.

We're on the list of those who are marked. We're on the list of those to be disposed of if we don't get a move on, if we don't lift our feet higher.

We've made some headway. We look at the sky. Just our bad luck, the weather wears its frowning face. Still, we hope to find shelter from the rain under some tree.

Tomorrow
the sun will stage one hell of a dézafi.

The dew oozes pink
on the tree leaves at dawn.
        We're already wide awake
        before the cooking fires are lit.
We walk quite a distance
before the sun rises.
        So many dreams clashed in a tangled mass in our
heads as we slept.
We forget them in a heartbeat.
They burn up in the heat.

We haven't seen each other face to face; our mouths met a long time ago.
We have never talked to each other; our voices are tangled into a tight bundle.
We love each other to death; we are one body.
The devil starts beating his wife; high noon, rain, love.

They choke us, they chafe us.
They rip us, they rumple us.
They chop us, they chip us.

They rob us, they disrobe us.
They frig us, they fuck us.

We laugh inside
We laugh in our bones.

They're readying the rusty daggers to castrate the zonbis.
A bunch of folks hightail it deep into the bush.
The lasigouav monster scares only little children and the feeble-
minded.
As for us, we stand fast by a smoking fire.

> *Seated in the cool dusk, we pull down the stars*
that are blinding us.
> *The night is thick, the night is long; we count the*
falling stars.

> *A gang of aloufa fall on a pregnant woman;*
they slice open her belly; they pull out her baby. But the sun will
rise tomorrow. We hear a woman's voice. We rush to take a look.
A bright light is shining where the navel should be. New grass is
growing.

Every morning we stick a picket into the ground; we're counting
the days. We talk by ourselves. We talk to ourselves

Lightning wounds us like a machete. The light trembles; the
water quivers; bones get smashed; the earth bleeds. We shudder to
our marrow.

Our heads feel all woolly; our shoulders are dislocated; our
hands are limp; our hips are lopsided; our legs are crooked. We
wear a mask. We are crippled. We're turned inside out. We walk
with a drag. We walk with a gimp.

Are we playing games?
Which is our real face?
Have we really changed?
Have we changed for good?
Or are we faking it?

The wind slices the tongues of those who jabber on the street.
Our mouths are all black; they say we're crazy. Iron swords are
drawn. We gird our loins. Our guts are wrenched. We hear a wom-
an's scream. We vomit a stream of blood; we're covered with our
own blood.

Night catches us in a dangerous ravine. Weapons are drawn at
the cockfight. Brand-new machetes are wielded. Dangerous beasts
lie in wait in our path.

False words scatter in the wind. We need patience to dig up the
sun's corpse. We dream our fingers have metamorphosed into pass-
keys.

We tickle life; death turns around. We meet our shadow; it
doesn't look like us at all. We talk to it; it doesn't answer. We're
cold to our very bones.

In our sleep needles break, eggs shatter, birds fall dead. We
hit the road; we go sniffing around for food; we swallow air; we
lie down to sleep in the damp after rain; we've forgotten the way
home.

Conspiracy. Our tongues are tied. Our lips are under lock and
key. Woop! We stand up. We stomp our feet. We roll on the ground.
We bounce up and down. We free our necks from their nooses. Our
voices rise up to the sky.

We wash and rub our rags; the soapy foam rises; the soapy foam spreads.

A troublesome wind rises, churning the trash around; we're covered with dust; a whirlwind surrounds us.

A cat jumps over the fence.

> *Lightning words*
> *Thunder words*
> *Words have feet*
> *Words have wings*
The light dies
> *We don't know why*
We fly high
> *We're not human!*
Baka, out of the way!

At midnight sharp
> *A noise at the door*
We're startled
> *We hold our breath*
We hear a scream
> *They're speaking in langay*

We don't remember anything
> *Clews of worms have hollowed out our brains*
Our memory has fled abroad
> *Our memory has broken its tether*

The eighth round has started / spurs split open many a game-cock's chest / gamblers spit blood / pockets are turned inside out / Siltana spent a sleepless night / hardwood stick blows rain on the zonbis' backs / Zofè beats up Klodonis / opened veins / dislocated shoulders / smashed mouths / biting words / fires lit on the zonbis' backs / the earth covered with suppurating wounds / derailed trains / overturned boats / sky rent / Jéròm has learned to live alone in the attic / misery stomps us / hunger stabs us / death has a strong smell / Kamélo and Filojèn are still watching out for scammers at the cockfight / they've come to the dézafi to win . . .

The days fly
We cuddle rag dolls

We climb up a tree. We hang head down. The branch shatters. We fall to the ground face down. The earth feels our weight.

We're carried far away by raging floodwaters; we get burned in fire. Crabs feed on the entrails of dead animals; the smell of corpses is overpowering; the stench of rotting carcasses spreads.

Oh, earthly beings! The cross of misfortune is abroad. Lock your doors up tight! Making faces before a mirror attracts death.

We throw words to the wind. We collect andaki words. We open our eyes wide. We look for some small opening to catch a sliver of light; we find a borderless shadow.

We've been digging. Our fingers are now dull; our fingers have lost their edge. We dig like crazy.
Tèktègèdèk!

No wasting time / tar glue / lime dust / twirling smoke / a woman's coffin / rob the graveyard / steal a woman / steal a soul / zonbis in the swamp / Siltana's lost her mind over Klodonis / Zofè is suspicious / Sintil keeps fielding a pintadin gamecock in the cockpit . . .

The moon's face is pockmarked
Life and death are twins

We've been hauling such heavy loads that our lower backs have caved in / the neighbor's cock is reeling from two quick spur hits / pinched lips / swollen jaws / lighted fires / bleeding rocks / Zofè assaults the zonbis with his bullwhip / Jéròm is in a foul mood up in the attic / he wants to get out / he wants to drink a bitter cup of coffee with Sintil, have it out with him . . .

Love is weighing anchor; hold your breath or else death shall sink you.

A hurricane is raging
        We swallow loads of words
Many, many words are repressed
        We keep our hopes under our skin
The hurricane is rampaging out there
There's a storm brewing in our hearts.

A massacre. We cross the river. Roots of underwater plants under our feet. Bro Piè's pian-plagued flat feet bleed blood.

The roof of our house has burned down; the sky is now our blanket. Someone's sprinkled itching-pea powder all over the yard; someone's sprinkled powdered black pepper all over the cockfight arena. We scream. We scream so much that our voices turn raw.

A single match. The bridle catches fire. We talk. We take a heavy load off our chests. Escape. We forge ahead.

The lamp's wick's been lighted
        The secret is out.

Life and death worship in the same ounfò.
We sweat blood.
                           Broken bottle shards lie at the bottom of still waters.
          Polished stones lie smooth in spring water.
                           The shark's teeth are like a sharp saw under the sea.
                           We're just learning how to live.

Big cat

                    Blue balls

Beast of burden

                    Bag of nails

Butt ugly

                    Bite tongues off!

Star dust

                    Slit veins

Smoking candle

                    Old folks grumbling

Torture room

                    Bone-crushing mill

    Corpses are piled up two rows deep; zonbis' corpses are inciner-
ated. Dark and malodorous clouds lick the sun's belly, sweep over
the mountain peaks. A mute boy raises his head to look up; he's
sucking his gossipy forefinger.

A gazillion people start talking all at the same time. We turn away at once. We have no time for talk that is neither male nor female.

They come after us in the middle of the night. We don't fall into two-bit traps nor do we get caught in half-assed snares. We've been untying gordian knots and unraveling tangled ropes since we were born. When we get tired we change places with one another. That way we manage to catch our breath.
        Head backwards . . .

        Eyes rolled back . . .

Deadly games . . .

We're on the job season out in season out. We've walked for so long in the sun that our skin is coarse as tanned leather, our heels burnt, our ankles swollen, our legs stiff. A ferocious hunger is gnawing our insides.

Days go by. We bathe in an infusion of green leaves. We wet the tips of our tongues. We gargle with spring water.

During the day we speak out loud, we talk in code. At night we speak in a low voice, we speak clearly, we speak the truth. In the presence of the enemy we speak in signs, we talk in one another's ears, we whisper, we spread rumors and gossip.

To get rid of the idiots and bigmouths who linger too long in our house, we sprinkle a few grains of salt under their chairs and stand a broom upside down behind the door. This is why some people say we're sorcerers. The rumor mill spreads the smear. They say we're lougarou who fly in broad daylight.

Ninth round / the roosters have been released / they've allowed cockers from far away to pitch pintadin roosters in the cockpit / two-bit cheating players and gamblers / Filojèn and Kamélo scream / they shout stop thieves / they shout catch 'em / they shout stop 'em catch 'em! / several players and gamblers react / we make haste as we walk in the country sun / the ninth round breaks up . . .

Our joints hurt; seasonal fever has turned our skin inside out. Our horses are neighing at their tethers. Our yard is packed full of skinny starving dogs with droopy eyes.

Each time we see the sea we think of slaving in the salt marshes. Each time we see a flock of birds in the sky our hearts become heavy.

The trees are rotting. Their leaves droop. The flowers are wilting on their branches. The mangoes drop to the ground before they mature. The tree roots dry up in the ground. Ill winds blow us into the darkness. The power we got from the dark side is driving us mad; we made a bargain with the devil and now we're paying the price.

Weird dreams fragment our sleep. We scream in our nightmares. When we wake up we find some bitter medicine to drink. False hopes. Rusty daggers. Burnt meat. We're tired of going to sleep only to dream of masquerades. We're tired of swallowing purgatives.

A blinding light shines over the mountain peaks. We follow our shadows. The sun burns our eyelids and leaves no scars. Temptation. The sun grates our tongues and leaves no residues. We burn bitter words deep inside our hearts.

Weevils rampage through our gardens. Rapacious pests eat mud, lick cadavers, dig into rotten navels, suck up and spit out the dead's flesh, stink up the graveyard. We quickly plug our noses.

Dusk falls. The earth bends its knees. We embark on death's pelvis-grinding boat. We haul a pelvis-churning coffin. Spurs are thrust right and left. We gallop faster than a galipòt horse. Flowers get crushed under hooves. Blood flows. We become baka for once to save our children.

The corners of our mouths are rotting. The pain is like a piercing arrow. The pain is like a club smashing our bones to the marrow. The pain is like burning coal in our veins. We're not horses, we're not livestock, we're not mules. Why do they want to stamp us with a branding iron? Life has already ground our flesh.

Mosquitos and blackflies bite our children as they sleep. Mosquitos play their grating music. Ferocious critters practice scales for the night's ears.

Beware zonbis!

We shake our bodies. Our roots are a tangled mass. Our roots have no beginning and no end. We let our dreams marinate inside our heads. We climb up stairs, we climb up ladders, we climb up mountain peaks. We ride naked on an immense cloud. We travel at full speed to the end of the earth, to the fabled land of the sanmba, where we catch rose-colored fishes, where we trap birds of gold. Our ten fingers wide open, we pluck the purple stars. All hot and eager, we lie down to caress Lasirèn Diaman.

The river is full of junk / its waters overflow with rubbish / Kamélo is talking nonsense at the cockfight / Filojèn makes a long face / we're thinking / we don't wish to run into trouble / we stand up / we mull things over / we dodge / we pretend to have supernatural powers / we speak in langay / words are uttered in whispers / many bets are placed at the dézafi on the other side of the tracks / we talk nonsense / we make a gazillion occult signs . . .

The house's roof has caught fire
            The flames grow horns
Lips stiffen
            We're getting roasted
Fences are overturned
            The women start complaining
Our tails grow longer
            Our ears hang lower
Our heads are in turmoil
            We've turned into monstrous beasts
The house collapses
            The sky's floodgate opens
The rain pours down like a deluge
            We're wet as sponges
The sun flickers its tongue
            We come out onto the street

Avocado season. Mango season. Maize season. Millet season. Sugarcane season. Off season. Hog-tying season. Round and round we go.

The lasigouav monsters are out; mothers will suffer much.

Rain. Mud. Sun. Dust. Hunger. Misery. A calvary of martyrs. A calvary of miracles. A tortuous calvary. A vicious circle of a calvary. A calvary full of uncertainty.

When are we leaving?
            Let's go!

The sound of footsteps
            The rumble of thunder
The roar of the wind
            Turtledoves taking flight

Wild cats hiding in the bush
            Avocadoes falling off the trees
The moon is pockmarked
            The stars are hanging from the sky
Rusty daggers are out
            We cut poles to pull down the clouds
Brains splatter
            All hands on deck
We dream of Tèt-san-kò
            Hold the knives by their handles

The trees have been sparring with the wind until they've lost their leaves, their flowers, their branches, and their birds. We barely finish combing our hair they start uncombing it. They pull our hair. They uproot our hairs. The streets won't regain their colors anytime soon; we'll be combing our hair for a long time yet.

As we wait for daybreak we chain-smoke; the tobacco tastes bitter as bile in our mouths. Even water is tasteless. Our tongues are raw. We lie alone, fetus-like, by a pile of rocks. We hear the crickets' music; we regain our strength. We have a word with the creatures of the woods. The cow's udders are swollen with milk. Butterflies alight on our shoulders. The sky scowls under our nails. Stone crusher. Iron breaker. Mountain slasher. The hawk closes its wings. We rise. We keep walking. We dive into a river. We swim lightning fast like the slippery eel. We arrive at the sea; we swim below the surface. We find the secrets of the conch. We have a word with the creatures of the water.

The trees are playing with the wind.
            A brawl ensues.
We see the color of the sky under our nails.

They may build a wall around us, our dreams will vault over it be it seventeen leagues long, seventeen leagues high.

Our dreams have wings.
We shout for help
         The owl's shadow slips away
The cheers now go to the other side
         Who's devoured the tiger's cub?
The plates are turned over
         Who's had any beans to eat?

We lick the corners of our mouths. Why are our gums bleeding? Why are our teeth hurting? We're guilty of nothing; we bear no responsibility for the spices, nor for the sauce, nor for the scandals. Besides, we've been in hiding, out of circulation.

Smoke is rising from the other side of the fence; the neighbor sets a pot on the cooking fire every day; one hears the sizzle of meat in hot oil over there. As for us, we've been tightening a rope around our guts for a long time now. Who's had any beans to eat? Who's butchered the tiger's cub?

We're thinking hard. We remember . . .
         We remember the sound of the iron swords. The abattoir stench. The smell of death. We make a turn into a narrow alley. A pack of hungry dogs are fighting over a garbage heap.

         It's been raining. Offal and all sorts of junk are floating all the way down to the sea. Baskets full of holes. Crushed basins. Rusted fence wire. Bits of cloth. Rags. Beat-up cooking pots. Bottomless chamber pots. Meat fat. Chair legs. Old soles. Lots of torn shoes. Mouldy hats. Bottle bottoms.

         Handymen, tinsmiths, cooking-pot makers, chitterlings and junk peddlers form a hustling swarm on the sidewalk. Street urchins are fighting in the open sewers over bits of roofing tin and pieces of cardboard.

Which way is the scale leaning?

Bottle bottoms and glass shards crown the walls. Nails and thorns are strewn in our path. We're plodding through mud. But our dreams have wings. We don't allow our dreams to falter.

They may build a wall around us, our dreams will vault over it be it seventeen leagues long, seventeen leagues high.

Our feet have been set afire. The ship is about to leave port. The smoke floating over the sea is pulling us. We sail at full speed and reach the river mouth. We look up, we look down. We shake our heads. Our hearts become heavy. We don't want to cross the river.

We stumble against sharp stones. The wounds are deep. We sprinkle crushed salt on our legs. We get thirsty; our mouths are dry. We drink water from holes in the sand.

We spread dust on a white bedsheet; we haven't found a size to fit our age. Even if we yawn with a gnawing hunger, we will not cross the river.

Wooden horse
    Donkey's jaw

Bald mountains burnt savanna smelly codfish rainfall sprouting mushrooms failed millet crop stunted corn plants the wind blowing everywhere.

We laugh. We make fun of crippled old people. The witch suckles the sun with her left breast to curse impertinent children.

In the narrow alleys of the city the dogs have been barking all night. We ask no one to pour libations neither with water nor with rum. We get hold of our wooden sticks. We simply say, watch out!

Gossipy forefinger. Trouble finger. Danger finger. A circle has been drawn at the cockfight. Blows for blows. Sudden death. Threatened fights. The game turns bloody. The game turns wild.

And exactly how long have we been playing?

We're tired to our bones. We've been getting nowhere so fast that sweat has pooled in our armpits. Bandits cross their legs at our door; they won't let us in. Some days we wake up depressed, full of doubt, full of disgust, full of repugnance. We get ready to go out; the sun lies to us, the rain disappoints us. We're forced to sit down and wait.

Dream dust lies thick on our heads. The wick of an idea is lit. Ashes scatter. Smoke rises. We see . . . . . . trouble. We go inside ourselves. An untamed horse starts champing at the bit inside us.

Before we travel, we think long and hard.

The tenth round opens / love makes Siltana soft in the head / Klodonis can't understand anything / roosters face off in the cockpit / chickens are sacrificed / we bind all insolent loua / Filojèn and Kamélo are watching out / Zofè is enraged at all the zonbis / Gaston almost dies in La Gonave searching for buried jars of gold / marasa voices / we glance at the sea / we reject all nonsensical ideas / Jédéyon's gone gaga in the old two-story house / spurs are thrust right and left / Jéròm wants to get out / Jéròm wants to drink a cup of bitter coffee with Sintil, to have it out with him . . .

Bearer of death. After three days the thunder roars, the sky's dam opens. Forty rows of teeth grow inside the two-footed baka's mouth.

Insolent children in a hurry wear their right shoe on their left foot . . . Lost in the dark separated pairs are frantically looking for their twins. Come this way, cross over the other side, we'll meet, our paths will cross. Wild dancing. But on which foot shall we dance at the tinginding crossroads?

Three handfuls of salt

are dissolving

in a pot of hot water

Craven players whisper into calabashes / Zofè whops any restive zonbi's ass / lightning is a magnet . . .

> A rebellious zonbi is hanging upside down from the rooftop of Sintil's péréstil.

No quarter . . .

> They've sprinkled juju powder in front of our door and put miskadin in our food.

Two mean and fearless roosters are facing off in the cockpit / our hearts are heavy with anxiety / cockspurs here there everywhere / shouts rise after a killer spur hit / our hearts are jacked up . . .

> Jédéyon is not well. He just lies there gaga inside the crumbling two-story house. His stomach heaves. From time to time Rita brings him a pill to swallow.

Juju signs and magic spells all over the cockfight arena / the *koudjay* street band and dancing crowd are out / a fight breaks out / our rooster gets knocked out / Kamélo and Filojèn are watching out for low blows and scams in this dog-eat-dog contest / Sintil attends the dézafi every day / spur jabs and slashes from midday until late evening . . .

> Jéròm and Alibé have been talking all night, trying to get to the bottom of things.

"Jéròm! How does Sintil manage to get his zonbis at the graveyard?"

"Zonbis are people like us. Sintil feeds them some doped-up food that takes their will away."

"Why doesn't Sintil want them to taste anything with salt in it?"

"Alibé, my brother, salt gives soul. When salt gets into a zonbi's bloodstream, it slaps his body, shakes up his guts, wakes up his brain. Once a zonbi gets a taste of salt, he stops being passive, he becomes a bouanouvo, he sees clearly, he becomes strong. That's when he gets enraged and wants to break loose. You understand, Alibé? You understand why Sintil says salt is poison?"

"I sort of get it now."

"But, my old brother, salt is life."

We need a scaffold to build life on the back of death!

The fight is heating up / a rooster stumbles and reels from a spur thrust / feathers fly / we bet on the aggressive cock . . .

Won't we crossbreed the animals in our yard with jackass stallions anymore?

*In the middle of the night
death locks its door.*

We jiggle our fingers in the keyhole; we pick the lock and open to let life in.

Love lights a fire in our hearts, a huge fire. We were bent and awkward; the sun's light has straightened up our bodies.

Putting on a show, the stars break their tether; the stars explode and fill up the sky; the stars shower down on the island.

The tin lamp's wick flares up and down; our shadows dance a wild dance on the wall. Rain drizzles down; we look for the root of light in each water drop. Several massive clouds break up; we wet the tips of our tongues with the moon's spit.

We haven't quite opened our eyes yet.
Festering wounds still plague our memory.

> They've sprinkled ashes on our heads. Our brains are boiling and foaming. We roll in the dust.

The weather is still dreary. A blind dog is leaning on its tail and barking its hunger.

> The silk cotton tree has been shedding its leaves one by one in Jédéyon's yard. An albino sun is winking in the sky. Jédéyon has been coughing nonstop. Rita has been handing him pills for his heart disease and his joint pain for so long she's become a doctor.

> The weather wears a frown. The sun has set. The rain falls hard all night long.

Try to discover the weak points of tyrants. One blinding slap. The enemy gets out of our way.

Gaston is tired . . .

> Gaston is tired of dragging his wings throughout Port-au-Prince. He's been thinking of going back to Ravin Sèch. He's been gnawing on his thumb. He's been going to bed hungry and waking up hungry. He's tired of wasting his life in the city.

A wayward wind
A ne'er-do-well wind
A wandering wind
        A wild wind
        has been winnowing dust
        on the face of every living earthly creature
Katchoumbonmbé!

Life has burned us
        Life has flayed us
They've surrounded us
        Hideous beasts encircle us
Our heads throb with pain
        Katchoumbonmbé!

Sorcerers have set their eyes on our children. Baka are dancing the kalinda at the crossroads. The sorcerers are abroad; the children cower under their bedsheets.

Playing lago with eyes closed
        Playing lago with eyes wide open
Trouble
        Katchoumbonmbé!

We parse our dreams every morning; our sleep is troubled; our minds are confused.

        Pain sticks to our tails
        Pain won't leave us be

Killer blow

        High noon sun
        Upright sun

Burning sun
Poisonous sun
Strafing sun

A cooking stove is turned over face down
   Who dropped a handful of dirt in our clay water jar?

A bed-wetting dream. We dream of rain. Hide and seek. Tur-
moil. Vertigo. We're feeling groggy.

   Our dreams are packed full of crazy birds

Until it gets cut off
The head keeps hoping for a hat

   We go to bed and we wake up destitute with the
twins poverty and misery in our house.

When we love, we breathe hard, we have the hiccups, we shiver
with fever in the middle of the day.

The darkness of night hangs heavy over Sintil's yard.
The dogs have been barking continuously. Siltana can't
sleep a wink. Her belly wrapped tightly with a length
of cloth, she bites her pillow, weeps, and slams her
body on the bed. She wants to pluck the moon from
the sky, she wants to sink her teeth into the stars.

A tangle of massive clouds are coughing like consumptives; a
gaggle of scraggly clouds are coughing like starvelings.

Some mischievous children jumping rope with a rotten cord
fall flat on sharp jagged stones; they start a fight. They spit blood.

Baka are putting on a show. Bizango are dancing the kalinda at the crossroads.

Butterflies are playing hopscotch on the sunflowers. We hear a woman's voice. We've lost our way chasing skirts. We've gone astray chatting up women. We turn back in a hurry. We glue our eyes to a crack in the window to take a look outside. Life itself is knocking at our inner door. We must open the door a crack to let some light in.

Hunger
Guts twisted into a painful knot
Sad long faces
The wind sprints forth unrestrained
We use our teeth to untie our tethering rope.
The moon or the sun
Which is more beautiful?
Which do you love more?
Children play
Grown-ups display

They've diverted the stream away from our garden. Cow dung litters the ground in front of our house in big fat piles dry on top and wet on the bottom. Horse piss has collected into thick foamy puddles. Carcasses of rats that died of constipation lie on top of garbage heaps. It's time we cleaned up our yard.

Our memory has been caught in a trap.

Wherever there's a wall blocking the path of light, we rise up, we shout. Our voices soar high. All shadows lie flat in the dust. Owls and hawks scram to safety.

Death plot
　　　　Swirling smoke
The rain beats a kata beat on the tin roofs
　　　　　The wind blows its vaksin bamboo horns
Houses collapse
　　　　Death dances on its toes

Sun-like water
　　　　Mirror-like water
Eyes are set on fire
　　　　Mouths spit flames
Fingers turn into pinewood sticks
　　　　Fingers throw sparks
　　Halt, Marshal Death!

Words are stuffed into the oven. Words are taken out of the oven. Our dreams are browning under the ashes. We dig holes in the rocky ground.

Along the cliffs the journey turns
harrowing. They interrupt us
as we speak. Our tongues are
gummed up in the dark.
　　　　　How many breaststrokes must we do to ford the
flooding stream?

Killing lust meets with death wish to plot mischief. A perfect storm.

For our part, we hold death by the collar to give love some breathing space. We pluck the stars wide awake. We pluck the stars in our dreams. We never pause.

Our words have become incoherent. We light a fire, we use a hot iron to scrape the hardened crust off our vocal cords. We make our voices strong. Our words shine bright now. Our words have become silky smooth. Our words match our dreams. Our words and our thoughts are intertwined.

Vinegar has been sprinkled on the ground; laggards must walk faster now.
   Noise in the water
         Shakes up the soul
   A light shining in the night
         We bind the wings of the evil air.

We didn't love well. We loved piecemeal. In bits and pieces. We were aware of love only through the burning pain it inflicted, through the blood it caused to spill. We don't know how to love yet.

Our hearts are reeling in pain. There's a taste of ash in our mouths. There's a taste of burnt food on our tongues. A heavy weight is crushing our guts. Love just won't die. We wait for the bad weather to pass; we start loving again. We're learning to love so life can grow new feathers.

We plumb the depth of the water with a thick rope before rushing to cross the river. We ignore the nonsense coming out of the mouth of fools. We hear the sound of the drum; we try to get the beat right before rushing to dance to that weird music.

We send our hearts ahead to look around for sustenance.
      We want to live
      We sniff the air.

We've long turned our backs on death in anger; we won't fall for some undertaker's maneuvering. Midnight tolls. A scream from the neighbor's house. We wake up startled. More screams. We're about to go crazy. We've lost our minds.

We're roasting in the midst of huge flames; right then our minds conjure up water.

We've been raising and training roosters for the cockfight for a long time now. Our cooking pots are turned upside down. Not even the carcass of a dead gamecock; they give us no alms. Day in day out we lick the lightning, we swallow the thunderstone. Rain's on the way.

Rats bite then blow on the wound
       We're vigilant
The candle's flame shines bright
       Shadows dance on the wall
The sun weighs anchor
       The fight starts in earnest

The flooding waters roll down carrying garbage, banana trees, stones. The drumbeat always tells the truth. Mud covers the ground in everyone's garden. Tomorrow we'll have to measure everyone's field again.

We haven't had anything to drink. We haven't had anything to eat. We haven't slept a wink. We're waiting for the cockfight. Our faces look gaunt. We've become as thin as dry twigs. A night owl's hoot pierces our eardrums. A flock of birds flies away. We're waiting for daybreak. The sun rises wielding its twin razor-sharp spurs to slash off the horns of inauspicious stars.

Throw a rock
Hide the hand

      We're keeping watch

The sound of rabòday music fills the air. We hear a woman's voice calling us. What's our dog name?

Danger in the air
The path is thorny
    Don't count on woman

The mangooses are on the prowl. Our hens are sitting on their nests. Our corn harvest is drying in the sun. We're keeping watch. We hear a woman's voice calling us from the rabòday. We answer quickly. But what is our real dog name?

A mere rivulet of water
for a whole bunch of mouths
    Our hearts are windmills
    We use them to pump water up

If our eyelids are tarred shut by darkness, why don't we clap our hands to limber up our bodies? Death has crossed the railroad tracks. Knock on pots and pans and raise Cain around the grave-yard!

Severed legs. Severed hands. Broken backs. Severed heads. A gang of sorcerers has surrounded our house.

Thorny ants, fire ants, red ants, crazy ants have invaded our brains. Our memory is full of stairs that go nowhere. Our veins are full of inside-out corridors and crooked ladders.

    Our dreams are confusing labyrinths
    Our thoughts are incoherent shreds

All the way to Guinea the native speech flowers and fruits on our tongues, moves us to our very entrails. Our umbilical cords have budded; countless native flowers bloom all over our bodies.

The midday sun slashes the impudent clouds. Skinny starving dogs show their teeth as they bark.

We walk around observing
 We carry a cooking stove on our heads
Our memory is a patchwork of mismatched pieces
 Misery has shredded life to pieces

Much straining to make our memory lucid again! The sun is showing its gums; it's getting ready to smile.
 We get up to extinguish the firefly lamp.

Words of wisdom: shut your eyes, cover your ears, clinch your jaws, lock your doors, shut your windows. A gutless man always loses the battle. You can't eat hot gumbo with limp fingers. The feebleminded should eschew dangerous games. A savanna rooster's beak is useless in a close cockfight.

We slept so long our brains conjured up a maize-and-mushroom dream for winning lottery numbers, a raging flood carried away our dreams.

Someone threw water
 Who got wet?
The wind is barking
 Watch out!
We don't go poking our fingers into anyone's eyes.

The wind whirls puffs of dust on the streets and lifts the women's dresses up to their waists. Watch out. Take care. But remember: don't curse the wind if it lets you glance a scandalous spectacle!

Every day we swim behind death's roots to keep life afloat.

They've tortured us, stuck fingers down our throats, shaken up our branches. The birds fly songless. The birds fall dead disoriented. Through it all the trees remain steadfast.

Fish die and leave the sea behind
Birds fly away and leave the trees behind
Corpses rot and leave speech behind

            We're swimming behind death's roots to keep life
afloat.

We're sleeping in a ravine, lying down on the edge of a cliff.
Clusters of stars are sprinkling sand over our hair, blowing dust on
our faces. The moonlight bathes our bodies. Love possesses us.

The night is so long we wake up before time. We mull things
over. We wrack our brains; it's impossible to count the number of
stars left rotting in fishing nets. We stand up. We stretch our bodies
to get rid of our cramps and loosen our joints.

Days go, days come. Many days go by. The land hungers after
the sun. The moon licks the land's behind.

Grandma's bones
Old folks' bones

           Rusty daggers
           Skinning daggers

Wound and kill
Kill and die

           How high is the sun at dawn?
           How much road have we covered?
           It's the head that guides the feet on the road.

           We're swimming behind death's roots
to keep life afloat.

           The cockpit is always open
           The dézafi never ends

Cooking pot voices
Tin pot voices
Rattle voices
Awakened zonbi voices

> *We've barely begun to speak*
> *We've barely begun to scream*
> *We've barely begun to sing*

Our voices are now unleashed. Our voices now scatter words abroad. Our voices hold the earth in a tight embrace, then rise up to wander with the wayward wind.

We weigh our shadows in the dust. We want to somersault to the other side of the night. We talk to ourselves as we walk on the street. We talk to ourselves as we stand in a corner. We talk until daybreak. We must raise our voices so we can be heard at the ends of the earth.

Our bodies have been skinned raw by the sun's claws. Fires are lit. Fires are stoked. Ashes cover our skin. But our bodies are not hemmed in. Our thoughts have no limits.

We ponder the old folks' words, words that have teeth, words that meander, words thrown to the wind, andaki words. Vertigo seizes us. Words that speak of death and resurrection are ageless.

Love games
> *Death's fingers*

The sun has set. It has been raining for a long while. Unrelenting pain has been wracking Jédéyon's body. He's been lying stiff on a dilapidated bed. He hasn't spoken in three days; he hasn't slept a wink.

Rita is sitting by the bedroom door awake and watching. She spends half the night watching. From time to time she catches a few winks. After midnight she falls asleep. Her dream carries her all the way back to Ravin Sèch. She jumps in the river to bathe, dives under the sea, rolls, leaps, dances with Lasirèn on the sandy beach, and walks leisurely throughout a palace bathed in multi-colored lights.

Rita stumbles through a sequence of confusing dreams. At one point, two neighborhood roosters start crowing and trading shrill horn riffs. Rita suddenly finds herself clinging to the back of Lasirèn Diaman; the swell grabs her, roils her and carries her far away. She wakes up startled, her face wet with sweat. She stands up and walks toward the bed . . . Jédéyon is lying there stiff. Rita looks at him, talks to him, shakes him, touches him. Uncle Jédéyon doesn't respond; his body is colder than the nose of a dog out in the damp at dusk.

Tears suddenly start flowing down Rita's cheeks. After a while she opens every door and window in the house. A light drizzle is falling on the street. The weather's face is dark under a yellowish sun straining to climb a patchy sky. Rita lets out a shrill scream.* In the time it takes a startled cat to jump, the neighbors have gathered in the house. Several stand around Jédéyon's bed, holding their sad faces in their hands. Before you count to two, the house is emptied, swept, washed, dried, and made ready to welcome Marshall Death.

After the last prayer has been said Rita returns to Bouanèf to live in her late father's cousin Alibé's house. Its front gate roped up, its windows nailed shut, its doors barred, the old two-story house stands abandoned in utter loneliness.

---

* According to custom, when a death occurs in a house, a woman lets out a piercing scream to announce the news to the neighborhood.—Trans.

The river is rolling down, raging and roaring as if possessed. A wild wind is buffeting and shaking the trees. The straw-covered shacks crumble under the torrential rain. No one dares venture outside. A woman's voice calls us. A hand gestures to us. Our horses are tied on the other bank of the river. How shall we ford this furious flooding stream?

We have an understanding with Grinn Pronminnin: rendez-vous with Tèt-san-kò at midnight's crossroads. We don't linger in bed sleeping and snoring.

"I'm going to fly!"

"Go ahead and fly! Just don't come down to roost on our branches."

"I'm going to curse!"

"Go ahead and curse! Just don't curse at our kinfolks."

"I'm going to throw up!"

"Go ahead and throw up! Just don't vomit phlegm into our cooking pot."

"I'm going to kill!"

"Go ahead and kill! Just don't cut and slash our children's bodies."

"I'm going to fall!"

"Go ahead and fall! Just don't wreck and smash our rooftop."

"I, Tèt-san-kò, I laugh at the words of the living. Tonight you're lucky my belly's already full. I'm on my way to sleep in my village."

"Tèt-san-kò, you're lying! We won't fall for such an obvious con. The season is changing. The season is turning around. You're about to lose your wager. You're looking for some way to trap us, to catch us in your net. Well, you won't succeed, Tèt-san-kò! We've stopped listening to nonsense."

"I, Tèt-san-kò, I'm laughing out loud. My belly's full. I'm on my way to sleep in my village."

"You're lying again, Tèt-san-kò. You never laugh out loud. You only know how to smirk and show your teeth. Your gullet is leakier than a sieve. You have no intestines. You're always hungry, you're always greedy. You have no entrails; you're pitiless. You can't imagine a mother's pain. This time we just won't sleep at all. We'll stay awake all night. We'll keep watch till daybreak."

"I say, I'm heading to the right of that dead body!"

"You'd better find your way to your village instead to pick up rotten meat scraps at the slaughterhouse to patch together a mismatched body for your head. Go hustle over there! Go scratch your itch over there! Go hawk and rattle over there! Go and die over there! Go ahead and hook yourself to that dead body. But don't you dare look in the direction of our house. Death's mouth! Stinking mouth!"

We reject both misbegotten facile dreams and impossible dreams. To conquer death we suckle life. The veins in our foreheads are stretched taut. Our memory is filling up. We place a light in front of a mirror; our faces are regaining their color; our hearts are beating. The lamp's wick throws its light on the path to our dream to keep us from falling over the ravine's edge. The lamp's wick is soaking wet with our blood. The lamp's roots are intertwined with the earth's veins. The lamp's light cannot be extinguished; it's already spawned millions of smaller lights. The birds themselves have metamorphosed into flames, yet their wings are not burned; they'll be flying here there and everywhere forever.

We've forded many a treacherous current on a perilous journey. We don't waste our time looking in fright at our deformed faces in a cracked mirror. To the contrary, we've learned to look far ahead; we've stopped walking around dragging our feet spreading ourselves thin for a single reason (which is worth a load of reasons): our shadows keep fooling us / our shadows are at odds with our bodies / our shadows are full of defects on uneven roads / our shadows are like big-bellied horses / our shadows enjoy lingering on the way sniffing around eating grass, especially when we are in a hurry . . .

We get angry and decide to ignore our cursed shadows so that we don't linger on our long journey.

We're tired of moaning. We're tired of complaining. We'll endure our pain in silence.

Misfortune has been shackled: we can move on now; we can make some headway. However, even if our ideas and our words have wings, we will never fly away and leave our bodies behind.

Our memory may fly aimlessly like a kite in a whirlwind, but it won't get waylaid. Our memory has roots like the rhizomes of a vine; its roots go deep so we can always remember what we leave behind.

The journey is endless. The journey is arduous and dangerous. Death may nibble now and then on our edges, but it will never succeed in gutting life's core.

Instead of weeping in the dark, let's open our eyes to draw in and hold the light of the stars. Such orgasmic delights when we put our hands on her belly and caress the golden skin of the moon! Such boundless joy when our hands reach and grasp the lightning! Such wonder when our dream couples with the thunder! The rain falls and soaks our bodies. The sun rises shining bright and new behind the mountain. Tomorrow we will gather at the crossroads; sparks will fly as words collide.

Day and night are playing lago
Lago hide

Lago catch
           Lago run around
Open season
           We're thinking hard

In the blink of an eye life blooms and changes its colors.

One big-mouthed cockfight fan forgets his place and starts sing-ing pointed songs aimed at us right there in the middle of the cock-fight. We talk back and say: "Please! We've always walked behind bright lights; we're not about to pay attention to some crude oil lamp now." Then we shut up. We say no more. There's no need to say more. The reach of our hands is the reach of our actions is the reach of our tongues.

When the wind blows, it grinds all words; it chews and spits out those words that have no substance, those words that have no roots.

Death yawns with hunger; we hide our children under our wings. Death has so many tricks up its sleeves, so we stay vigilant.

Detour. Tortuous road.
If life moved onward and upward, straight like a palm tree, all dreams would be straightforward. If there were no obstacles to cir-cumvent, life would be boring.

A stir-crazy shadow has been running around seeking an infirm body. Who would dare laugh at such misfortune?
           Laughter brings on a toothache sometimes.

Running around and jumping over fences like a tomcat all over the place, as he has been doing for a long time, Pastor Pin Kris eventually finds himself in trouble. He's never been able to uproot that habit of his of frigging his friends' women. One night around midnight one of Pastor Pin Kris's Protestant brothers catches him straining and sweating climbing up Mount Sinai. Gall-bursting anger. A smashed bed. Mother hens scramming for shelter. A machete drawn. A head slashed off. The rest of Pin Kris's body is found leaning against a fence post, an old frayed Bible on his crotch. The news soon spreads topped up with plenty of rumors. Quite a few dyed-in-the-wool faithful tear up their flags; quite a few Gospel fanatics burn their Bibles. Churches shut their doors. Shacks are pulled down. The loan sharks stop all easy-terms money lending.

Gaston's freeloading days are over; he has to find some other branch to perch on.

We hustle and manage to put down a few bets at the cockfight. We lose several wagers, but we still hope to win eventually. The dézafi never ends. We have many gamecocks in training; moreover, we have lots of kinfolk. The roosters have just begun to face off in the cockpit. Life is limitless. Life is endless. Why do you want to count gamecock carcasses on the ground? Why are you complaining and counting tombs in the graveyard? Come what may, life bounces back in every drop of water, in every spoken word, in the veins of every tree, in every grain of sand on the seashore, in every twirling puff of smoke, in every dusty gust of wind, in the blinks of the stars, in the glow of the moon, in the light of the sun, in the embrace of lovers, in the dance of the birds, in the cry of every newborn, in every child's game of hide-and-seek.

There is no surveyor's tape nor yardstick with which to measure the length of life. There will never be a cemetery for burying life!

We trek to every remote corner of the land, wander in every wood. We speak in langay. We burst out in songs. We play music. We shout. When we get tired we let the people around us take over the shouting. The rara bands are out on the plains. The vaksin bamboo horns resound in the mountains. The lakou dwellers gather. We're going to cross the river. The sanmba at the head of the band raises his voice; the women chorists in the back respond with gusto; voices in the crowd join in. We roam through the bush, wander through every alley. In the end we remember many uttered words, many forgotten dreams. Our memory dances the dance of the loua with every print our toes make in the dust, with every hole our feet dig in the mud, with every vèvè we draw at the crossroads to keep death from having a hold on life.

One dangerous crossroads! A curse on children who disrespect grown-ups. We look up . . . We look down . . . We're going to cross no matter what.

Ground maize

Akasan siro! . . .

(He who gives the blow forgets, he who bears the scar remembers.)
Teeth know how to bite flesh but they don't know how to count
bite marks.

Siltana is on her knees, her arms hooked around Klodonis's legs, crying. Her hair hangs loose on her face.

"Klodonis!"

"Wee waan!"

"How many times have I begged at your feet like a dog?"

"Wee waan!"

"You just won't give me any hope."

"Wee waan!"

"We're in hell. I'm tired. Let's escape together. Let's go far away from here. Let's go to some other place, far, far away."

"Wee waan!"

"Let's run away from this house and leave Sintil and Zofè behind us."

"Wee waan!"

Siltana keeps on weeping and moaning and biting Klodonis's leg. Nothing works.

"So much suffering, good Lord! Aye, mother! What is this ragged cross I'm dragging!"

"Wee waan!"

"Please, talk to me so I can taste life again. I just want to have a life with you, Klodonis."

"Wee waan!"

"Klodonis, I want you for my man. Make me your woman. Klodonis, kill me! Spit on me!"

"Wee waan!"

"You really don't understand a thing, do you? Give me some reason to love you. I have a taste in my mouth more bitter than bile."

"Wee waan!"

"Just say one word and I'll run away with you. Tell me you love me, and our lives will change right away. Please, Klodonis. Answer me."

"Wee waan!"

Klodonis just stands there, his limp and lanky body wrapped in a burlap shabrack, his shoulders lopsided, his face twisted and his head bowed, staring at the ground. Siltana rises and, crying as she wraps her arms around Klodonis's waist, starts caressing him.

"Klodonis, we're alone in the house. Sintil went to the cockfight on the other side of the tracks. Zofè's out getting drunk on tafia. Talk to me, Klodonis. I'm tired of suffering, tired of the sleepless nights. That's no life. The sun is about to set. Hurry up and answer me before it's too late. Talk to me . . ."

Just then Siltana hears a voice clanging from the yard like a rusty tin can. She rushes to peer through a crack in the window. It is a drunken Zofè filled to the gills with tafia, stumbling about, cursing to high heaven, about to fall into the canal. Siltana leaps out. Turning the key quietly, she locks Klodonis inside the room, then she fixes her hair and with a hard look of resolve on her face she walks up to the péréstil's potomitan.

Zofè stumbles against a tree stump and almost falls flat on his face. He then limps up to the potomitan, bumps against Siltana, and tries to touch her breasts. Siltana recoils with an air of disgust. She walks backward all the way to the ounfò's door.

"Get a hold of yourself, Zofè. Know your place."

"Siltana, it looks like you're upset to see my face. You seem unhappy I had a few drinks."

"Now you're really out of line. It's none of my damned business. I couldn't care less."

"Siltana, please! Give me a break! Just a little taste! Don't worry, I won't tell a soul. Please, just a little taste!"

"Being drunk is no excuse for bad behavior. You just wait, when my dad comes home tonight you'll see how much hell you'll catch. Such disrespect! You must be crazy! You must be possessed!"

Zofè walks up to Siltana. He starts cracking his knuckles. His eyes are blood red and look on fire. His jaws move like a mill as he chews and grinds his teeth.

"Siltana, I know what you've been up to . . . Why are you spurn-
ing me? . . . You've got nothing to fear . . . There's no reason to be
afraid . . . No reason at all . . . I've always been nice to you . . . I've
been serving your family loyally for a long time . . . I'm a strong box
for keeping the family's secrets . . . I'm a heavy gravestone over a
tomb in the cemetery . . . I don't talk . . . I've been hard at work in
this lakou for a long time . . . I've always kept my mouth shut . . .
You, for instance, I've always suspected you . . . From the very first
day Klodonis got here speechless and soulless . . . I've never said a
word to Sintil . . . I've never confided in anyone . . . I've known for
a long time you've been madly in love and pining after Klodonis
the zonbi . . . "

Siltana suddenly starts shaking as if in the grip of a fever. She
looks ill. Her lips are paralyzed and she can't mouth an answer.

"Some bosal loua must be riding you!* You, impertinent drunk!
The klérin must have turned your brain to mush. Why don't you go
sleep it off?

"I know what I'm talking about. I've been spying on you for a
long time, Siltana. Now I've caught you and have you against a
wall."

Zofè grins, his open mouth showing chipped teeth like those of
an old saw sawing a piece of hardwood. He clears his throat. His
eyes turn even more red than they were. He spits out a thick and
slippery gob of green phlegm mixed with saliva against the wall of
the house, where it slithers down to the ground.

"You're such a sly little bitch! Such a slut! When I unload on Sintil tonight, you'll hear everything you've done . . . The ant's entrails
will be out in the open . . . We'll settle all accounts . . . You've been
weaving a rotten sisal rope in the house for a long time . . . Sintil
doesn't know what you're capable of . . . Tonight, that's it, the cat's
shit will come out . . . I'll slice open the clever horse's belly . . . The
donkey smiles as he brays . . . Klodonis has his backside on a burning stove . . . I'll whip that impertinent zonbi's ass good and hard
. . . Let me through! Let me through!"

---

* To be possessed by a *loua* is to become the *loua*'s horse.—Trans.

Shoving. Tumbling. Pushing. Wrestling. Zofè throws Siltana on the ground. He blows into the house like the wind and comes out wielding a fetish wooden club. Siltana stands up, grabs a chair, and tackles Zofè. Zofè brings his stick down. The brawling gets wild. Shoves. Slaps to the face. Chair snapping. Body blows. Bites. Kicks. Throws. Siltana picks up a pestle and lays Zofè down stiff on the ground.

Without a pause, looking like a wild mare, Siltana puts a pot filled with water and vegetables on the cooking stove. It's an old, busted-up, all caved-in and smoke-blackened pot. She drops three handfuls of salt into the pot. When that salty soup is ready, Siltana unlocks the bedroom's door. She funnels a tumbler full of broth down Klodonis's throat. Klodonis makes a gargling noise as he takes three swallows in a row.

Suddenly Klodonis feels dizzy. Painful cramps grip his stomach as if it were being pounded by galloping horses and crushed under a heavy steamroller. His brain feels like an ants' nest, a raw wound, about to burst. He grabs his head in his hands. His whole body is dripping with sweat. Disoriented by vertigo, he stumbles into a corner and falls flat on his face. Siltana rushes to Klodonis and starts wiping his face with a wet towel. She dabs his face, massages his temples, rubs his waist, feels his lower abdomen, pulls on his toes, scrapes the bottom of his feet, scratches his underarms, tickles his ribs, bites him all over his body.

Klodonis wriggles. His now open eyes shine like those of a fat sun lizard. He tries to stand up on his two feet. His knees collapse under him and he stumbles as he hurries to lean on the bedroom's wall. Then he starts having visions. His whole life unfolds before him in bits and pieces as in a dream: a calabash perched on his head / bathing at the spring / playing hopscotch / roasting corn /

falling down and getting up / hide-and-seek among the plantain trees / playing football with an avocado seed for ball / a rags ball rolling in front of the Calvary cross / fumbling love in the dark / a shy and trembling kiss behind the house / two-bit soldiers in the school yard / grammar lessons / dictations / the rule of the past participle / a boumba wooden boat overturned in the river mouth / dugout canoes / wild ducks / the Bouanèf pond / diving in the water / mother's caresses / father's grumbling / the streets of Port-au-Prince / raging floods / rendezvous behind the Cathedral / a loud commotion in the Croix-Bossales market / salt fish / ponyak plantains / Madan-Kolo standing tall and straight at the intersection of rue Macajoux and rue du Peuple / drinking coconut water / swirling smoke rising from the sugar mill in the direction of the plains / the Mouzin lakou / the Bois-de-Chêne bridge / a melee at the sugar mill / the SHADA Company sisal plantation / a loud commotion at the Salomon market / wandering around hungry / Hornets Gate / leisurely walks in Frésino / brawling with brass knuckles / the MacDonald train station / tchaka soup / free movies on a wall in the Bel Air neighborhood / sneaking inside a dance hall for free / a rabòday band in full swing in Champ-de-Mars Square / the Bizoton brothel bars / walking around hungry / the electric poles in Place Bicentenaire / the sea in Ravin Sèch / end of third semester school exams / school reports / July vacation / fun and games / playing the young dandy / an awkward young man / a self-assured young man / Ravin Sèch gives Klodonis a standing ovation / an indefatigable young stud / a champion gamecock / Bouanèf is in a festive mood / the villagers are happy / bravos for Klodonis / Sintil's heart is bitter / Sintil is furious / Sintil is angrier than a cornered snake / Sintil wants to kill someone / Sintil wants to turn someone into a zonbi / Zofè is lurking surveilling that strutting self-assured young man / danger hangs over Klodonis's head over my head! / Sintil catches me in a head trap . . .

While he was taking shelter from the rain in Fabi's shack, a poisoned lemonade caused that loud-mouthed Bouanèf young man's gizzard to burst. Sintil cannot stand educated people. Klérin rum and herb mixtures, keep-away lotions, madness-inducing poisons, zonbi cucumber, beware-the-dusk-moisture, wait-and-see, energy-sapping water, three-drops, limb-crushing leaves, fast-walk powder, soul-taking cigarettes, poisoned lemonade, Sintil knows all sorts of concoctions for putting anyone under a spell. The moment he hits you, sleep overcomes you and brings you to a state resembling death. After the burial he becomes a body snatcher. He goes into the cemetery, opens the grave, and administers a vial of rise-up water to the dug-up body. He now has a zonbi he will set to work growing rice in the swamps. A zonbi has no memory. A zonbi has no life force. A zonbi is forbidden ever to taste salt, for he must always remain passive, without any desire to escape.

Sintil hated Klodonis for his smarts and his learning. Zofè went to work and fixed a special lemonade. Klodonis had come to spend his vacation in Bouanèf. One evening, as he was sheltering from the rain in Fabi's shack, Klodonis fell into a trap. His stomach ached excruciatingly, as if someone was sawing and hammering nails into it. Sintil smirked. Three days later, the traditional scream that announced a death in a house was heard. A band of cloth to tie shut the arrogant young philosopher's jaws. Get going! Get going, I say! You're going to the swamps to plant rice! Klodonis, I say, move! Let's go meet Zofè!

The salty broth stirs Klodonis's blood, and he begins to understand the unfortunate events that have interrupted his life. Suddenly he feels alive again. He glimpses in his mind all the trials and tribulations he suffered under Zofè's claws. Lightning flashes from his eyes. Thunder rumbles in his head.

Klodonis is raging mad. He lets out a shout like the bellow of
an angry bull. He hits Siltana with a bone-breaking bone-crushing
bone-shattering body-felling backhanded slap. He jerks open the
bedroom's door. He dives down, picks up the pot full of salty stew,
and runs across the yard. Each and every zonbi gets to taste the
salty broth. Klodonis is out of control!

A jumble of shouts and screams and yells erupt from the zonbis' throats as they go through a sudden change after tasting their
share of the salty stew. Their heads reel; they're about to see more
clearly; they're about to become bouanouvo. A rumble of cacoph-
onous voices fills Sintil's lakou. Foolproof padlocks are broken.
Strongboxes get smashed and their secrets exposed. Bridles and
bits come off and mouths are freed. Words popping like corn kernels and salt exploding. It's a new day.

The moon is waning / the earth's belly is swollen / a burning
brand in a festering wound / katchoumbonmbé / a prize cattle is
kept tethered / rural policemen are demanding their pay / two man-
sharing women in the same lakou / big scandal about beds getting
trashed and broken / Sintil is greedy / many donkeys are kept in
the communal park / Sintil steals souls / rara for three seasons in
a row / heaps of sea turtle eggs hatching in the sand by the sea at
Ravin Sèch / the first millet harvest has started / three bitter taro
roots / two swollen cow's udders / water in which ouari seeds have
been boiled whitens the skin / Sintil is a shameless thief / Zofè is a
ferocious shark / tumbling fall / twisted ankles / early January coffee / the sound of laundry beetles at the fish pond / piles of cay-
man eggs hatching on the lake's shore / we'll get to the mill before
daybreak / a wooden bowl of cooked mazoumbèl leaves upended
on the MacDonald railway tracks / the savanna denuded / the bald-
headed mountain showing its teeth / two sets of twins born to bring

more gut-wrenching misery / stomachache like birth pangs / the corrupt sindik has cut off the irrigation water / the canal stays dry for more than three days / nights of lovemaking under the roof of one's main woman / strong doesn't mean more / two calabash bowls of shrimps at the Saturday market / the north wind storms hit hard in the last days of August / wooden boats smashed in the Saint-Marc Channel / ships plying the coast in big trouble / a few rolls of the dice in Fabi's shack / the old dress suits come out on Three Kings' Day / the villagers are dressed to the nines / Bouanèf villagers are sharp and cool / Bouanèf villagers walk funny / envy and jealousy all around / Zofè goes around gossiping and speaking ill / Sintil has his eyes on every Bouanèf woman / vitriol on a festering wound / nitrate powder foaming on a horse's suppurating wound / drops of candelabra cactus sap fall into the drifter's eyes / gossipmongering winds spread the news / a donkey with its mouth skinned raw / the breastfeeding woman's milk has slipped into her blood / flocks of blackbirds are pillaging the crops in the fields / Sintil has a rendezvous with a woman under a silk cotton tree at midnight / the owl's hoot prophesies misfortune / an ill wind rises and comes to rest on the thatched roof / Sintil steals the villagers' women / the loua has manifested herself inside the temple / boulé zin / the big family ceremony has swallowed up quite a lot of money / désounin ceremony / who's slurped down the food of forgetfulness / the liquor flows on the other side of the railway tracks / be careful in the dusk's damp air! / Sintil saddles girths bridles paws the ground on the high road / gird up your loins and tighten your belts / hard labor in the swamps / Zofè brings down his whip / Zofè pounds cuts crushes bone joints / pig meat roasts on fire stones / zobòp sorcerers drink blood from a calabash bowl / vlingbinding sorcerers bump and grind at the Tuesday night dance / ominous crossroads / dangerous crossroads / bewitching crossroads / swirling smoke / the greedy aloufa stand up in a hurry / buzzards are sniffing the air . . .

The wind is wearing new feathers, dancing the kalinda, jumping over the railroad tracks, grinding its hips, as it rushes down from the top of the mountains to the sea. All the zonbis now have a fresh face, all speak with a new voice. All the zonbis have turned into bouanouvo. Pandemonium in Sintil's lakou.

Shoving. Pushing. Doors, windows, bug-infested pallets, bull-whips, wooden clubs, désounin-water bottles, rough-hewn couches, bedding rags, whips for slashing veins, razor-sharp daggers for stabbing, leg-cutting chains, pruning knives for popping gallbladders, hooks for crushing throats, razors for slicing the skin, graters for peeling the skin red, brushes for spreading vitriol, wooden clubs for crushing bodies, scissors for castrating, pliers for breaking jaws, hammers for pounding fingernails, mills for grinding testicles, hot plates for burning backsides, saws for sawing bones, smoking pipes for rendering passive, iron picks for piercing eyes and stabbing guts, bags for giving bouziyèt enemas, all sorts of junk is thrown pell-mell over the fence to be scattered on the ground. The bare walls collapse. Flames engulf their wooden slats, devour the rotten planks. The roof caves in.

Zofè crawls on his belly, drags himself on his knees, then starts running toward the gate. A band of bouanouvo surround corner grab slap beat dispatch Zofè before he can even whisper peep. Jaws, teeth, arms, legs, forehead, spilled guts, ears, hands, Zofè lies scattered in bits and pieces in the high road's dust. A thunderous shout goes up. The ears of the villagers in Bouanòf and Ravin Sèch ring like a struck gong.

Machetes, chair legs, cattle horns, sickles, broken bottles, conch shells, stone-filled straw bags, pickaxes, fish traps, iron swords, rough ropes, hardwood clubs, wooden beetles, hatchets, hammers, pestles, all sorts of old tools and sundry objects become handy weapons.

A band of bouanouvo are running down the road, a disorderly mass, looking like a pack of mad dogs sniffing around for food. A crooked road. A raping road. A wild road. An anything-goes road. A brawling and rioting road. A bone-shaking danger-filled road.

The Bouanèf and Ravin Sèch villagers are in shock, ears strained, eyes wide open, watching the big commotion with their hearts in their mouths. Without stopping and with a sense of urgency, Klodonis raises his voice to speak to the bouanouvo: "Where are you going? Where do you think you're going? Why are you so scattered and aimless? You don't go very far on a horse that loiters and paws the ground on the savanna. All of us bouanouvo we need to come together and join the villagers. I've just heard Sintil has been sneaking pintadin gamecocks into the cockfight. Pull yourselves together and gather up your courage to tackle Sintil. He's enjoying himself right now at the dézafi on the other side of the tracks."

All of a sudden the villagers recognize Klodonis. Shock. Ringing shouts. Rejoicing. Hugging. Weeping. Scarves are tied around waists. Sleeves are rolled up. Machetes are pulled out of their scabbards. Pinewood torches are lit. The villagers join the bouanouvo in a single mass. Hand in hand, in a tight formation, they start out in earnest for the other side of the railroad tracks.

From behind Lakataou Mountain an albino moon shines over Bouanèf.

Stiff as a rod with fatigue from bending straining crouching patiently watering a hard and reticent soil, Alibé is shuffling home from his farm plot. Plantain and banana leaves, peapods, rice grains, millet spikes, loads of sweet potatoes, green wood, measuring tins full of lemons are dancing a jig in his head. His shadow precedes him dancing a soulless tolalito dance in jagged clickety steps.

Way up there on the flanks of Lakataou Mountain a wandering wind, a gossipmongering wind, a loudmouthed wind brings a rumble of discordant voices to Alibé's ears: died and came back to life / crops destroyed / bouanouvo on the way / Zofè dead / Siltana ran away / salty stew / salt all around / Klodonis got to taste salt / he gave salt to all the zonbis / zonbis transformed into bouanouvo / Zofè's guts hanging on a fence / fire in Sintil's lakou / meat barrel overturned / pintadin gamecocks sneaked into the cockfight / Sintil at the dézafi / Let's go rip Sintil's ass! . . .

Alibé is anxious. He cocks his ears to catch the broken words, the confusing utterances thrown to the wind. He hurries over Zabriko Hill, rushes down the valley, takes a shortcut, and suddenly finds himself before a wild-eyed mob chanting in unison: "Let's go chop Sintil up! Let's go cut Sintil's balls off! Let's go fillet Sintil! Let's go skin Sintil! Let's go crush Sintil! Let's go slice and pound Sintil's guts! . . ."

Suddenly Alibé understands. He leaves at a sprint and rushes like the wind to get home.

"Jéròm! Jéròm!"

"Alibé, my brother! What is that wind that's blowing swirling tumbling through our village?"

"It hasn't got a name yet. The christening will come later. Come on out, konpè Jéròm, you don't want to miss Mass."

"Really?"

"The earth trembled to its core. A hurricane blew through Sintil's lakou, then rolled through Bouanèf and Ravin Sèch. The zonbis tasted salt. The zonbis passed the salt around. The zonbis stuffed themselves with salt. Every single zonbi has become a bouanouvo. They've joined as one with the villagers to go beat up Sintil at the dézafi on the other side of the tracks."

"Is that the truth?"

"Siltana escaped in the confusion. Zofè's guts are hanging on some fence. Sintil's in big trouble, his coffee has got coffee grounds in it."

Without wasting a second, Jéròm slides down the ladder so fast a few bars shatter and, with Alibé at his side, makes a beeline for the dézafi on the other side of the tracks.

Since Pin Kris's death, Gaston has been like a game-cock reeling from one of those spur hits to the chest that lift and slam a fighting bird to te ground. Pulling a handcart, carrying heavy loads, being a yard boy, bathing foreign dogs (doberman pinschers, sheepdogs, german shophords, saint bernards, bulldogs), washing and polishing late-model cars, begging in front of stores, being a guide and errand boy for foreign tourists, loading and unloading trucks, hustling around always hungry and looking sickly, Gaston has become a gaunt figure of misery. Life in Port-au-Prince has given him a real beating.

When you run out of luck even a malanga leaf will cut your finger. But then again, if you don't wash and scour the clay jar yourself, you will not have clean water to drink. As you make your bed so you lie in it. Gaston wiggles until he manages to set himself free. One afternoon, he resolves to take the road back to Bouanèf. He catches a ride on a Texaco truck that drops him halfway, then he takes a shortcut through the bushes all the way to the lakeshore. When he arrives on top of Jonjon Mountain, his heart almost stops. Ravin Sèch is in turmoil. He stops, looks, and says out loud: "Goddamn! Bouanèf is up in arms! This mahogany wood is too hard; I don't think I'll be able to saw it. This baby doesn't even own the hairs on his back. I'd better go and hustle elsewhere."

Gaston keeps staring, his hands on his cheeks. He takes two halting steps. He turns around and starts walking in the direction of Port-au-Prince.

The village is in uproar. Alibé, Klodonis, Bouanèf villagers mingled with bouanouvo arrive at the dézafi on the other side of the tracks like a stampeding herd: Let's go cut Sintil's balls off! Let's go pound on Sintil! Let's go dispatch Sintil! . . .

Discreet as a cat, Sintil sneaks away, threading his way through the crowd, getting ready to fly away from the cockfight. Kamélo and Filojèn reach for him and grab him by his shirt. They punch him, kick him, slap his face, and throw him on the ground. Sintil begs for mercy. Sintil moans and begs for his life. A bunch of bouanouvo, enraged and out of control, stomp pound tear Sintil's body into tiny bits and pieces.

Benches, chairs, tables, fried food trays, dice cups, playing cards, cooked foods, eating bowls, klérin bottles, all sorts of junk is getting thrown to the other side of the road.

In the midst of all this wild commotion, Jéròm is running hither and thither preaching salty words, magical words, uplifting words, soaring words, words with teeth, words with wings: "Just one grain of salt under your tongues and you'll start suckling at life's tits. Before you dip your feet in the water, purge your souls, get rid of the bad spirits in your heads, of the old dank matted hairs in your armpits. The journey is long. The journey may last many harvests, the journey may have many ups and downs. You must get it all off your chests, vomit all the phlegm, fill up your calabashes with clean water, steel your wrists to fend off every ferocious beast that tries to rip off your gizzard on the high road. At every crossroads, draw vèvè signs in the dust with your toes so that those who follow you will know on which foot to dance. The dézafi never ends. The dézafi has no limit. Gamecock owners will forever groom their roosters. Life is but one huge dézafi. We mustn't let bad sleep bring us close to death . . . "

The few stars still loitering in the sky finally weigh anchor. The sun is about to rise. Bouanèf has started to wash itself clean. On the Ravin Sèch road, hand in hand, like two turtledoves, a young man and a young woman are walking on their way to the spring to bathe together.

GLOSSARY

akasan cornmeal mush traditionally sweetened with molasses

akasan siro molasses-sweetened cornmeal mush served as offering to Vodou deities

aloufa a greedy, all-devouring person

andaki coded, cryptic speech, to be understood by the person for whom it is intended and not by other listeners

ason a ritual object used by the Vodou priest during a ceremony—a small rattle made with a dried pear-shaped calabash covered with a loose net of stringed colored beads and snake bones

assorossi bitter melon, a tropical vine whose fruit and leaves have medicinal properties

avé a plant whose roots are used as insecticide particularly against bedbugs; also reputed to have abortive properties

Ayibobo an exclamation used to punctuate a Vodou song or to signal the end of a ritual performance, meaning amen; may also be used to express praise or approval

baka a demon in the form of a midget of extremely repulsive appearance

balansé-yaya a children's song with a swinging rhythm

bayakou a professional latrine cleaner

bizango members of an occult society of the group of sects called "red sects" who practice ritualistic human sacrifice

bòkò a sorcerer, or a Vodou priest, who engages in harmful magical practices

bosal a neophyte's wild *loua* that has yet to be tamed through a special Vodou baptismal rite

bouanouvo literally, "new wood," a *zonbi* who has consumed salt and regained his or her full faculties of will and cognition

bouapini a knotty hardwood used to make walking sticks or clubs

boulé zin   Vodou ritual in which an *ounzi* is elevated to the level of *kanzo*; see the term "*ounzi kanzo*"

boumba   a dugout canoe

boustabak   a species of black birds

bouziyèt   a poisonous shrub with a toxic milky sap and leaves that trigger rashes and swelling at a mere touch

Chaloska   a mardi gras figure wearing an army officer's costume and mocking a brutal and boastful early twentieth-century general named Charles Oscar, responsible most notoriously for ordering the mass murder of prisoners in 1915 on the eve of the United States' occupation of Haiti

chòché   sorcerer

dégi   a little extra added to a purchase by a vendor as a gesture of appreciation for the customer's patronage

démanbré   family gathering to honor ancestral Vodou spirits; sacral plot of land in which family ancestors are buried

désounin   a ceremony during which the Vodou priest removes the personal *loua* from the head of a recently deceased Vodouist and takes back the secrets the latter had received at initiation

dézafi   cockfight tournament; cockfight

djipopo   hurdle, obstacle, danger

gagit rooster   a fierce gamecock with nail-sharp spurs

galipòt   mythical animal resembling a wolf or a monstrous horse

goud   Haiti's currency unit

gouden   a coin or combination of coins worth 25 cents of the *goud*

govi   a clay jug in which a Vodou priest keeps spirits or a dead person's *loua*

Grinn Pronminnin   name of a mythic figure who wanders ceaselessly; used as a metaphor, it means "wandering seed," "rolling stone," "wanderer," "vagabond"

kalinda   a dance consisting of bumps, grinds, and spectacular somersaults

karang   louse; type of ugly and aggressive fish

kata   a rhythmic sound made with a stick against another stick or against the side of a drum to accompany a drum beat

katchoumbonmbé   trouble, clash, messy confrontation

klérin   popular cheap white rum

kòb   money, coin

konpè   term by which a godfather and the father of the child call each other; also used as a term of respect and camaraderie

koudjay   a moving music and dance fete in which the dancing crowd follows the band through the streets

Koumatiboulout!   an exclamation of amazement or admiration

lago   hide-and-seek game

lakou   traditional extended family compound in the countryside; a high-density compact working-class urban neighborhood with tightly close dwellings and narrow alleys

lamayòt   a carnival game in which a mardi gras–costumed figure is paid a small fee to allow a member of the public to guess the contents of a closed box, usually a snake or a toad, or some other small animal or object

langay   esoteric language used by an *oungan* in Vodou rituals or by a Vodouist possessed by a *loua*; sometimes referred to as "langaj"

Antouan Langonmié   early twentieth-century Vodou priest from southern Haiti renowned for his legendary gift of prophecy and clairvoyance

lasigouav   a mythical monster with a wolf's head and a metallic body

Lasirèn   a female sea deity

Lasirèn Diaman   one of the iterations of the female sea deity Lasirèn

loua   Vodou spirit or deity

lougarou   a sorcerer with supernatural powers or a shape-shifting demon who preys on people

lycée   a public secondary school

Mabouya lizard   a fat black-and-yellow-striped lizard

Madanbrino   carnival figure in the form of a grossly obese woman carrying a male manikin on her back representing a cuckolded husband.

Madan Kolo   landmark nineteenth-century statue of a generic female figure by a public fountain in the Bel-Air section of Port-au-Prince, so named by the population of the time after a renowned woman shopkeeper, Clorinde or Madame Colo, who had her business in Bel-Air; sometimes used to refer to Bel-Air as a whole

madlèn snake   a small common and harmless grey striped snake

malanga   a root vegetable; the large heart-shaped green leaves are also edible

malfini   a species of hawk that preys on small wild birds and domestic fowl

mannil   a heavy, fat gamecock

marasa   twins

mayanba a children's game in which players toss porcelain or ceramics shards

mazoumbèl a root vegetable; the large heart-shaped green leaves are also edible

miskadin a love potion, a charm

moundong loua the deities in the Congo-Petro category of Vodou *loua*

ouari a large red bean or seed used to make poison, a skin-bleaching concoction, or in divination

ounfò the Vodou temple complex that consists of the *pérestil* and the *loua*'s chambers; the *ounfò* is considered the *oungan*'s family patrimony

oungan a Vodou priest

oungévé a large necklace of snake bones and beads in a variety of colors worn as a protective talisman

ounzi kanzo the *ounzi* is the Vodou priest's assistant; the *ounzi kanzo* is one who has undergone initiation by fire

pérestil the rectangular-roofed court in front of the *ounfò* where public Vodou ceremonies take place

pétévi a frail, passive, and stupid person

piastre the alternative name of Haiti's currency unit, the goud ("pias" in Kreyòl)

pintadin a chicken and guinea fowl hybrid

ponyak a variety of plantain or banana

potomitan a sacred pole at the center of the *pérestil*; it is considered the ritual axis of all Vodou ceremonies

rabòday a roaming carnival band whose characteristic music consists of the polyrhythmic honking sounds of bamboo horns of different sizes and a rolling drumbeat

rara a country carnival that takes place from Ash Wednesday to Easter Monday

sanmba a storyteller, poet, composer, and singer

sindik an official who supervises the irrigation system in a particular area and ensures a fair distribution of water to the farm plots under his responsibility

sòlòkòtò a sorcerer

soubréka a lackey, a flunkie

tafia the cheapest and lowest grade of white rum

tchaka   a thick soup made with bits of pork, corn, and several kinds of beans.

Tèktègèdèk!   an exclamation used to emphasize the inevitability of a situation or event, or the futility of an action

Tèt-san-kò   literally "Bodyless Head," a mythic creature who is just a head rolling on the ground and wandering at night to prey on humans for his missing body parts

tinginding   an adjective meaning preternaturally dangerous

tolalito   a children's game similar to tag

vaksin   a horn made of a length of bamboo

vèvè   esoteric symbols of the Vodou deities drawn on the ground with corn flour or wheat flour by a Vodou priest during a ceremony

vlingbinding   members of a secret society of sorcerers who practice human sacrifice and who roam the city streets and the countryside at night in search of victims

yanvalou   a Vodou dance mimicking the undulating movements of a snake

zinga   a large aggressive gamecock, a bruiser

zobòp   members of a secret society of cannibalistic sorcerers

Zoklimo   a Vodou deity in the Petro family of *loua* traditionally considered particularly fierce and aggressive

zonbi   a person brought back to life from a state akin to death induced by a concoction administered by an *oungan*; alive but without free will and cognitive faculties, the *zonbi* is used as a slave and can become a complete person again only by ingesting salt

AFTERWORD

On the English Translation of *Dézafi*

Jean Jonassaint

Franketienne's *Dézafi* (1975) is the first novel published in the Haitian language but not the first narrative written and published in the Haitian vernacular or in other so-called Creole languages of the Caribbean.[1] Through WorldCat, for example, we can find Carrié Paultre's *Ti Jak*, a thirty-three-page-long illustrated story apparently published in 1968 in pocketbook format. But this undated short narrative, like the Haitian poet Georges Sylvain's *Fables de La Fontaine racontées par un montagnard haïtien et transcrites en vers créoles* (1901) or any short story for that matter, cannot be labeled a novel in any language or literary tradition, despite the publisher's identification of the work as a novel on its cover page, a claim relayed by Thélyson Orélien, a *Huffington Post Québec* blogger, in a post on "the first novel in Haitian Creole."[2] Orélien is not the only critic to express such confused views about Caribbean literature. The eminent French linguist Marie-Christine Hazaël-Massieux showed a similar misunderstanding in the appendix to her 2003 article "Creole in the French Caribbean Novel of the 1990s: From Reality to Myth?"[3] Among the "Principal Works of Fiction Published Wholly in Creole in the Caribbean," she lists not only works written in French, such as Justin Lhérisson's *Zoune chez sa ninnaine* (1906) and Tonton Dumoco's *Les Mémoires d'un Vonvon* (1905), but also short narratives written in "Creole" that are not novels at all, such as Carrié Paultre's *Amarant* (1976, 48 pages) and Gilbert de Chambertrand's *Dix bel cont avant cyclone* (2nd ed., 1976, 62 pages), the latter clearly identified by its title as a collection of folktales.

The label "novel" might fit other works better. For example, in 1885, the Guyanais writer Alfred Parépou published *Atipa*, a two-hundred-page work of fiction subtitled "*roman guyanais*" (a Guyanais novel), which is considered the first "Creole novel." Further-more, by 1974, Émile Célestin-Mégie had completed the " *prémiè épòk*" (first part) of a novel in Haitian to be published by Éditions Fardin. The publisher, Dieudonné Fardin, made the deliberate decision, presumably with Célestin-Mégie's consent, to publish Frankétienne's *Dézafi* before releasing the first volume of Célestin-Mégie's *Lanmou pa gin baryè* at the end of 1975. The novelist, who was also Fardin's colleague, would subsequently praise the publication of *Dézafi* in a short article in Haitian, "Dézafi krazé défi" (*Dézafi* met the challenge),[4] written under his pseudonym To-giram. Fardin's decision to publish *Défazi* first ultimately bestowed on the work a unique position among Haitian literary productions both in Haitian and in French. Its publication was, as emphasized in the title of the special issue of Fardin's journal, *Le Petit Samedi Soir*, devoted to the novel's release, "Un événement sans précédent dans l'histoire des lettres haïtiennes" (An unprecedented event in the history of Haitian literature). Nonetheless, *Dézafi*'s fame does not derive from these nonliterary factors but rather from its es-thetic qualities, which surpass all expectations for a text in a Ca-ribbean language, with Frankétienne's novel achieving for Haitian what, centuries earlier, Cervantes's *Don Quijote* did for Spanish and Dante's *Divina commedia* for Italian. Quite appropriately, Togiram's review emphasizes the groundbreaking significance of Frankétienne's novel: "Here is a book that has brought me great delight and ineffable intellectual stimulation. . . . Here is the liter-ary treasure Haitians with a Haitian soul have been expecting for a long time."[5] For his part, Émile Roumer, another poet and ardent defender of the Haitian language and culture, commented about the novel: "*Dézafi* is an engrossing book. I spent a whole afternoon under the irresistible charm of a story that unfolds like the cantos of Dante Alighieri's poems, fascinated by a mystery that resists a self-absorbed urban dweller's understanding. . . . Personally, I am proud that a Haitian could write such a masterpiece. If you don't have a library, start one and make Frankétienne's novel, *Dézafi*, the first book on its shelves."[6]

The first volume of a Haitian library, according to Roumer; a foundational text of a literarity in the Haitian language, according to the Franco-Haitian scholar Rafael Lucas,[7] *Dézafi* is a unique venture in the history of literature in new vernacular languages of the Americas. Frankétienne was fully conscious of this situation. Indeed, he was so conscious that, for the first time, he asserted his authorship rights over one of his published works: "No one in any country may translate, reproduce, or adapt in whole or in part the text of the novel *Dézafi* without the author Frankétienne's permission."[8] This statement highlights a striking contrast with the position that the novelist expressed years before on the cover page of his *Ultravocal* (1972), asserting that "the work belongs to no one; it belongs to everyone." Written in a new language born from the transatlantic encounter in the Caribbean, *Dézafi* interweaves a number of traditional Haitian narrative forms (*voye pwent*, proverbs, sayings, lodyans, etc.). But, as surprising as this might appear, the novel also integrates some of the most modern Western narrative forms, elements of which can already be found in Haitian popular discourse.[9] Thus, it is possible to identify in *Dézafi* elements of the French *nouveau roman* in the multiplicity and nonlinearity of the reported stories; aspects of John Dos Passos's cinematographic storytelling in the montage of textual sequences in different typographical characters indicative of specific discursive forms or narrative series; or Joycean stream of consciousness, notably in the sections in italics or boldface.

NATIONAL AND TRANSNATIONAL CONTEXT(S)

Dézafi is also the story of a perception shared by Haitians, both inside and outside the country, of their sociopolitical situation in the 1960s and 1970s. Frankétienne implicitly alludes to this commonly held notion—that an autocratic regime was oppressing the entire population and that liberation could only come from the top or the center—by rewriting the myth of zombis released by the salt provided by a woman, houngan's mistress or daughter. The choice of this well-known grand national narrative, which is already present in W. B. Seabrook's *The Magic Island* (1929),[10] is both judicious and significant as it allows the writer to explore certain realities without addressing them explicitly. Thus, the plot of *Dézafi* projects and foreshadows the fall of the Duvalier regime in 1986 and the ensuing popular reactions, notably the *dechoukaj* (literally, "uprooting"—a violent overthrow of an oppressive regime), without exposing the author to the risks that would have been associated with publishing a more explicitly referential narrative. This particular posture is one that may be called *andaki*, to use a term found in both Frankétienne's text and peritext, as the novel is presented by the publisher and the narrator as "paròl andaki." The *andaki* discourse, a Haitian mode of expression in which a speaker encodes the communication to have different meanings for a general audience and the person or group of persons for whom the words are intended, thus made it possible for the book to circulate in a restrictive political environment, on the one hand, and to carry a polysemy that would inspire some of its critical reception abroad, on the other. I refer in particular here to Max Dominique's Marxist critique of *Dézafi* and to the exchanges both oral and written among the *"action patriotique"* Left in the Haitian diaspora.[11]

Even commentators who may question *Dézafi*'s political values—mainly its revolutionary content or its service to the cause of the masses—nevertheless acknowledge that the novel reflects problems that have affected and still affect Haiti and Haitians. Examples include the problem of underemployment and unemployment alluded to in the dialogues between Gaston and his aunt Louizina and other characters (pp. 46–47, 63–65); and the omnipresent gambling, as in the cockfighting at the center of the novel or in Fabi's gaming shack, where Gaston's fate takes a turn (pp. 44–45). There are also the issues of both internal and external migrations evoked in the stories of Rita and Gaston (in Port-au-Prince), of Jédéyon (abandoned by his family who reside in New York [p. 41]), and of Fabi (who left for the Bahamas [p. 90]). The evocation of these socioeconomic realities, explored in such earlier novels as *Mûr à crever* (1968) and *Ultravocal* (1972), shows that *Dézafi*, although written in the Haitian language, falls within the continuum of Frankétienne's literary production.

Beyond Frankétienne's personal creative agenda, *Dézafi*, written in part as a response to a challenge from the activist and journalist

Jean Dominique to produce a novel in Haitian,[12] was born in the broader context of the valorization of the Haitian language and literature, which had the tacit but active support of the Haitian government, a fact that is often forgotten or silenced, as well as the support of both Catholic and Protestant churches, particularly in the wake of the Second Vatican Council, which encouraged the use of the vernacular in liturgical practices. Indeed, the inclusion of Haitian literature in the secondary school curriculum, decreed in an October 26, 1959, memorandum by the minister of national education, the Reverend Father Hubert Papailler—who was himself a writer and the author of, among other works, *Fleurs d'ombre et paillettes d'écumes* (1954) under the pseudonym Jean-Hubert Mariamour—brought positive national developments. Among these, it is worth mentioning the production of Haitian literature textbooks, the most important of which were *Cours d'histoire de la littérature haïtienne à l'usage des élèves des classes de 4e, 3e, 2e et 1ère, des lycées et colleges*, vols. 1–4, by Dieudonné Fardin and Hérard Jadotte (1961–63); *Histoire de la littérature haïtienne (de l'Indépendance à nos jours)*, by Ghislain Gouraige (1960); and *Manuel illustré d'histoire de la littérature haïtienne*, by Les Frères de l'Instruction Chrétienne (1961).[13]

Following the release of this latter textbook, the historian and scholar Leslie F. Manigat published a brochure with the approving title *Une date littéraire, un événement pédagogique* (1962) that signaled the significance of the Haitian state's educational initiative. Another important work published in that decade is René Piqui-on's *Manuel de négritude* (1966?), a volume of some three hundred pages that is a sequel to his earlier work on Aimé Césaire, Léon-Gontran Damas, and Léopold Sédar Senghor, *Les Trois Grands de la négritude* (1956?).[14] It is worth recalling as well such equally significant undertakings as the republication and promotion of several works by the newspaper *Panorama* and the publishing house of the same name owned by Paul Blanchet, minister of coordination and information in the Duvalier government, and his brother Jules; and the release of a series of books by Éditions Fardin and the publication of the weekly *Le Petit Samedi Soir*, both under the leadership of Dieudonné Fardin, a top-level civil servant in the

Office National d'Alphabétisation et d'Action Communautaire (ONAAC), a government institution responsible for rural education in Haitian and for the study and promotion of the language. It should be pointed out that it is actually the ONAAC-designed spelling system that Frankétienne used in *Dézafi*, the same system that was followed with some degree of accuracy in such Protestant periodicals as *Bon nouvèl* and *Boukan* and in the reading materials developed for the government's literacy program.

In summary, it is worth recalling that *Dézafi* was written and published in a national context of great cultural effervescence both in Haiti and in the Haitian diaspora. The signs of this effervescence included the publication of Jean-Claude Charles's *Négociations* (1972), René Philoctète's *Le Huitième jour* (1973), René Depestre's *Alléluia pour une femme-jardin* (1973), Jean Jacques Honorat's *Enquête sur le développement* (1974), Raphaël Berrou and Pradel Pompilus's *Histoire de la littérature haïtienne illustrée par les textes*, vols. 1 and 2 (1975), Alain Bentolila et al.'s *Ti Diksyonnè Kreyòl-Franse/Dictionnaire élémentaire créole haïtien-français* (1976), and Hubert de Ronceray's *Projet expérimental sur le bilinguisme créole-français au niveau de l'enseignement primaire en Haïti* (1976). The productions of the theater troupe Kouidor in New York (from 1969 onward) that involved such writers and actors as Syto Cavé, Georges Catera fils, Jacques Charlier, and Josaphat Large were of similar cultural significance.[15] Finally, a number of periodicals contributed enormously as well to the cultural ferment of the times, among them the journal *Nouvelle Optique* in Québec (1971–73), the reborn weekly *Le Petit Samedi Soir* in Port-au-Prince (1972), and the newly launched journal *Dérives* in Montréal (1975), which published excerpts from Frankétienne's *Ultravocal* in its inaugural issue, a first for this home-based writer.[16]

ON DIFFERENT EDITIONS OF THE NOVEL

There are two different editions of Frankétienne's novel in the Haitian vernacular: the 1975 edition, with an *accent aigu* on the letter "e" in the title *Dézafi*, and a 2002 edition, without the accent on the "e" in the title *Dezafi*. The text of the first edition, published in

Port-au-Prince, is 312 pages long (about 31,400 words) and follows the orthographic system of the time, the so-called ONAAC spelling system. The second edition, released in France, is a revised and expanded version of the novel, 295 pages long (more than 34,200 words), that uses the official spelling approved in 1980 by the Jean-Claude Duvalier government. In addition to its length and to changes in the spelling, mainly the use of the article "yon" (a, an) instead of the earlier "youn," this second text is rather different from the 1975 text in several respects, notably in its typographical layout. A quick visual comparison of random pages from the two editions shows that, in the 2002 edition, phrases entirely in capital letters are introduced, a greater variety of fonts and type sizes (from 12 to 24 points or more) is employed, and the use of boldface is abandoned. It should be noted as well that the nineteen short sequences typeset in 10-point Helvetica or Calibri and laid out in columns on the right side of certain pages in the second and third section of the 1975 edition are not reproduced *in extenso* in the 1979 French adaptation of the novel by Frankétienne, *Les Affres d'un défi*, or in the 2002 edition in Haitian. In fact, with a couple of exceptions (S75: 1975 p. 150; 2002 p. 143), these sections no longer form autonomous typographical blocks; rather, they simply blend into the flow of longer narrative, poetic, or discursive sequences set in roman or italic type.[17] Further analysis shows that, in addition to the orthographical distinctions, there are fundamental differences, both textual and typographical, between the 2002 *Dezafi* and the 1975 *Dézafi*. For example, the text on page 228 of the 2002 edition, a rewritten version of the text on page 241 of the 1975 edition (see figure 1, S143 and S145), contains at the top of the page a sentence in capital letters set in 24-point type on five lines; the same sentence in the 1975 *Dézafi* (p. 139) stands alone on the page and announces the third part of the novel. At the bottom of the page there is an eleven-line paragraph, justified and set in 12-point or 14-point type, that reproduces the four sequences found in the 1975 edition (see figure 1) without the original typographical differences, but with additions, elisions, and displacements.

Another interesting example (see figure 2) is found in the contrast between page 233 in the 2002 *Dezafi* and page 247 in the 1975

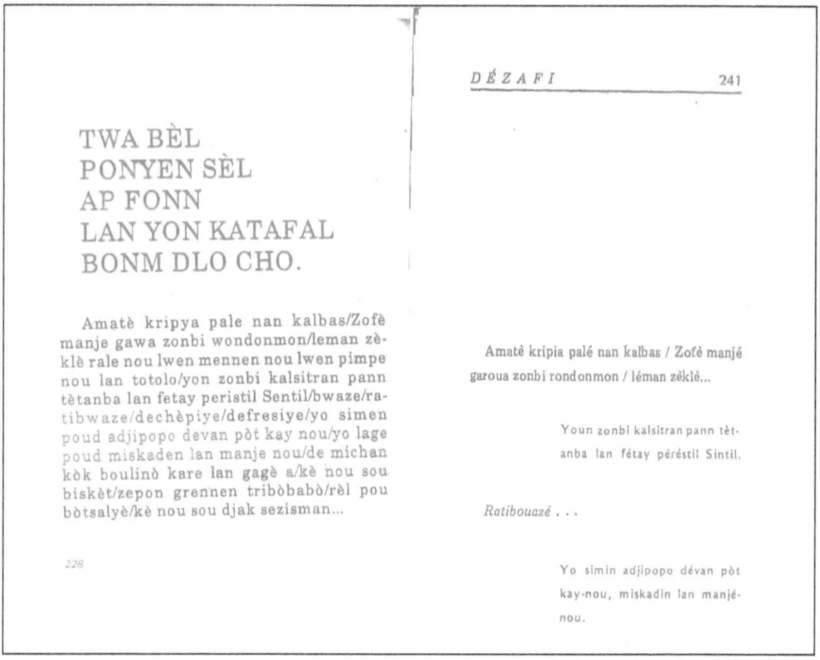

DÉZAFI   241

TWA BÈL
PONYEN SÈL
AP FONN
LAN YON KATAFAL
BONM DLO CHO.

Amatè kripya pale nan kalbas/Zofè
manje gawa zonbi wondonmon/leman zèklè rale nou lwen mennen nou lwen pimpe
nou lan totolo/yon zonbi kalsitran pann
tètanba lan fetay peristil Sentil/bwaze/ra-
tibwaze/dechèpiye/defresiye/yo simen
poud adjipopo devan pòt kay nou/yo lage
poud miskaden lan manje nou/de michan
kòk boulinò kare lan gagè a/kè nou sou
biskèt/zepon grennen tribòbabò/rèl pou
bòtsalyè/kè nou sou djak sezisman...

Amatè kripia palé nan kalbas / Zofé manjé
garoua zonbi rondonmon / léman zéklè...

Youn zonbi kalsitran pann tètanba lan fétay péréstil Sintil.

Ratibouazé . . .

228

Yo simin adjipopo dévan pòt
kay-nou, miskadin lan manjé-
nou.

Figure 1

Dézafi (S161). In the 2002 edition, the sequence concludes a longer sequence that begins on the preceding page. As with sequences
143 and 145 analyzed above, the text has undergone a number of
transformations, some of which change it from an open, polysemous text into a closed text. For instance, in the first sentence,
the adverb "toutbonvre" (really) followed by a period replaces the
ellipsis in the earlier text and thus compels a univocal reading. In
other words, it is no longer possible for the reader to wonder about
Gaston's fatigue or to imagine him from other possible angles.
Similarly, in the last sentence, the word "lavil" (in the city) is re-
placed with the phrase "lan koridò bidonvil" (in the alleys of the
slum), thus closing up the space completely. As a result, whereas
the reader of the 1975 text is given to imagine that Gaston wanders
through every neighborhood in Port-au-Prince, the reader of the
2002 version can only see him confined to the closed universe of

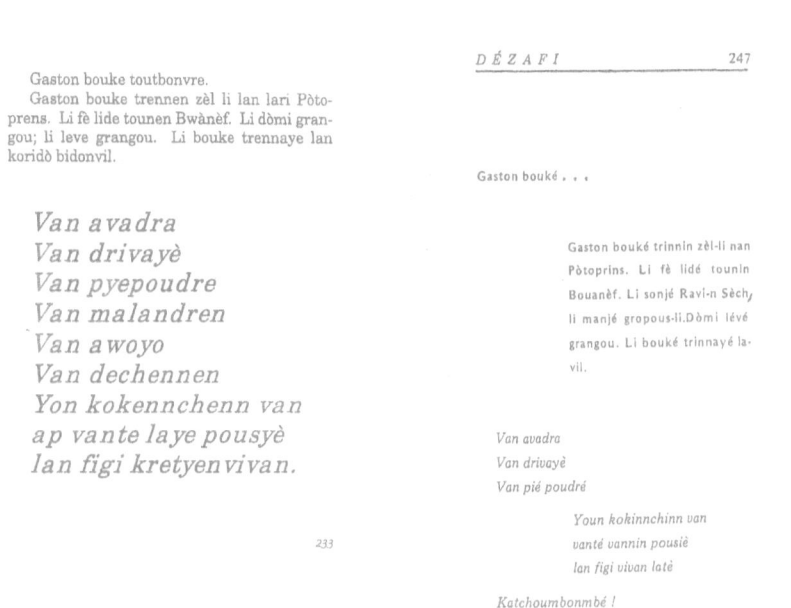

Figure 2

narrow alleys in the slum, as if the latter had no points of contact with the rest of the city. A similar closing occurs with the rewriting of the original text on page 241 of the 1975 edition. Instead of keeping "*Ratibouazé . . .*" as a one-line paragraph framed by two blank spaces, Frankétienne now submerges the verb in a long sequence, framing it between two other verbs that contextualize it and make its meaning more explicit: its opposite, "bwaze," and its effect, "dechèpiye." This explanatory strategy, like some other writing practices found in the 2002 text, shows clearly that the target readership of this version of *Dezafi* is neither primarily nor exclusively Haitian, unlike the anticipated readership of the 1975 *Dézafi*. Here is another convincing example of rewriting that suggests different intended readerships for the two texts. The powerful sentence "*Dòmi lévé grangou*" (Sleep wake up hungry) in the 1975 original (S161) now becomes "*Li dòmi grangou; li leve grangou*"

(He goes to sleep hungry; he wakes up hungry). This transformation from a sentence that incorporates the very poetic essence of the Haitian language into a most prosaic phrase exemplifies the fundamental differences between the two versions of the novel and indicates the author's intention to reach a readership beyond native Haitian speakers. It is important that Asselin Charles elected to offer readers the English translation of the original *Dézafi*, a text that is much more poetic and more profoundly rooted in the Haitian popular narrative traditions and the poetics of the language.

Based on the 1975 Haitian text of *Dézafi*, Frankétienne wrote a French version of 240 pages (nearly 68,000 words with a glossary of Haitian terms), *Les Affres d'un défi*, published in 1979 in Port-au-Prince. Although longer, this French re-creation of the novel has fewer typographic sequences (135 against 177). With some orthographic corrections and two more or less similar layouts, the French iteration of the novel was reissued twice in France, in 2000 and 2010. In all the different editions, the story has the same characters evolving in the same places according to the same narrative modes. Except for the 2002 edition of *Dezafi*, we also have more or less the same typographic design of the 1975 text. However, the three section-heading pages (3, 73, 123; 1975 ed. pp. 9, 143, 239) and the white pages that frame or follow them, as well as the illustration of a coffin with its cross on page 281 of the original (p. 145 this edition) are not repeated in any subsequent edition. The Haitian-Canadian scholar Mae-Lyna Beaubrun's interesting master's thesis, "Structure et stylistique de *Dézafi* et de *Les Affres d'un défi* de Frankétienne" (2002), highlights the similarities and differences between the two works.[18] The American critic Mollie McFee also published an insightful comparative article on these Frankétienne books, "Beyond Translation: The *Matrice* of Frankétienne's *Dezafi*" (2017).[19] The Brazilian scholar Celina Scheinowitz published an entire volume, *Les Affres de l'inhumanité: Défi romanesque de Frankétienne* (2012), that analyzes *Les Affres* in detail, both at the textual and typographic levels.[20] In spite of possible reservations, these three works offer the interested reader stimulating insights that may help them to better grasp the differences between the two books. They make it particularly clear that the poetic intentions of *Les Affres d'un défi* are not those of *Dézafi*. Indeed, while the more concise text of *Dézafi* (1975) tends toward the gnomic and the enigmatic, and calls for complicity between reader, narrator, and characters to decode this *andaki* discourse, the text of *Les Affres d'un défi* (1979) is rather explicit, seeking to inform or convince the reader.

Dézafi (1975) is a Haitian narrative in Haitian, for Haitians, the story of the resurrection of zombis brought about by ingesting salt. In contrast, the French version, *Les Affres d'un défi*, targets a dual national and transnational readership, Haitian and Francophone, as is made evident by the addition of a glossary of Haitian terms at the end of the volume and by Franketienne's own statements in a 1986 interview that he had created this "adaptation" in response to the "wishes of some Haitian and Caribbean friends" as "a way of putting the work within the reach of non-Creole-speaking communities, [to] give the work a chance to be read in Francophone circles."[21] It is the original Haitian version of the novel, translated by Asselin Charles, that is the focus of my remarks. That is a text that explores the limits of Haitian expression, both syntactically and lexically. The first sentence of the second paragraph in italics of *Dézafi*, "*Dòmi lévé gadé maché manjé lanbé taté souflé tonbé kouri ralé jounin grangou*" (p. 11), clearly demonstrates such a writing strategy. This string of verbs without subject or complement, without any punctuation, for the reader who can find its rhythm of diction, is presented as a long portmanteau word describing a long day in the life of the hungry poor. It is an original verbal creation that is not to be found in any lexicon or dictionary, or in any oral or written expression. It is comprised of neither neologisms nor archaic words but of everyday terms arranged in a new, unexpected way, pushing the limits of the genius of the language. The "*patasouèl krazébrizédémantibiléblayividé*" administered to Siltana by Klodonis at the end of the novel (p. 295) is another striking example of Franketienne's verbal inventiveness. Agglutinating five past participles—*krazé* (crushed); *brizé* (broken); *démantibilé* (dismembered, put into pieces); *blayi* (thrown); *vidé* (hollowed out, poured)—Franketienne creates an adjective that gives more force to the slap Siltana received than would a more usual sequence of these qualifiers.

In the novel of Haitian tradition in French,[22] the writer tends to interpret or translate typical Haitian words or situations for its dual readership, Haitian and foreign. In *Dézafi*, in contrast, Frank-étienne provides no translation or interpretation of the compound phrases and many other similar expressions scattered throughout the novel, leaving readers free to come up with their own interpretations. This radically different writing strategy for a national, if not exclusively Haitian, readership makes the novel, especially in the 1975 edition, more difficult to read or interpret, even for Haitians. It is Anglophone readers' good fortune, therefore, thanks to Charles's translation, to be able to access, even indirectly, the 1975 text rather than the 1979 French adaptation, *Les Affres d'un défi*, or even the 2002 Haitian version, *Dezafi*. In fact, the French edition of the 2002 Haitian text at times follows the common explanatory practice, the most obvious example being the substitution of the graphic on page 281 by a text that tends to follow the French version of 1979: "*La violence meurtrière de l'assassin attise notre soif de vengeance. Nos cicatrices bourgeonnent. Les dents du bourreau mordent impunément la chair de nos enfants. Qui aura su compter nos blessures* [1] *à ce dangereux carrefour de déséquilibre où tant d'infortunes pèsent sur nos épaules ?* [2] *Après avoir sondé les quatre horizons, nous sommes décidés à enjamber le fossé des vieilles malédictions, à briser la croix du malheur.* [3] *Nous avons pilé du maïs;* [4] *immanquablement nous mettrons l'acassan au feu.*"[23]

Thus, instead of a graphic representation of the symbolic *madoulè* (painful) coffin and the cross of the Haitian crossroads drawn on the page,[24] Franketienne proceeds as he does in the French text of 1979, *Les Affres d'un défi*: he first recounts, contextualizes (*Memwa nou pran danse lwa lan chak mak zòtèy nou trase lan pousyè*), then explains both the aims and modalities of the "Nou" narrator (*lan chak vèvè nou simen lan kalfou pou lanmò pa gen priz sou lavi*). Finally, he translates by reformulating the popular Haitian proverb at the bottom of the page into a proverbial phrase of his own, which he also capitalizes: "ZODAN KONN MÒDE VYANN, LI PA KONN KONTE MAK."[25] The insistence on the historical injury to the slave's or the zombi's scarred body ("*Bay kou bliyé, potémak sonjé*") can be read as a desire to remind the reader that the myth of zombification, for the most part, is a reminiscence or reiteration, in the independent postslavery Haiti, of the long transatlantic crossing in the holds of slave ships and of inhuman treatment on Saint-Domingue plantations. In this regard, the anthropologist Alfred Métraux writes: "A *zombi*'s life is seen in terms which echo the harsh existence of a slave in the old colony of Santo Domingo."[26] Indeed, zombification, as described in *Dézafi* and other narratives, notably René Depestre's *Hadriana dans tous mes rêves*,[27] shares two characteristics with slavery: first, the involuntary displacement of the subject, who has become an object, movable property, from his place of origin to an unknown space, the *habitation* of a master; and second, the subject's imprisonment and forced labor in the field or in the house under duress or torture and a deficient diet.

THE 1975 HAITIAN TEXT

The first thing that strikes the reader, especially one who is unfamiliar with contemporary experimental novels, is the diverse typography of the book, whether the version at hand is the original *Dézafi*, or Asselin Charles's English translation of same, or the 1979 French adaptation, *Les Affres d'un défi*, or else the revised and expanded French edition of the 2002 Haitian text, *Dezafi*. As in a film montage, in addition to the three pages in script characters delimiting the three parts of the novel, the text shifts from a series of blocks in Times italic type, to others in Helvetica or Calibri roman type, and to passages in Times boldface or roman type. The printing quality of the 1975 edition is somewhat uneven, so I follow here the French text of 1979 and opt for the boldface type used in the Charles translation. Moreover, the italic/boldface contrast allows one to better underline the differences between two symbolic universes of the novel, one global, the other specific, but both anchored in everyday modes of expression, such as the contrasting "Nou"/"Yo" (evoking a rather urban but also metaphysical world) and the "**boulay**" (round) of the cockfighting arena (of a rather rural, concrete world). Finally, these typographic choices are better suited to the discursive forms they convey, an enigmatic descriptive or philosophical poetry that unfolds like sea waves, and a no less enigmatic narrative poetry that telescopes various conflicting or parallel narratives within the same sequence. Analyzing the distribution of the boldface and italic type in *Les Affres d'un défi*, the Brazilian scholar Celina Scheinowitz argues that the italic and boldface type are more related to the expression of "emotions and inner visions," whereas the roman type transmits above all the "linear plot linked to the unfolding of the story told."[28] Whereas such an analysis may apply to *Dézafi* (1975), it may not necessarily work for the 2002 book, *Dezafi*, whose typo/topo/graphy is much more complex. While the two texts share some common traits in this respect, the differences are numerous—sometimes obvious, sometimes rather subtle, as shown by the brief analysis of the term "**boulay**" in *Dézafi* that follows.

Indeed, it is important to pay attention to the Haitian word "**boulay**," which I retain rather than an equivalent in French or English, such as "combat" (fight), a word used by Frankétienne in *Les Affres d'un défi* (1979) to translate indifferently "**boulay**" and "batay"—"premier combat" (first round [p. 95]), "coqs de combat" (fighting cocks [p. 10]), "combat de coqs" (cockfighting [p. 155]), or "troké kòn" (confrontation [p. 11]).[29] On the one hand, a careful analysis shows that "**boulay**" is strictly reserved for the enumeration or brief descriptions of cockfighting rounds in the context of a *dézafi* and is found only in boldface sequences of the second and third parts. I have inventoried thirteen occurrences: once to qualify respectively the first, second, third, fifth, sixth, eighth, and tenth "**boulay**" (pp. 145, 154, 157, 167, 181, 214, and 236; this ed. pp. 75, 80, 81, 86, 92, 109, 120); four times to narrate the seventh "**boulay**" (pp. 191, 192, 197, 199; this ed. pp. 98, 101, 102), and twice about the ninth "**boulay**" (pp. 222; this ed. p. 114). It should be noted that the text does not mention the fourth "**boulay**," just as it says nothing about the fourth and tenth "combat" (round) in *Les Affres d'un défi*. Indeed, the reader of the French text is not aware of the tenth "**boulay**"; for him, there have been only nine rounds of cockfighting. Here we can see how the analysis can diverge even on factual elements according to which of the texts is taken into account. Ultimately, *Les Affres d'un défi* (1979), the best-known and most studied version of this story of zombis liberated by ingesting salt, is neither *Dézafi* nor even a replica of it in French.

Moreover, the word "boulay" is taken in a particular sense—"a series of fights," "a fighting round," or simply "fight." Although these meanings are not fully accounted for in any dictionaries consulted,[30] the word is understandable for Haitian-language speakers and those familiar with the cultural practices that it names or describes. It thus appears that this term may be considered as a distinctive feature of the Haitian text of 1975, and to a lesser extent that of 2002, compared to the French text (1979, 2000, and 2010). In this regard, in using the English word "**round**" exclusively for "**boulay,**" Charles has made a judicious translation decision, one that is consistent with the author's obvious intention. Because of this distinctive feature, the English translation is aligned even more closely with the original text. It is perhaps a detail, but an important one that shows how Charles was, in this process of transformation, attentive to various nuances of Frankétienne's text and his typo/topo/graphy, a profuse and significant typography that a reader should not underestimate at the risk of completely missing the complexity of *Dézafi*.

From the first sequence of paragraphs in italics that opens the novel, the reader stumbles onto intriguing confrontations, in an unidentified indefinite space, between a narrator simply designated by the pronoun "Nou" (we) and a character or group of equally impersonal characters designated by the pronoun "Yo" (they): "*They would rather say we're short a few leaves; they hurry to shut us up. Days go by. Nights go by. A strange season. We remain befuddled in a dream full of bad omens. A dream punctuated by nightmares. Wind. Lightning. Thunder. We shake our bodies a little. Between sleep and wakefulness, we open one eye. We remember. We forget. We remember a little. But we forget a lot . . . in the dream*" (pp. 5–6).[31]

If the reader is not completely diverted by this discursive mode modeled on the Haitian tradition of the "voye pwent,"[32] but rendered in a form that recalls the poetic prose of the opening of Jacques Stephen Alexis's *Compère Général Soleil*,[33] he discovers, in the following sequence in roman type, this time in a clearly identified urban space, Pòtoprins, another pair of characters: a rather tyrannical and spoiled master, Jédéyon, and his malnourished little maid, Rita, alone in an old house, facing the hostility of a frightened neighborhood. If he is paying attention, and especially if he knows the Haitian language well, the reader realizes that this story involves the same "Nou" narrator/character or possible narratee/ character of the opening sequence in italics. Indeed, this Haitian "Nou," both first- and second-person plural, like the "Yo" (both "They," "We," "He or She"—since Haitian pronouns do not reflect gender), carries an ambivalence difficult, if not impossible, to render entirely in English or French, to refer to the two foreign languages in which a translation and a self-adaptation of *Dézafi* exist.[34]

On the other hand, by opting for the pronoun *"Nous"* (We) instead of *"Vous"* (You), although the French *"Nous"* as well as the English "We" can include both the speaker and the person spoken to, the French text erases the ambiguity and can only be read as the narrator's discourse: **"Enchevêtrement de branches d'arbres au fond d'une vieille cour. Terre dure aux veines emmaillées de pierres et de sable. Tripes encouleuvrées/lovées par la faim. Entrailles sanglées par la douleur. Chaque jour, le ventre vide, Rita s'échine dans les travaux domestiques. Enfermé dans sa maison, sans trêve, Gédéon lance des injures. Au milieu de la nuit, des cris déchirants nous vrillent le tympan, nous dardent la cervelle."[35]**

In his translation, just as Frankétienne does in the French text of 1979, Charles opts for "We"/"Our," thus removing the ambiguity of the "Nou" in the narrative: "A clump of gnarled trees with tangled branches loom at the far end of an old yard. Stones and grains of sand clog up the earth's veins. Guts all twisted up. Rita breaks her back working all day long without food. Jédéyon curses as he wanders around the house. In the depth of the night an ear-piercing scream for help stabs our brains. We shudder to our blood. Our stomachs rumble. Our hair stands up on our heads. We bolt up" (p. 6).

This is a correct choice, consistent with the intention of the author, who thereby revives a feature of the novel of Haitian tradition that tends to make of the narrator a national "we"—which includes the entire society of the novel: narrator, characters, narratee, potential or virtual reader—rather than a singular "I" enunciator.[36] A much earlier and very convincing example of this narrative strategy is the last paragraph of Fernand Hibbert's *Les Simulacres* (1923): "Haitian mothers, cultivate your children in the right way, and the Motherland will not perish! The day of glory will come! White Simulacra as well as Black and Yellow Simulacra will volatilize; and we will remain masters of the inheritance of the fathers, thanks to the new virtues, the science and the courage that you will inculcate to your children, who will not need anyone anymore for the development of their country by the Freedom, the Work, the Science and the Arts."[37] Retaining this narrative mode, Charles avoids the risk of misinterpretation while giving English-language readers access to a certain Haitian perspective despite linguistic differences. For, if Frankétienne had wanted to maintain some ambiguity about this or these anonymous character(s), he could have used, as Michel Butor does in *La Modification* (1957),[38] the "Vous," which in Butor's text can be read as a "You" who is the narrator/main character, or simply a main character.

Again, in this second sequence in roman type,[39] in the following paragraph, moving without any transition from the city to the countryside, appears another group of characters who, in accordance with Haitian tradition, are simply identified by their first name and/or their status: the houngan Sintil; his daughter, Siltana; and his assistant, Zofè, facing a horde of zombis and the terrified peasant populations of Bouanèf or Ravin Sèch. These two stories form a chiasma. Rita's domesticity (answering "yes uncle" on any subject just as the zombis utter "Wee waan!") and the fear that Jédéyon inspires in his neighbors in some respects echo the terror in which the zombis live on Sintil's plantation. Similarly, the death of Jédéyon, which frees Rita to leave Port-au-Prince to return to Bouanèf to live with her late father's cousin Alibé (p. 138), recalls the murders of Sintil and Zofè that liberate the peasants from their tyranny. These are also the two main narrative axes of the novel. Moreover, it is the second story, that of the zombification proper, that contains the most decisive episode for the denouement of the novel: the story of Siltana's love for the new zombi Klodonis, to whom she feeds the liberating salt, suddenly rousing him, at the end of the novel, from his lethargy and his submissiveness. The Klodonis character, more than the salt, is the disruptive element that allows the transformation of the narrative. Indeed, the very arrival of Klodonis at Sintil's *péristil* disturbs and transforms Siltana's attitudes toward her father's practices from the first moments of their encounter (pp. 67–68, 69–70). Desperately in love with the young zombi and conscious of the disruptive impact of Klodonis's presence on her previously predictable life, Siltana confesses to him, "I lost my bearings the first night you came into this house" (p. 71).

Furthermore, one could postulate that if Klodonis had been pleased with Siltana's desire for him, he would not have transformed himself, through the salt, into a subject in search of his own object of desire, his freedom and that of his own group, and the novel would have had a very different ending. In other words, if Klodonis had accepted Siltana's proposal to flee, rather than sharing the revitalizing salt with the other zombis, who, becoming bouanouvo, unleash their rage for revenge on Zofè and Sintil, whom they slaughter (pp. 155, 160), and on Siltana, who escapes (pp. 158–59), the populations of Bouanèf and Ravin Sèch probably would not have been able to put an end to their tyranny, and the initial situation of oppression would not have changed into the final moment of liberation and hope that closes the novel: "The few stars still loitering in the sky finally weigh anchor. The sun is about to rise. Bouanèf has started to wash itself clean. On the Ravin Sèch road, hand in hand, like two turtledoves, a young man and a young woman are walking on their way to the spring to bathe together" (p. 161).

In addition to these two core stories, the novel contains a number of other plots that alternate in the text. They may be found first in the sequences in roman type and then, in synoptic or fragmentary form, in the sequences in boldface punctuated by slashes, for the typographic complexity is further enhanced by a proliferation of plots. Indeed, if one is to have a more or less complete view of the novel, one needs to take into account not only the narratives built around the conflicting "Nou"/"Yo" but also the other microstories.

The first important micronarrative is that of the endless wandering of Kamélo and Filojèn from one *dézafi* to the next, tracking

Zofè and Sintil along the ten *boulay*, reported in boldface type, which punctuate the unfolding major clashes, symbolic or real, between various actors of the novel both in the closed space of the cockfighting arena and in the rural areas of Bouanèf and Ravin-Sèch or the capital, Port-au-Prince. These two characters are also the ones who prevent Sintil's escape from the cockfighting arena (p. 160), thus allowing the crowd of peasants and *bouanouvo* to cut the houngan's throat. The couple Kamélo and Filojèn are explicitly described as stronger than "grinn pronminnin" (1975 ed. pp. 28–29; this ed. pp. 13–14), the mythical figure with great knowledge of the different social actors, crossing the Haitian space from end to end, beyond the barriers of clans or classes. This duo of characters recalls Vatel in *Ultravocal* (1972), who is "condemned to wandering," and who forms a couple, oppositional certainly, with "Mac Abre, the incarnation of evil" to quote the front page of Frankétienne first "*spirale.*" Interestingly, it is this same Haitian folk figure that Michel-Rolf Trouillot chooses two years later to narrate his history of Haiti, *Ti-difé boulé sou istoua Ayiti* (1977), the very first historical work written in the Haitian language. This scholarly masterpiece, like *Dézafi*, initiates a new Haitian literarity, that of a national historical discourse in Haitian according to a typically Haitian narrative model, and at the same time appropriates and transforms a popular intertext, the legend of Grinn Prominnin, into one of the most important from a social science perspective.

The second important micronarrative in *Dézafi* is that of the very complex relationships between the chronically unemployed Gaston and his aunt Louizina in Ravin Sèch, and subsequently between the village native and the great womanizer Pastor Pin Kris in Port-au-Prince, where he migrated after defeating the reputedly invincible and diabolical Antonin at a dice game at Fabi's. Gaston, even though he is a secondary character, is interesting , being a significant figure in the denouement of the novel. Indeed, this character (namesake of a figure of power in *Mûr à crever*[40] [Ready to burst]) allows Frankétienne to highlight two different social issues. First, Gaston's story shows another side of the rural exodus in Port-au-Prince, quite the opposite of Rita's situation, the reality of the hungry poor, of the homeless, of the precariously employed, and others left behind in the capital. Second, subtly, Gaston's story critiques both Christianity and Vodou by making the Protestant Pastor Pin Kris (a very significant surname, Christ's penis), a sort of clone of Sintil—each one in his own way abusing poor people, both murdered at the hands of their victims. Although narrated in a very brief paragraph of 474 characters on page 278 of the 1975 edition (pp. 142–43 this ed.), the killing of the pastor prefigures that of the houngan and is a turning point in the outcome of the novel, a first indication of a possible victory of the weak against the strong, the final reversal to come. Moreover, it should be noted that, apart from the murder sequence, the only three important passages on Pin Kris and Gaston are indented on the page (pp. 76–77, 77–78, 159).[41] This emphasis—or marginalization, according to the point of view adopted—is not without meaning: it attracts the reader's attention. Charles's English translation fortunately respects this layout, which invites English-speaking readers, as well as their Haitian counterparts, to focus on a couple of characters who might otherwise go unnoticed in the tangle of the stories in roman type as in *Les Affres d'un défi*.

Finally, one cannot forget the cloistered existence of the politician or militant Jéròm in the attic of his peasant friend Alibé.[42] His status is not obvious, especially since he is the last character to express himself, in the penultimate paragraph of the novel, preaching a consistent political message in Bouanèf, one made up of "salty words, magical words, uplifting words, soaring words, words with teeth, words with wings" (p. 161). At more than six hundred characters in the 1975 edition, Jéròm's is the longest direct speech of any character in the novel (pp. 311–12; pp. 142–43 this ed.). Is it a satirical or serious portrait of these politicians hidden somewhere, in town or in the countryside, awaiting the end of the storm, like the slippery leader satirized in Frédéric Marcelin's earlier novel *Marilisse* (1903)? The few sequences (twenty-one) referring to Jéròm and his inseparable friend Alibé are too brief (on average one page or less), especially in the Haitian texts of 1975 or 2002, to allow a clear interpretation of Jéròm's character.[43] On the other hand, the 1979 French text, *Les Affres d'un défi*, has a long se-

quence focused exclusively on Jérôme that describes him as a sea-
soned and tortured activist (pp. 195–197, after the ninth round).
This is either a flashback or a nightmare. Again, it is hard to decide
one way or another, but based on this passage, Scheinowitz argues
that "Jérôme is a character who fulfills a political and ethical function in the novel" (p. 155). This opinion, more than any other by
the Brazilian scholar, illustrates the risk of confusing *Dézafi* (1975)
and *Les Affres d'un défi* (1979), of taking one for a duplicate of
the other. Frankétienne is quite right to insist that they are two different works, although one is the hypotext of the other, this latter,
hypertext (in the sense that Gérard Genette grants to these terms
in *Palimpsests*) produced in an attempt to join the Other,[44] to fill
even this desire to please the Other who sees in us, Haitians, his
"imaginary barbarian."[45]

In fact, this long scene, which to a certain extent is reminiscent
of Gérard Étienne's *Le Nègre crucifié* (1974)[46]—with a character
suffering torture and humiliation—does not seem to make sense,
either in the structure of the novel, where the flashbacks are rare
and brief, or from the standpoint of narrative logic. It is not quite
clear how Jérôme could have escaped from the prison world of his
executioners, and readers may well wonder whether he would have
been pardoned without having betrayed his comrades. To a certain extent, Jérôme's story may be seen as a mimetic recovery of
anti-Duvalierist commonplaces, or perhaps simply as a fantasy of
self-defense or self-justification. Whatever the interpretation, one
must understand that the micronarrative of Jéròm's "*boisé*" (literally, wooded),[47] the Haitian term for going into hiding, as politicians in Haiti often must, as well as the micronarratives of Kamélo
and Filojèn, and of Gaston and Pin Kris, are but fictional recon-
structions or representations of a Haiti that Frankétienne wants to
question rather than describe.

POSSIBLE READING MODES

It is critical to insist on this willingness to question "the real"
rather than to describe it. Indeed, more than a description of the
state of the City, one can read *Dézafi* as a *questioning* of the state

of the City. Although the novel shares some features of the novels of Haitian tradition, the "Nou" of *Dézafi* is not an informed narrator but one who keeps asking questions, who keeps wondering. The novel's enigmatic narrative mode is less that of a riddle than of a philosophical quest. The narrator doubts and strives to know, not to educate like the narrators of Frédéric Marcelin's narratives or Jacques Roumain's novels, who tend to explain Haitian peculiarities or singularities for their dual native and foreign, national and transnational readership.[48] Otherwise how else to explain or justify these questions, concerned or not with the "Nou," uttered by an anonymous "Kilès" (Who), which punctuate the sequences in italics in particular: *"Kilès pami nou k-ap viv toutbon? Kilès?"* ("Who among us is truly alive? Who?" for example [p. 5; 1975 ed. p. 12]); or in boldface, **"kilès ki manjé pitit tig?"** (**"Who's devoured the tiger's cub?"** [p. 87; 1975 ed. p. 169]); and to a lesser extent, in roman type, "Kilès ki lòtè éskandal piblik?" ("Who is responsible for this noisy fracas?" [p. 78; 1975 ed. p. 151])? These questions, like a *"pwent,"* the Haitian insinuative provocative phrase, unlike those of the narrator in Frédéric Marcelin's *Marilisse* (1903), for example, remain unanswered, but they imply a knowledge or a common doubt between narrator and narratee or potential reader. Thus, ignoring that the question **"kilès ki manjé pitit tig?"** echoes Jean-Claude Duvalier's famous slogan, *"pitit tig se tig"* (the child of the tiger is a tiger, or, in other words, "like father, like son"), one cannot understand its full scope.

Undoubtedly, faced with such complexities in a text recounting multiple plots variously embedded—a text sometimes segmented into blank-verse stanzas or punctuated with slashes, sometimes unfolding like a theatrical dialogue in a language at the heart of the deep country (the *parole des grands fonds*, to borrow the term coined by Kouidor),[49] a text composed and laid out in a variety of typographic characters—the foreign or Haitian reader may be intrigued or intimidated. In either case, the important step is to enter the book, read it. But how? How to read *Dézafi?*

Like any printed volume, Frankétienne's novel may be scanned or read in the order in which the words, sentences, paragraphs appear on the pages—a normal, traditional reading from beginning to end. But the layout in distinct typographic blocks also makes possible a different reading—by types of sequence. For example, one might first read the italicized sequences to delve into the metaphysical and poetic universe of the work; then one might move to the sequences in boldface for an overview of the various stories recounted in the novel; finally, one might focus on the sequences in roman type for a better understanding of the key intrigues of the narration. Readers more interested in the plots will venture first into the sequences in roman type for the main micronarratives that make up the novel. These readers will then explore the narrative poetry of the sequences in boldface that go beyond the world of the cockfighting arena to telescopic snapshots of a cast of characters in various settings. Finally, they will enjoy the purely poetic parts of the work in italics. Readers who want to experience the dual poetic and narrative registers of the novel will start with the sequences in boldface, then switch to the italics or roman type, depending on whether they want to explore more thoroughly the universe of the characters or the metaphysical poetry of the work.

All of the options for reading but the first, the customary way of reading, can be altered to create other decoding paths. For example, one could first alternate between the sections in boldface and those in italics, then move on to the sequences in roman type, or vice versa. One could also alternate between the boldface and roman passages and then read the sections in italics, or vice versa.[50] Ultimately, the polyphony and polygraphy of *Dézafi* make possible a variety of reading paths, including the random reading that one does with a great book of poetry. Regardless of one's reading preference, though, it is important to avoid seeing *Dézafi* as a sociological or ethnographic documentary for understanding Haiti, and to remember Franketienne's own take on his work: "*Dézafi* was first of all for me an aesthetic literary experience at the level of the Creole language. *Dézafi* is first and foremost the novel of the Haitian language, but as a language is indissolubly linked to the becoming, to the destiny, to the lived situation of a people, so a novel of the language which, inevitably, must also have been the novel of the Haitian people: the novel of the possibility, the eventuality or the probability of a liberation."[51] In other words, like James Joyce's *Ulysses* (1922), *Dézafi* is a quest into language, a deep exploration of Haitian discursive modes (with their commonplace or syntagmatic and paradigmatic particularities, their lexical fields, and so on), and the stories or cultural practices they convey.

ON ASSELIN CHARLES'S TRANSLATION

More than any previous text by Franketienne, *Dézafi* is an open work, one that allows different readings but also various reading paths. Charles's translation, a first in Haitian studies, the only translation of this magnitude of a narrative in the Haitian language, allows the English-speaking reader to have a reading experience along the variable paths embedded in the text itself. This is one of its merits, and not the least.

The fact that this first translation of a novel in Haitian into a foreign language, more specifically into English, is published in the United States is not pure coincidence. This American edition is part of a long tradition dating back to the first-known Creole texts, *Idylles, ou essais de poésie créole* (Idylles, or essays of Creole poetry), first published anonymously in New York in 1804 by "a settler from Saint Domingue," then reissued with some changes in Philadelphia, in 1811, by "an inhabitant of Haiti," under the title *Idylles et chansons, ou essais de poésie créole* (Idylles and songs, or essays of Creole poetry). It was also from New York, during the calypso fever era of the 1950s, that Harry Belafonte introduced the English-speaking world to one of the great classics of poetry in the Haitian language, Oswald Durand's "Choucoune" (1883), better known under the title of its musical iteration by the Haitian American composer Michel Mauleart Monton, "*Tizouazo*" (in Haitian) and "Yellow Bird" or "Do Not Ever Love Me" (in English).[52]

Similarly, it is not by accident that this English translation of Franketienne's *Dézafi* is published in the CARAF Books series, one of whose former series editors is Dr. Carrol Coates, translator of Jacques Stephen Alexis's and René Depestre's fiction published in this prestigious collection. Finally, we can only thank the University of Virginia Press, especially Assistant Director Eric Brandt; the series editors of the CARAF Books, Professors Renée Larrier and Mildred Mortimer; and also the translator Dr. Asselin Charles, who, in 2000, gave us the English translation of the 1885 masterwork by Anténor Firmin, *The Equality of the Human Races (Positivist Anthropology)*,[53] for having made possible the release of a work by the great Haitian writer and artist Frankétienne that affords readers further and deeper insights into Haitian creativity.

NOTES

This afterword is part of the larger framework of a current genetic edition of *Dézafi* and *Les Affres d'un défi*, undertaken on demand and with the support of the Institut des Textes et Manuscrits Modernes (ITEM, a research unit of ENS and CNRS, Paris). Preliminary results of this research have been published notably in "Édition génétique de *Dézafi* et *Les Affres d'un défi* de Frankétienne," in *Rencontres scientifiques 2013–2014* (Nantes: IEA, 2014), 64–72; and "Des éditions génétiques haïtiennes: Pourquoi? Pour qui? Comment?" *Genesis* 33 (2011): 79–91. Moreover, this publication would not have been possible without the generous help of Mrs. Lélia Lebon and the staff of the Interlibrary Loan of Syracuse University, whom I thank warmly. I would also like to thank my colleagues Dr. Jean-Robert Cadely and Dr. Meera Lee for their thoughtful advice and comments, and the students of my fall of 2016 seminar "Haiti, Myth and Reality" at Syracuse University, especially Clémence Fabi, whose questions and comments have helped nourish my research on *Dézafi* and *Les Affres d'un défi*.

1. I share the now widely held view articulated by Nanie Piou in her article on the subject, "Linguistique et idéologie: Ces langues appelées *créoles*" (*Dérives* 16 [1979]: 13–30), that the terms "Creole" and "Creole language" are not scientifically valid concepts for identifying the language spoken by Haitians. Consequently, except in quotations, I will use the terms "Haitian" and "Haitian language" to refer to the Haitian vernacular commonly known as "Creole" or "Haitian Creole."

2. Carrié Paultre, *Ti Jak* (Port-au-Prince: Comité Protestant d'Alphabétisation et de Littérature, n.d.); Georges Sylvain, *Cric? Crac! Fables de La Fontaine racontées par un montagnard haïtien et transcrites en vers créoles* (Paris: Ateliers haïtiens, 1901); Thélyson Orélien, "La vérité sur le premier roman publié en créole haïtien," *Huffington Post Québec* (2014), http://quebec .huffingtonpost.ca/thelyson-orelien/litterature-la-verite-sur-le-premier -roman-publie-en-creole-haitien_b_5777962.html.

3. Marie-Christine Hazaël-Massieux, "Creole in the French Caribbean Novel of the 1990s: From Reality to Myth?" in *The Francophone Caribbean*

Today: Literature, Language, Culture, Studies in Memory of Bridget Jones, ed. Gertrud Aub-Buscher and Beverley Ormerod Noakes (Kingston: University of the West Indies Press, 2003), 82–101.

4. Togiram, "Dézafi krazé défi," *Le Petit Samedi Soir* 114 (1975): 11.

5. Ibid.: "Min youn liv mouin fèk koumansé ap totòt ki mété léspri-m an pinpian é fè m-santi-m ozanj. . . . Min youn boulchans tout ayisyin nan nannan t-ap tann dépi diktlantan."

6. Émile Roumer, "Dézafi vu par É. Roumer," *Le Petit Samedi Soir* 115 (1975): 6: "Dézafi, cé youn enchantement et m'passé toute apré-midi a gé m'collé la-dansl' sans m'pas cab départi chapitres m'ta rhélé cantos com Dantes Alighieri poème qui rende mystère oun vie moun la ville pas comprende car cé seulement pellicules tête yo représenté. . . . Personnellement m'sentim'fier oun Haïtien cab produi oun pareil chef d'œuvre si l'pas gain oun bibliothèque comment fè youne ac Dézafi, liv Frankétienne la."

7. See, among other works, Rafael Lucas's "La littérarisation de la langue haïtienne," in *Typo/topo/poéthique: Sur Frankétienne,* ed. Jean Jonassaint (Paris: L'Harmattan, 2008), [123]–46), which shows how and why *Dézafi* initiates and establishes this Haitian literarity.

8. See Frankétienne, *Dézafi* (Port-au-Prince: Éditions Fardin, 1975), copyright page: "Dépi sanmba Frankétienne pa bay dizon-li, piès mounn, lan ninpòt péyi, pa gin laloua sèvi ak paròl nan roman « DÉZAFI » pou tradiksion, réprodiksion ak adaptasion."

9. On this latter point, it is important to recall the words of one of the eminent figures of the Spiralist movement, Jean-Claude Fignolé, in an interview with Dieudonné Fardin: "At the strictly theoretical level, we have chosen to follow the modern novel in its refusal of the action's uniqueness. Because such an approach is consistent with our conception of a total genre: neither novel, nor poetry, nor theater, but all three at once. This conception is not foreign. It is Haitian. Take the trouble to go to the countryside. If, by chance, the peasants gather under the arbor to tell stories in your presence, you'll be easily convinced. The narrative structure of the folktales is often broken. . . . The story becomes theater and show (dialogues, songs, dances). The listeners intervene, cutting the story into improvisations outside of the plot—we call them fugues—through which the poetic and inventive genius of our peasants is revealed. There is a participation of the listeners outside the limits of the narrative that prohibits a linear development of the narrative." My translation of Fignolé's words: "Au niveau strictement théorique, nous avons choisi de suivre le roman moderne dans son refus de l'unicité de l'action. Parce qu'une telle démarche est conforme à notre conception d'un genre total: ni roman, ni poésie, ni théâtre, mais les trois à la fois. Cette conception n'est pas étrangère. Elle est haïtienne. Donne-toi la peine d'aller à campagne. Si par chance, les paysans se réunissent sous la tonnelle pour tirer des contes en ta présence,

tu t'en convaincras facilement. La structure narrative des contes est souvent
éclatée. . . . Le conte devient théâtre et spectacle (dialogue, chant, danses) Les
auditeurs interviennent, coupant le récit en des improvisations en dehors du
récit—nous les appelons fugues—par où se révèle le génie poétique et inventif
de nos paysans. Il y a comme une participation des auditeurs hors des lim-
ites du récit et qui interdit, par là même, le développement linéaire du récit"
(Dieudonné Fardin and Jean-Claude Fignolé, "Dialogue à bâtons rompus sur
le spiralisme," *Le Petit Samedi Soir* 13 [1972]: 23–24).

10. W. B. Seabrook, "Dead Men Working in the Cane Fields," *The Magic
Island* (New York: Literary Guild of America, 1929), 92–103.

11. See "Oun ti ralé sou DEZAFI, roman Frankétienne," *En Avant* 6 (1976):
11; and "Oun dezièm ti ralé sou DEZAFI, roman Frankétienne," *En Avant* 8
(1976): 14–15. These anonymously published texts are indeed by Max Dominique and Jean Jonassaint, respectively.

12. See Marc-Yves Volcy, "De Franck à Frankétienne: Fragments de mémoire fraternelle," in *Typo/Topo/Poéthique sur Frankétienne*, ed. Jean Jonassaint (Paris: L'Harmattan, 2008), 182.

13. Published under the name "Frères de l'Instruction Chrétienne" (F.I.C.),
this volume was conceived and written by Dr. Pradel Pompilus and Brother
Raphaël Berrou.

14. These two volumes by Piquion were published without dates; I record
the dates given on WorldCat.

15. On Kouidor, see Kouidor, "La Présentation (Notes pour un travail),"
Nouvelle Optique 9 (1973): 121–47.

16. See Frankétienne, *Ultravocal* (extraits), *Dérives* 1 (1975).

17. To better understand our demonstration, see the table of correspon-
dences of the short sequences in columns in *Dézafi* (1975) and their insertion
in *Dezafi* (2002): [2nd part] S73, p. 148; p. 141/S75, p. 150; p. 143/S88, p. 162; p.
155/S92, p. 165; p. 158/ S98, p. 168; pp. 160–61/S101, pp. 170–71; pp. 163–64/
S107, pp. 176–77; p. 169/ [3rd part] S143, p. 241; p. 228/S145, p. 241; p. 228/
S147, p. 242; p. 229/S149, p. 243; pp. 229–30/S153, p. 244 ; p. 230/S155, p. 245 ;
p. 230/S157, p. 245; p. 231/S159, p. 246; p. 232/ S161, p. 247; p. 233/S163, p. 250;
p. 237/ S174, p. 292–94 ; pp. 280–81/S176, p. 308; pp. 291–92. Please note that
this numbering of the sequences of the 1975 text does not take into account
the three pages in script, which mark the different parts of the book. If we consider each block of text in the same font, type treatment, and size (for example,
a Times or Helvetica font in roman, boldface, or italic, 12 or 10 points) as a
sequence, we have 177 sequences, of which a majority are boldface or italic,
which shows the enormous weight of the poetic over the narrative in *Dézafi*.

18. Mae-Lyna Beaubrun, "Structure et stylistique de *Dézafi* et de *Les Affres d'un défi* de Frankétienne" (master's thesis, Carleton University, Ottawa,
2002).

19. Mollie McFee, "Beyond Translation: The *Matrice* of Frankétienne's *Dézafi*," *Comparative Literature Studies* 54, no. 2 (2017): 381–405.

20. Celina Scheinowitz, *Les Affres de l'inhumanité: Défi romanesque de Frankétienne* (N.p.: Éditions Avenir, 2012).

21. See Jean Jonassaint, "D'un exemplaire créateur souterrain: Un entretien avec Frankétienne," in *Écrire en pays assiégé—Haïti—Writing under Siege*, ed. Marie-Agnès Sourieau and Kathleen M. Balutansky (Amsterdam: Rodopi, 2004), 276, 277: "[. . .] je me suis soumis aux vœux de certains amis haïtiens et antillais. . . . [Cette adaptation], c'était simplement un moyen de mettre l'œuvre à la portée des milieux non créolophones [de] donner à l'œuvre une chance d'être lue par des milieux francophones."

22. On this set of Haitian publications from the 1900s to the 1960s and their distinctive features, see Jean Jonassaint, *Des romans de tradition haïtienne: Sur un récit tragique* (Paris and Montréal: L'Harmattan and Cidihca, 2002), mainly the introduction and chaps. 1 to 4.

23. Frankétienne, *Les Affres d'un défi* (Port-au-Prince: Imprimerie Deschamps, 1979), 207–8. My translation: "The murderous violence of the murderer stirs our thirst for revenge, our scars sprout, the executioner's teeth bite the flesh of our children with impunity. Who would know how to count our wounds [1] at this dangerous crossroads of imbalance where so many misfortunes weigh on our shoulders? [2] After having probed the four horizons, we are determined to span the gap of old curses, to break the cross of misfortune. [3] We have crushed the corn, [4] we will inevitably put the acassan on the fire." To facilitate the comparison with the Haitian text of 1975, I have numbered the phrases that are translations of the original text. The first two sentences describe or contextualize the page, and are, by the way, additions.

24. In rural Haiti there is usually a cross at each crossroad, called the cross of the crossroads, which is different from the cross found in cemeteries. The cross of the crossroads is believed to protect the traveler and help him find his way, but it also marks a place to rest and pray.

25. Frankétienne, *Dezafi* (Châteauneuf-le-Rouge: Vents d'ailleurs, 2002), 270–71. Charles's translation: "Teeth know how to bite flesh, but they don't know how to count bite marks" (p. 146).

26. Alfred Métraux, *Voodoo in Haiti*, trans. Hugo Charteris (1959; New York: Schocken, 1972), 282; translation of *Le Vaudou haïtien* (Paris: Gallimard, 1958), 251. "L'existence des *zombi* vaut, sur le plan mythique, celle des anciens esclaves de Saint-Domingue."

27. René Depestre, *Hadriana dans tous mes rêves* (Paris: Gallimard, 1988), translated into English by Kaiama L. Glover as *Hadriana in All My Dreams* (Brooklyn, New York: Akashic, 2017).

28. Scheinowitz, *Les Affres de l'inhumanité*, 40.

29. The complete sentence is: "Lavi ak lanmò pa janm sispann troké kòn"

(self-translated by Franketienne: "Unceasing fight between life and death" [11]). But it is important to note that the phrase "troke kòn" is generally used to describe verbal, nonphysical clashes between two or more women; it does not really refer to the meaning of physical and violent clashes of the French word "combat." Of course, in this case, the clash (between life and death) is metaphysical.

30. In the Haitian lexicon, the term seems versatile, and dictionaries do not agree on its meanings. For Bryant Freeman and Jowèl Laguerre in their *Haitian English Dictionary* (2002), "boulay" refers to "round, sequence (sports); odd job; low-paying job"; for Prophète Joseph in *Diksyonè sinonim lang ayisyen/ Dictionnaire des synonymes de la langue haïtienne* (2001), "boulay" is synonymous with "dife, boukan, chalè" (fire, smoke, heat). As for the dictionaries of Jules Faine, *Dictionnaire français-créole* (Montreal: Leméac, 1974), Antoine Bentolila et al., *Ti Diksyonnè Kreyòl-Franse/Dictionnaire élémentaire créole haïtien-français* (Port-au-Prince: Éditions Caraïbes, 1976), Albert Valdman et al., *Haitian Creole-English Dictionary* (Bloomington: Indiana University/ Creole Institute, 1981), Féquière Vilsaint and Jean-Evens Berret, *English Haitian Creole Dictionary*, 2nd ed. (1991; Coconut Creek, FL: Educa Vision, 2005), and Max Manigat, *Mots créoles du Nord d'Haïti: Origines-Histoire-Souvenirs* (Coconut Creek, FL: Educa Vision, 2006), they do not mention it. In fact, it must be little used. It does not appear in dictionaries conceived or published before 1975, and Haitians consulted claimed not to know it. The few who recognized it associated it with the expressions "Ou nan boulay" (tèt chagé, problèm—difficulty, problem) or "Yon ti boulay" (yon ti job—low-paying job). Moreover, for some informants, it seems that the word "boulay" would be a variant of "batay." Of course, both are in the paradigm of substantives with the suffix "ay"—like *tray, travay, déblozay, tripotay, radotay*—usually associated with ordeals or negativity.

31. Frankétienne, *Dézafi* (1975), 13: "*Yo pito di nou manké pliziè fèy; yo présé fèmin bouch-nou. Jou alé. Nuit pasé. Sézon tolalito. Nou rété gaga lan youn rèv badé mové zè. Youn rèv tchaké ak kochma. Van. Zèklè. Loray. Nou souké kò-nou tikras. Ant somèy-révèy, nou louvri youn grinn jé. Nou sonjé. Nou bliyé. Nou sonjé tigout. Min, nou bliyé anpil . . . nan rèv-la.*"

32. "Voye pwent": short sentences, if not phrases, to insinuate, assert without affirming, to point fingers while denying it, as a formula often associated with these language performances expresses it well: "m voye dlo, m pa mouye pèsòn" (I throw water, I don't wet anyone), different from "paler andaki" (coded language), and "yodi" (gossip).

33. See "Prologue," *General Sun, My Brother*, by Jacques Stephen Alexis, trans. Carrol F. Coates (Charlottesville: University Press of Virginia, 1999); original French edition, *Compère Général Soleil* (Paris: Gallimard, 1955), 3–16.

34. There is an Italian translation by Annamaria Coppola of *Les Affres*

d'un défi but not of *Dézafi* (*Galli da combattimento* [Naples: S. Pironti, 1996], 214 pages). As of now, Charles's translation is the only one of the 1975 Haitian text.

35. Frankétienne, *Les Affres d'un défi* (Port-au-Prince: Imprimerie Henri Deschamps, 1979), 3. An English translation of this paragraph by J. Michael Dash: "A tangle of branches of trees in an old yard. Tough earth, veins hardened by stone and sand. Serpent entrails/coiled in hunger. Entrails knotted with pain. Each day, stomach empty, Rita slaves away at her chores. Locked in his house Gedeon spits out his curses. In the middle of the night, shrill cries pierce our eardrums, penetrate our brains. Fear in our guts, we tremble to our roots. Electrical shiver. Our hair stands on end. Suddenly, we leap out of bed." Frankétienne, "Defiance and Dread," *Callaloo*, 15, no. 2 (1992): 393–94.

36. See Jonassaint, *Des romans de tradition haïtienne: Sur un récit tragique*, chap. 2.

37. The capital letters are in the original French text by Fernand Hibbert, *Les Simulacres* (Port-au-Prince: Imprimerie Chéraquit, 1923), 102: "Mères Haïtiennes, cultivez vos enfants dans le sens indiqué, et la Patrie ne périra pas! Le jour de gloire arrivera! Les Simulacres blancs comme les Simulacres noirs et les Simulacres jaunes se volatiliseront ; et nous resterons maîtres de l'Héritage des pères, grâce aux vertus nouvelles, à la science et au courage que vous aurez inculqués à vos fils,—qui n'auront alors plus besoin de personne pour le développement de leur pays par la Liberté, le Travail, les Sciences et les Arts."

38. The translation by Jean Stewart of Butor's novel was published under two different titles: *Second Thoughts* (London: Faber and Faber, 1958); and *A Change of Heart* (New York: Simon and Schuster, 1959).

39. It is important to note that in the 1979 French text, the first appearance of the couple Jédéyon/Rita is in a short three-line sequence in boldface (p. 3), not in roman type as in the 1975 Haitian text. It may be a typographic mistake, for this use of the boldface in a short paragraph to introduce a couple of characters is not in line with the structure of the work.

40. Frankétienne, *Mûr à crever* (Port-au-Prince: Presses port-au-princiennes, 1968), translated into English by Kaiama L. Glover as *Ready to Burst* (Brooklyn: Archipelago, 2014).

41. For the record, the list of sequences concerning Pin Kris and Gaston: S73* (p. 148), S75* (p. 150), S86 (p. 160, a short sentence, rather enigmatic for a reader unfamiliar with Haitian affairs, on Pin Kris followed by another on Gaston: "Pastè Pi-n Kris sézi/Gaston pèsè Lagonav al chéche ja"—Pastor Pin Kris is shocked/Gaston lands on La Gonave island to look for a buried jar of gold), S114 (p. 184, "Gaston ap férayé ak pastè Pi-n Kris pou grinn diri sinistré"—Gaston is crossing swords with Pastor Pin Kris over charity rice), S116 (p. 185, "Gaston ak Pi-n Kris se kòkòt ak figaro/ yo koupé douk ansanm"— Gaston and Pin Kris are thick as thieves/they hatch plots together), S169 (p.

278, the killing of the pastor), S176* (p. 308). Asterisks indicate sequences composed in smaller point size and appearing like a newspaper column at the right side on the page.

42. When I refer exclusively or directly to the French text, I use the French spelling, "Jérôme." When I am referring to both texts, I use either the Haitian spelling, "Jéròm," or the French spelling.

43. See *Dézafi* (1975), pp. 40–41 (Jéròm alone), 63 (Jéròm alone), 69–71, 95–97, 155, 160–61, 168 (short indented sequence), 174 (Jéròm alone), 179, 181 (Jéròm alone at the sixth round), 185, 192 (Jéròm alone at the seventh round), 197 (Jéròm alone), 199 (Jéròm alone), 214 (Jéròm alone at the eighth round), 217 (Jéròm alone), 236 (Jéròm alone at the tenth round), 243 (short indented sequence), 269 (Alibé alone in relation with Rita), 305–7, 310–11 (penultimate paragraph of the novel).

44. Gérard Genette, *Palimpsestes: La littérature au second degré* (Paris: Seuil, 1982), chaps. 1 and 2; translated into English by Channa Newman and Claude Doubinsky as *Palimpsests: Literature in the Second Degree* (Lincoln: University of Nebraska Press, 1997).

45. See Laënnec Hurbon, *Le Barbare imaginaire* (Port-au-Prince: Deschamps, 1987), who shows how Haiti and Haitians have been seen over the centuries as "barbarians."

46. Gérard Étienne, *Le Nègre crucifié* (Montréal: Nouvelle optique, 1974), translated into English by Claudia Harry as *Crucified in Haiti: Narrative* (Montréal: Éditions du Marais, 2006).

47. Frédéric Marcelin gives an interesting description/definition of the phenomenon in *Marilisse* (Paris: Ollendorff, 1903), 307–8.

48. See Frédéric Marcelin's definitions in chapter 13 of *Marilisse* (Paris: Ollendorff, 1903) of some terms of the Haitian "political language," such as *secousses, Vindbindingues, couris, boiser*; or Jacques Roumain's portrait of the "père-savane" in *Masters of the Dew* (1947 translation by Langston Hughes and Mercer Cook [Portsmouth, NH: Heinemann/Caribbean Writers Series, 1978], 173–77); *Gouverneurs de la Rosée* (Port-au-Prince: Imprimerie de l'État, 1944), 292–97.

49. See Kouidor, "La Parole des Grands Fonds" (1973), in "La Présentation (Notes pour un travail)," *Nouvelle Optique* 9 (1973): [126].

50. These possible reading paths are more or less applicable to *Les Affres d'un défi*, but they are more difficult to take with *Dezafi* (without the accent on the "e"), the typographic layout of the 2002 book being much more complex.

51. See Jean Jonassaint, "D'un exemplaire créateur souterrain: Un entretien avec Frankétienne," in *Écrire en pays assiégé—Haïti—Writing under Siege*, ed. Marie-Agnès Sourieau and Kathleen M. Balutansky (Amsterdam: Rodopi, 2004), 275: "*Dézafi* a été d'abord pour moi une expérience littéraire esthétique au niveau de la langue créole. *Dézafi*, c'est d'abord le roman de la

langue haïtienne. Mais comme une langue est indissolublement liée au devenir, au destin, à la situation vécue d'un peuple, donc roman de la langue qui, forcément, devait être aussi le roman du peuple haïtien: le roman de la possibilité, de l'éventualité ou de la probabilité d'une libération."

52. On "Choucoune" and its fortune, see Jean Jonassaint, "Pour de nouveaux paradigmes: Haïti et nos humanités," in *Présences haïtiennes*, ed. Christiane Achour et al. (Cergy: Centre de Recheche Textes et Francophonies, Université de Cergy-Pontoise, 2007), 421–51.

53. See Anténor Firmin, *The Equality of the Human Races (Positivist Anthropology)*, trans. Asselin Charles (2000; Urbana: University of Illinois Press, 2002).

www.ingramcontent.com/pod-product-compliance
Lightning Source LLC
Chambersburg PA
CBHW020559030726
47497CB00007B/2010